Romantic Times praises Norah Hess, winner of the Reviewers' Choice Award for Frontier Romance!

LARK

"As with all Ms. Hess' books, the ending is joyous for everyone. The road to happiness is filled with wonderful characters, surprises, passion, pathos and plot twists and turns as only the inimitable Norah Hess can create."

TANNER

"Ms. Hess certainly knows how to write a romance . . . the characters are wonderful and find a way to sneak into your heart."

WILLOW

"Again Norah Hess gives readers a story of a woman who learns to take care of herself, fills her tale with interesting, well-developed characters and a plot full of twists and turns, passion and humor. This is another page-turner."

JADE

"Ms. Hess continues to write page-turners with wonderful characters described in depth. This is a wonderful romance complete with surprising plot twists . . . plenty of action and sensuality. Another great read from a great writer."

DEVIL IN SPURS

"Norah Hess is a superb Western romance writer. . . . *Devil in Spurs* is an entertaining read!"

KENTUCKY BRIDE

"Marvelous . . . a treasure for those who savor frontier love stories!"

WINTER LOVE

"Come on, Laura." Fletch stood up and came toward her. "Stop pretending that you didn't love the things I did to you in the barn that time. Remember?"

Yes. I remember, Laura screamed inside. She could almost feel his hands and lips on her body now—making her lose control, doing things that had made her blush in the daylight.

She drew a shuddering breath, and Fletch's eyes lingered on the pulse throbbing in her throat. "Ah, Laura," he said with gruff tenderness, "I can't get you out of my mind. All the time I was gone I thought of you."

His hands came out to grip her elbows and draw her to him. "Why did you get yourself mixed up with Beltran?" And while Laura gazed up at him in openmouthed surprise, he bent his head and crushed her lips beneath his with a desperate hunger.

Other *Leisure* and *Love Spell* books by Norah Hess:
RAVEN
WILDFIRE
LARK
SAGE
DEVIL IN SPURS
TANNER
KENTUCKY BRIDE
WILLOW
MOUNTAIN ROSE
JADE
BLAZE
KENTUCKY WOMAN
HAWKE'S PRIDE
TENNESSEE MOON
LACEY
FANCY
FOREVER THE FLAME
STORM

WINTER LOVE

NORAH HESS

LOVE SPELL BOOKS NEW YORK CITY

LOVE SPELL®

February 2000

Published by

Dorchester Publishing Co., Inc.
276 Fifth Avenue
New York, NY 10001

ISBN 0-505-52365-5

Printed in the United States of America.

To my friend, Jim LaTour

WINTER LOVE

Chapter One

Upper Peninsula, Michigan
1887

Twilight is the best time of the day, Laura thought as she sat alone on the porch that ran the width of the cabin. It was a time to reflect back on the day, make plans for tomorrow.

As was her habit since she was a little girl, she ignored the three chairs placed along the log wall and sat on the top of the steps. From there she had a better view of the yard, the lake, and the encroaching wilderness.

She turned her black curly head to the right, her dark gray eyes looking down on a shallow valley. It was wrapped in shadowy mists, totally unlike it had been this afternoon when she had gone there searching for wild raspberries. The sun had shone bright on the birch trees then, giving their silver-white leaves touches of gold and making the small berries she sought look like little red gems.

She had picked enough of their juicy sweetness to bake two pies and a cobbler.

An affectionate smile curved Laura's lips. Taylor had made a pig of himself, eating two slices of pie with his coffee at the end of their supper of meat pasties.

Laura's gaze wandered off through the pines to where the fur post sat a hundred or so yards from the cabin. The long, low building had been there as long as she could remember. It had gone up shortly after the living quarters had been built.

The post was divided into two rooms, and right now the front room of the establishment smelled like spices, apples and pears, and cloth goods. Later, however, when it snowed and the trappers started bringing in their pelts, it would stink so much the housewives would shun it whenever possible.

Soft lamplight glowed from the store, as well as through the window of the back room where the men of Big Pine gathered to drink their whiskey and rum, and to discuss whatever might be on their minds.

Laura couldn't see it, but she knew there was lamplight coming from the cabin directly behind the posts, too. She had been ten years old when big, redheaded Bertha Higgins and her four whores descended on Big Pine. Bertha had made a deal with the single men of the settlement: Build her a cabin and her girls would pleasure them free as it went up. But, she had added, she wanted the building finished in a week. They were not to drag out the job so as to enjoy her girls longer.

There had been so many woman-hungry men who had rushed forward to take Bertha up on her offer that every night almost a dozen showed up at the tent that Bertha had erected for herself and her girls.

The wives of Big Pine had strongly objected to the loose women moving into their settlement, but when a vote was taken, Madame Bertha won out over propriety. She and the men agreed, however, that the whores wouldn't flaunt their trade; they would stay strictly to themselves, going only to the tavern part of the post, and to the store when necessary.

The whores had kept their word.

The honking of wild geese brought Laura's attention back to the lake. By the early moonlight reflected on the water she saw them as they flew in, their feet dangling limply as they coasted onto the lake. They would be leaving the area soon, flying to a warmer climate, she thought sadly. It was the end of October and the first snow would be falling in another month.

November. A bleakness came into Laura's dark gray eyes. Fletch had left Big Pine that month, going off with four men from a fur company. She had been on the verge of tears as she'd watched him ride away, and a hopeless grief had grown inside her. The night before, when Fletch had told his father that he wanted to talk to him about something very important, she had felt sure that he was going to tell Taylor he wanted to marry her.

She had been stunned speechless when Fletch said instead, "Pa, I've been asked to blaze a trail into Canada for a fur company who plans on setting up a post there. I'd be gone close to a year. What do you think about it?"

And while she wanted to cry out, "No, Fletch, don't go," Taylor had smiled and said that he thought it was a grand idea. Tears had burned in her eyes and she had hurried to her room where she could sob out her misery in private and wonder how she could bear not seeing him for a year.

The next morning, just at dawn, Fletch had shaken hands with his father, then giving her a fleeting look, said, "Take care, Laura." She and Taylor stood on the porch watching him ride away in the gray darkness to meet the four men whom he would guide into Canada. It was all she could do not to run after him, begging him not to go.

Now Laura leaned her head on the chair back, trying to make sense out of Fletch's hurried leave-taking. But she had barely began to muse on his motivation when the hungry cry of her infant daughter brought her to her feet, everything else forgotten.

Over at the post, Fletch was on Taylor's mind also as he prepared to leave the store. His son would be returning home soon. He hoped that fighting the elements, freezing his tail, shivering in his sleep as he blazed a hundred-mile trail had done for his son what all of his words and advice over the years had failed to do.

Even as a youngster Fletch had been on the wild side, running free through the woods with the Indian lads from the nearby Indian village. When his second wife, Marie, worried that the boy would pick up their heathen ways, he had told her not to worry, he could also learn many good things from the Indians. He had also pointed out to her that there were no white boys Fletcher's age for him to play with.

A couple years later, other families had come to Big Pine, bought land and settled in. In the group of newcomers there were three teenagers around Fletch's age. After that he kept only one Indian friend, a handsome young brave named Red Fox, son of Chief Muga. To this day he and Red Fox often went off into the woods, living off the land for weeks at a time.

Fletch's wildness continued as he and his white friends grew into young men. They started hanging around the fort tavern at night, drinking and carousing, visiting the whorehouse back of the post. And though his friends, including Red Fox, eventually chose wives and settled down and began to raise families, Fletch continued his wild ways.

He now drank and whored with the trappers.

That was until this past summer. Fletch had somehow become involved with Milly Howard, a whore if ever Taylor had seen one. Everybody in Big Pine knew what she was, that she'd slept with most of the single men, and probably a big share of the married men also. Taylor hadn't worried too much until he'd heard rumors that Fletch was going to marry the woman.

When his son had proposed the trip into Canada, Taylor could have cried with relief. Maybe Fletch would get his head on straight after a spell in the untamed wilderness, he thought, locking up the store and taking the path to the cabin.

A cheerful fire burned in the fireplace, its flames casting a ruddy glow on the windowpanes and on Laura as she nursed her baby. As Taylor sat down in the other rocker, she glanced at him, gave him a vague smile, then went back to gazing into the fire.

He wondered what she was thinking about, this young woman who was his daughter, and yet wasn't his daughter, his wife, and yet not his wife.

For although the legal relationship between them might be confusing, Taylor's feelings for Laura were clear.

As far as Taylor Thomas was concerned,

Laura had been his child since she was four years old.

The Thomas and Morris families had settled in the Upper Peninsula within a couple of months of each other, and had become firm friends. It had been only natural that the Thomases would take four-year-old Laura into their home and raise her as their own when her parents were killed by renegade Indians out of Canada.

Taylor leaned his head back, remembering that awful hot summer afternoon. He had been fishing along the lake, less than a mile from the Morris place. When the sun was well westward he had shouldered his fishing pole, his grumbling stomach telling him it was near suppertime.

He was wondering what Marie, his wife, would serve for dessert, hoping it would be blueberry cobbler, when coming from the Morris place he heard the yelling and shouting of Indians on the warpath. Throwing down his pole and the string of fish he'd caught, and grabbing up his rifle he'd leaned against a tree, he ran along the lake, racing toward his friend's cabin.

He had arrived too late. The Indians were gone, leaving behind the dead bodies of Cal and Nan Morris. Nan lay crumpled in front of the cabin, and Cal's broken body lay a few yards away. A pail of spilled milk told him that his friend had been in the barn milking the cow when Indians struck. Both bodies had been scalped, but thankfully Nan hadn't been raped.

But where was little Laura? He looked wildly around. Had the Indians taken her? She was such a beautiful child with her black curly hair. Her curls alone would appeal to the Indians.

Then he had heard the childish cries coming from inside the cabin. In two long strides he was inside the small building, frantically looking around. He had spotted her almost immediately, crouched behind her mother's weaving loom. He gathered the sobbing child into his arms. Thank God the heathens hadn't set fire to the building.

Keeping her small face pressed into his shoulder, hiding from her view the parents who stared sightless at the sky, he ran along the lake path calling Marie's name. Within minutes she and 14-year-old Fletch came running toward him. He explained what had happened as he handed the frightened child to Marie.

While she and his son looked horror-stricken, he ordered, "Lock yourselves in the cabin. Keep the firearms loaded and your eyes peeled at the windows. I'll be back as soon as I alert our other neighbors that the red bastards are on a killing spree."

Fletcher had insisted on going with him, but when he pointed out that he must stay and look after his stepmother and Laura, Fletcher had said no more, only hustled Marie along to the safety of their cabin.

As it turned out, only the Morris place was hit. Apparently, killing Cal and Nan had satisfied the Indians' anger at the whites who were invading their land in ever greater numbers.

After Laura's parents had been buried in the small community cemetery, the little girl settled into their lives as though she had been born into it. He and Marie doted on her, and Fletch adored his little "sister." Marie had passed away from pneumonia when Laura was ten years old, and only the young girl's presence had kept him and Fletch sane for the first few months.

After Marie's passing, he'd been faced with the problem of what to do with Laura while he went about taking care of business. If he took her to the post with him, she was subjected to the coarse talk of the whores, and the coarser language of the trappers that drifted into the store every time the tavern door was opened. He knew that if Marie was alive she wouldn't allow it for one minute.

But what alternative did he have? he had asked himself. It was too dangerous to leave her in the cabin alone. Renegade Indians still went on the warpath occasionally, especially if they got their hands on some whiskey.

When he voiced his worries to Fletch, he had answered that the solution was simple. "Keep the door locked that separates the two rooms. Let the men use the side door, the one the whores use to enter the tavern."

And so, until Laura was 14 and could keep

house and cook as well as any of the women in the village, also expertly handle a rifle, she helped out in the store. She waited on the female customers and kept the shelves neater than he had ever done.

Then one day Taylor noticed that more and more men began to show up in the store, lingering overlong on some small purchase. It hadn't taken him long to discover the reason.

They came to ogle Laura. It seemed that while he wasn't looking, her young, coltish body had developed soft curves and full, round breasts. She had been a lovely child and was growing into a beautiful young woman with black curls tumbling down her back, and gray eyes that could twinkle with mirth or grow as dark as storm clouds when she was angry.

She hadn't demurred the night he told her that from now on she was to stay home and keep house. "I didn't want to say anything, Pa," she had answered, "but lately I've been getting uncomfortable the way some of the men stare at me."

"I know, honey, and I'm sorry I didn't notice it sooner."

"Do you think the trappers will come to the cabin?" She had looked at him anxiously.

Taylor shook his head. "They know better. But even if they did, I don't think any of them would step out of line with you. The trappers are rough in speech and manners, but they know a decent woman when they see one and would act accordingly."

Although the trappers had never come to the cabin, the young farmers did, giving her great aggravation since they were always underfoot. Taylor's lips curved in an amused grin. The young bucks never stayed long when Fletch was around. One hard look from him and they were on their way.

Taylor and Marie had always hoped that Fletch and Laura would marry once the girl became a young woman. Marie had said with a wistful smile that they would never lose their little girl if she married into the family.

With a long sigh, Taylor came back to the present. Laura had married into the family, but not to the son. She had married the father.

He stood up and, touching Laura on the shoulder, said, "I'll see you in the morning, honey. I'm going to step over to the tavern and have a couple of drinks before I retire."

Laura nodded, hiding an amused smile. She knew that Taylor wouldn't set foot in the tavern. He would slip through the forest, bypassing the post as he made his way to the Indian village a mile away. There he would spend a couple of hours with the Indian woman he had visited once a week a year after mother Marie had died.

No white except for herself, and *maybe* Fletch, knew about his liaison with the woman called Butterfly. Laura knew only because she had followed Pa one night and had seen him take the widowed woman into his arms and kiss her before following her into her tepee. The Indians liked and respected Pa and they never spoke of the love affair outside their village.

She had seen the Indian woman many times over the years, mostly at the store. Laura had always looked away when Pa never took any money for whatever Butterfly had purchased. She also pretended not to see the smiles they exchanged, or how they would touch hands when no one was looking. She could understand why Pa was attracted to the young widow. She was a fine-looking woman with her smooth skin, bright black eyes, and regal bearing. No white man ever called out crude invitations to her, not even the trappers.

Laura had always thought it a shame that Pa and Butterfly had to keep their love for each other a secret. She leaned her head back and closed her eyes. There were so many secrets to be kept; from Pa and from Fletch especially.

Where was Fletch tonight? she wondered. Laura didn't know exactly when her "sisterly" love for a "brother" had changed into that of a woman loving a man. She thought it was around the time she turned 16 that she started feeling differently toward him. And that was the time Fletch's manner toward her had changed.

It seemed that one day he was his usual teasing self; then the next day he didn't want to be around her and he spoke to her only when necessary. More and more he began staying away from home in the evenings, not returning until way after she had gone to bed.

But she would still be awake up in her loft room when he would quietly enter the cabin, whiskey fumes floating up to her. She would sit up in bed and watch him over the short railing as he sat before the fire, staring glumly into the flames. She would wonder what bothered him but was afraid to climb down the ladder and ask him. His answer would probably be a black scowl.

There had been a time when she could have gone to Fletch at any hour and asked him anything. But these days she only received cool looks and short answers when she ventured to ask him something.

What puzzled her also was that sometimes she caught him watching her with a strange look in his eyes. Almost the same way as the young men did who came courting her. When she would gaze back at him he would frown and quickly look away.

In her confusion and unhappiness she took to flirting with the young men who came calling, cluttering up the porch. Occasionally she would walk out with one or the other, unconsciously trying to make Fletch jealous. She danced harder, laughed more gaily than the other young women at the parties that were often given to break up the monotony of the hard work demanded of the families hewing out a home in the wilderness.

When the dancing and flirting was over, however, and she had gone to bed, hot tears soaked her pillow. She felt nothing but friendship for those young men she led on, and she was ashamed that she had given them hope when there was none. It was still Fletch whom she loved.

Laura felt her insides clench. When she was 17, Fletch had started courting that awful Milly Howard. To say that all of Big Pine was shocked was an understatement. Everyone knew that Milly was a slut who raised her skirts for any man who came along. Pa and Fletch had many an argument over the woman.

There had come an evening when Laura decided that she couldn't go on asking herself questions. She had to know why Fletch had changed so radically toward her. Pa had gone for his weekly visit to the Indian village, and Fletch was in the barn, doing she had no idea what. She suspected he had gone there to avoid her.

The early November air had been chilly as she walked toward the log building that housed their farm animals, and she pulled the shawl closer around her shoulders. And though her body grew warmer, her teeth chattered from nervousness.

Laura reached the barn, and steeling herself for the confrontation with Fletch, pushed open the heavy door. In the light of the lantern he'd hung on the wall she saw him immediately. He was currying his stallion, Buckskin, his brow furrowed as he swept the long-toothed comb across the animal's broad back. What deep thoughts were on his mind that made him frown so? she wondered. Whatever it was, he was giving it deep study.

With a determined sigh, Laura pulled the door closed behind her, its bottom dragging on the gravelly soil. Fletch looked up at the scraping sound, and she gave him a weak smile as she came toward him.

His frown deepened in annoyance. "What are you doing out here at this hour?" he asked gruffly. "Meeting one of the dunderheads that's always underfoot?"

"I am not!" Laura answered sharply, her hands tightly clutching the shawl under her chin. "I've never sneaked out to meet any man in the barn."

Fletcher's eyes bored into hers. "Are you trying to tell me that when Pa makes his weekly visits to the Indian village you don't slip down here to dally awhile with one of those green young men—especially that good-looking blond-headed one?"

"Don't judge me by yourself, Fletcher Thomas," Laura bit out angrily. "Just because you have loose morals where women are concerned doesn't mean that I follow in your footsteps with the men I know."

"And what do you know about my conduct with women?" Fletcher narrowed his eyes at her, his hand going idle on the stallion's back.

Laura wanted to bring Milly Howard into the heated words between them but hesitated. She was sure Fletch would defend the woman, and it would cut her deeply.

She said instead, "It's common knowledge that you're like a rutting moose looking for a cow in heat."

She saw him flinch at her description of him and wished she could recall the sharp words. He was no worse than some of the other single men when it came to chasing women.

He let her remark pass, however, and asked brusquely, "What brings you down here then?"

Laura laid her hand on top of the short stall door. "I want to talk to you."

"Well, talk then," Fletcher said impatiently and resumed grooming the stallion.

"It's important and I'd like your full attention."

With an irritated scowl Fletcher tossed the curry comb onto a ledge and left the stall. When he had fastened the latch on the breast-high door he leaned back against it, his arms folded across his chest.

"All right," he said, eyeing her coolly. "What is so important you had to follow me to the barn to say it?"

His surly tone and the lack of warmth in his eyes wounded Laura to the heart. This wasn't the Fletch she had grown up with, the man she had loved since she was practically a baby. He had left her somewhere along the way, and it was a stranger who looked at her so unemotionally.

Suddenly she didn't want to discuss anything with this stranger. Giving Fletch a thin smile, she waved a hand, dismissing as unimportant what she had wanted to say. "I've changed my mind." Her chin went up proudly. "There's nothing we can talk about anymore." She turned away, blinking against the moisture gathering in her eyes. "I'm sorry I bothered you," she said, her back stiff as she walked toward the door. "Go back to grooming Brave."

At her words a change seemed to come over Fletch. He stepped away from the stall door and called softly, "Don't go yet, Laura."

Laura stopped, her hand on the barn door. "Why?" she murmured softly. "Do you have some more hateful things to say to me?"

"No." Fletch stepped up to her and turned her around to face him. "I'm sorry for the way I spoke to you." He looked into her tear-glittering eyes, then dropped his gaze to her soft, trembling lips. "Damn you, Laura," he rasped as if in pain and pulled her up snug against his body.

Fletcher held Laura so tight she could feel the thudding of his heart, and her body quivered in helpless reaction. Her arms slid up around his shoulders as his head lowered and his lips took hers in a searing kiss that went on and on. When she felt his fingers on her bodice, fumbling with the buttons, she removed an arm from around him and helped undo the small buttons. She was as anxious as he to feel his hands on her breast.

The shawl fell to the hay-covered floor; then Fletch was pushing her dress down around her waist. She felt the roughness of his fingers on the gathering ribbons of her camisole; then it followed the path of her bodice.

Fletch held her away from him, and his eyes grew deep with wonder as he gazed at her perfectly shaped breasts, the pink nipples that were little nubs of desire. Laura gasped her pleasure when he lowered his head and placed his mouth over one breast. As he tugged urgently on it, she made little mewling sounds and stroked her fingers through his black hair, pressing his head closer to her breast.

She became weak with the thrill that flowed through her when he switched to the other breast and slowly tugged at the nipple with his lips.

She was so deep in the wild, hot sensations running from her breast to the inner core of her, Laura wasn't aware of Fletcher's busy fingers ridding her body of her clothes until the cold air hit her bare flesh. When she shivered, Fletch released the swollen tip, and sweeping her up in his arms, carried her to a pile of hay and gently laid her down. He went back then and picked up the light shawl that lay with the other discarded clothing and spread it over her. He then hurried out of his own clothing.

Stripped bare, he stood before Laura, and she knew that he wanted her to look at him. She lifted heavy eyes to his desire-ridden face, then slowly lowered them to take in his broad shoulders, his flat stomach and narrow hips. Finally, she shyly looked at his man strength jutting proudly from a nest of curly hair.

Her eyes widened at the hard length that throbbed with a life of its own. There was no way her body could take it all; she was sure of that. As though Fletch read the doubt in her eyes, he came down on his knees beside her. "It will fit," he said huskily, taking her hand and laying it on his hungry member. He curled her fingers around his thickness. "Get acquainted with it first, feel how anxious it is to bury itself inside you."

Eager to please him, Laura did his bidding, marveling how the long length could be so hard yet feel like velvet as her fingers stroked over him. He lay down beside her, and as she continued to fondle him he smoothed a palm down her stomach, coming to rest on the black curls at the apex of her thighs. She made little purring sounds when he inserted a finger inside her and rubbed the little nub hidden there.

Laura felt herself grow hot and moist as Fletch stroked her. He withdrew his hand and gently turned her over on her back. "It will hurt at first, honey." He looked deeply into her face. "But only for a moment when I break your maidenhead."

Laura nodded, almost impatiently. She could only think about the relief her inner core was demanding.

Fletcher gently spread her legs and positioned himself between them. Eagerly, Laura lifted herself as he took his largeness in his hand and guided it to her.

Laura's surprised cry of pain was smothered by his mouth coming down and swallowing the sound.

As Laura's body remained rigid, her hands on his chest as though to push him off her, Fletcher held his body perfectly still, only dipping his head to suckle her breasts, one after the other. Gradually the stiffness went out of her. When her arms came up to cling to his shoulders, he took her mouth in a deep, soul-shattering kiss.

He slid his hands under her smooth cheeks and lifted her to fit into the well of his hips. His body rising and falling then, he thrust slowly and deeply. On his fourth drive he was spewing his seed inside her. He hardly broke his rhythm, however, and the wet heat only increased Laura's pleasure.

To her amazement, after only one more drive of his hips, Fletch was reaching the same crest again. This time his release was so strong and lasted so long he collapsed on top of her.

And though his body was bathed in sweat, his hair wet with it, he was not yet finished. When he began to move inside her again, Laura guessed that he was determined to control himself until she could have her own release.

It didn't take more than three minutes of slow, steady stroking before Laura tensed, feeling her feminine walls convulsing around him. He gathered her close, timed his movements to hers, and they climbed that hill together. Moments later the barn rang with the combined cries of their release.

Yes, she had known heaven that night, Laura thought. A heaven as intense as the hell she went through the next morning when Fletch left so unexpectedly for Canada.

A log burned through in the fireplace, scattering ashes on the hearth and waking baby Jolie. Laura soothed the little one back to sleep, scolding herself for remembering the night her daughter was conceived.

"It wasn't lovemaking we did," she said impatiently. "It was just plain old lust making."

Chapter Two

Laura lay in bed watching the moon move across the sky. To her annoyance Fletch was still on her mind. She had ordered him away a dozen times since putting Jolie to bed in her little cradle, then retiring herself. He had, however, persisted in returning, keeping her awake.

And always to drag her mind back to the night of passion they'd shared, and to the morning following it.

As the heat of desire left her she had shivered in the coolness of the barn and snuggled up to Fletch to share the warmth of his body, her mind willing him to put his arms around her. He had, instead, stiffened and said gruffly, "You'd better get your clothes on before you catch cold."

She had gone still, wondering what had happened to the soft loverlike voice that had whispered endearments in her ears as he stroked inside her.

After a moment she rose, blinking back tears when he didn't help her find her scattered clothes and help her into them. He had readily helped her out of them. But he had busied himself getting into his own clothes, hurrying her along, reminding her that Pa could be coming along at any time.

Her confusion had grown as they walked toward the cabin, he several steps ahead of her. She told herself not to put any importance on his now unloverlike attitude, that he was in a hurry to get into the cabin before Pa returned from visiting Butterfly.

When they stepped into the kitchen she waited for him to take her into his arms and kiss her good night. He had barely glanced at her as he said, "You'd better get up to your room. If Pa sees that hay in your hair and clothes, there'll be hell to pay."

Hurt, and still more confused, she'd watched Fletch enter his bedroom and close the door behind him without so much as a spoken good night, let alone a kiss.

With hot, painful tears gathering in her eyes, Laura climbed the ladder to her loft room. She stripped off her clothes, then cleansed her sore private parts before pulling a gown over her head and crawling into bed.

She was still awake when Taylor came home, moving quietly, humming softly under his breath. Every time he was with Butterfly he came home with a happy tune on his lips. She pictured Fletch stretched out on his bed. The son had acted as though the hour they had spent together had been disappointing.

Her eyes flew open with a sudden thought. Fletch could very well be disappointed in their lovemaking. It had been her first time and she wasn't at all experienced, unlike Milly Howard, for instance. Milly knew all the ways there were to please a man, Laura expected.

Fletch had seemed to want Laura though, she remembered as she finally drifted off to sleep. The soreness between her legs attested to that.

The next morning she was up at her usual early hour, eager to see Fletch. She put on one of her prettiest dresses and brushed her dark curls until they snapped and crackled. Could Pa look at her and know that she was no longer a virgin? she asked herself as she climbed down the ladder. She hadn't noticed any difference in her face when she had looked into her mirror.

As Laura made coffee and fried ham and potatoes, she told herself that a good night's sleep would make Fletch more like the man who had made love to her.

To her disappointment, Fletch hadn't appeared in the kitchen until after she and Taylor had sat down to eat. He grunted a good morning on his way to the washbasin, his whiskered face hard and brooding. When he joined them at the table and helped himself to the breakfast fare, he avoided looking at her. She told herself that he was afraid to look at her in case his expression might give something away to Pa.

She was sure of that when later they were having coffee and Fletch said, "Pa, I want to discuss something with you that's very important. I want your opinion on it."

Her heart had beaten like that of a frightened rabbit. He was going to ask Pa if he could marry her. What Fletch had said instead made her heart skip a beat. She couldn't believe what she was hearing when Fletch informed them he was going to Canada.

"I've been asked by a man from a large fur company to blaze a trail for them into Canada. Thing is, I may be gone close to a year. What do you think?"

And while she had felt as if she were bleeding inside, Pa had given Fletch his blessing. Fletch had left the cabin then, not returning until the next morning. The four men he would be traveling with accompanied him; they sat at the table talking to Pa and ogling her while Fletch went to his room to gather up his winter clothing.

He and the men left then, Fletch shaking hands with Pa, saying that he would probably see him this time next year. On the verge of tears, not believing what was happening, Laura had waited for him to say good-bye—and maybe some private word—to her.

She felt chilled to the bone when on his way out the door he said nonchalantly, "Take care of yourself, Laura." She ran to the window to watch him and the men strike off through the woods. "Couldn't you have at least looked at me, Fletch?" she cried inside. "Would it have killed you to smile at me even if you didn't mean it?"

For a month, in the lonely darkness of her room, Laura cried herself to sleep every night. Suddenly, then, a more pressing matter than Fletch's cold treatment came to plague her.

She had missed her menses. She was expecting Fletch's child. What was she going to do? she had asked herself over and over. After a week of worrying she had come to only one decision. Cold logic told her that she must tell Pa. A pregnancy could be kept secret only so long.

But she need not tell him who the father was, she had decided. It would break Pa's heart if she told him that his son had made love to her and then taken off to Canada.

She would never forget the day she got up the nerve to tell Pa that soon she would be bringing shame down on his head. She had spent the night before tossing and turning, with intermittent short periods of sleep, mulling over in her mind how to approach Pa about her pregnancy. She had arisen from bed the next morning with a headache and red-rimmed eyes. She also had her first bout with morning sickness. She had barely made it to the necessary before losing the remains of her supper from the night before.

Her stomach had calmed down considerably and she was able to make breakfast, feeling only a little nauseous at the odor of frying bacon.

She had picked at the food on her plate, however, having no appetite, and Pa had noticed right away. She had always been a big eater and he often teased her, saying that she had a hollow leg.

"How come you're playing with your food this morning, honey?" He frowned at her. "I thought I heard you vomiting in the necessary before. Are you coming down with something?"

Taylor's innocent question brought on a fit of hysterical laughter. Was she coming down with something? If only that were the case, she would be so happy. Even if it were death-threatening typhoid, she'd welcome that over what the next several months would bring.

When Pa gave her a puzzled look, she knew that there would be no better time than now to tell him of her true condition. She looked across the table at him and, with shame and grief in her voice, said, "I'm going to have a baby, Pa."

For several seconds, Pa had stared at her, thunderstruck, shaking his head in denial. She reached across the table and gripped his clenched fist lying next to his plate. "It's true, Pa," she said gently. "I'll be delivering sometime in August."

Taylor regained his speech with a roar. "Who is the bastard who did this dastardly thing to you?" he demanded. "Tell me his name."

Laura looked down at her plate; then in a voice proud and scornful, she answered, "Since I have no intention of marrying the baby's father, I see no reason to name him."

"Are you telling me that you let a man you didn't love have his way with you?" Taylor sounded scandalized.

Laura lifted pain-filled eyes to Taylor. "I thought I loved him, Pa. I thought he was everything I'd ever want in a husband." She paused before adding, "I was never so mistaken in my life."

"I still want to know his name." Taylor leaned across the table, his fork gripped in his hand. "I have a right to know."

"No." Laura shook her head stubbornly. "You'd only go after him, and tongues would wag more than they will when people discover I'm going to have an illegitimate child."

Naming her unborn baby a bastard brought tears streaming down Laura's cheeks. It wasn't the little one's fault that his mother was stupid and his father was a cold, no-good, woman-chasing wolf.

She looked at Taylor through grief-filled eyes, then dropped her gaze as she asked in desperation, "What am I going to do, Pa? I am so ashamed."

Taylor looked at her bent, black curly head, her shoulders slumped in despair, and wished that he could get his hands on the man who had maybe ruined the young girl's life. "Laura," he said gently, "you can feel disappointed in yourself that you loved unwisely, but don't be ashamed that you loved."

Laura made no response, and Taylor stared thoughtfully out the window before speaking again. "Although you've never mentioned it, I know that you're aware of the relationship I have with Butterfly. I want you to get dressed now and we will go talk with her. She will advise us what to do."

Laura lifted her eyes to Taylor, unable to hide her shocked disbelief. How could this Indian woman she didn't know help solve her dilemma? She wasn't going to drink some concoction that would kill her baby. What she had said to Pa about not wanting to marry the little one's father didn't mean that she didn't want it.

"I don't think that's a good idea, Pa," she said. "Butterfly and I don't even know each other."

"She knows you, Laura. I've told her about you through the years. She is a very wise woman and she'll know what we should do."

Laura started to object more strongly, then realized all of a sudden that Taylor was frightened. He had come onto something he didn't know how to handle. If mother Marie were still alive, they would ponder over their daughter's problem together. And since Butterfly was the woman in his life now, she supposed it was only natural he'd want to turn to her in an emergency.

She nodded and said, "I'll be ready in half an hour."

The sun was slowly burning off the heavy mist that hung over the lake as Laura and Taylor walked toward the Indian village. They avoided the beaten path that numerous feet had trod, keeping in the deeper forest adjacent to it. Only rarely over the years had Taylor gone to see Butterfly in the daylight hours. It had to be, as now, a matter of importance to chance being seen by his neighbors.

The village of between 20 and 25 tepees lay in a sunny meadow, surrounded by tall pines and shimmering birches. A small fire burned before each one, and the women tending the cooking fires looked at Taylor and Laura as they passed by, several bony-ribbed dogs yapping at their heels. Some spoke to Taylor; others only gave him a stolid stare. But it was plain they were all curious about Laura.

Butterfly's tepee sat apart from the others, and Laura wondered if that was her choice or if she had been ordered to keep a distance from the others because of her relationship with Taylor. She thought irritably to herself that it was always the woman who paid for loving a man.

When Taylor scratched at the rawhide cover of Butterfly's home, and she lifted the flap of the narrow entrance, if she had any curiosity as to why Laura was with him she didn't show it. She smiled with friendly warmth and said, "Welcome to my home."

A small fire burned in the center of the cone-shaped room, contained in a circle of carefully arranged rocks. Blue smoke drifted up from it and disappeared through the opening in the peaked roof where the supporting poles met and crossed.

The floor was covered with thick furs, and against one curving wall was a pallet made from several layers of bearskin. On top were two layers of soft beaver pelts between which Butterfly would sleep. There was no doubt that the Indian woman slept cozy and warm in the winter.

When Taylor sat down in front of the fire Indian fashion, Laura did the same. Then Butterfly sat down on his other side, their knees touching. He laid an affectionate hand on her shoulder and said, "I guess you know this is Laura. I've bent your ear enough about her all these years."

Butterfly smiled at Laura. "It is good that I finally get to meet your Laura."

"And I am happy to finally meet you, Butterfly." Laura returned the smile.

"Sadly, the cause of your meeting is not a happy one," Taylor said at the end of a long breath. "We have come to you with a big problem, Butterfly. I hope that you can help us solve it."

"I will gladly try, Taylor," Butterfly said quietly, "but first let me offer you and Laura a cup of herb tea. It calms the nerves and brain so that one can think clearly."

In a short while, Laura and Taylor were each handed a small gourd bowl. When Laura raised the tea to her lips she expected the tan-colored liquid to taste bitter on her tongue. She was pleasantly surprised at her first sip. The tea was strong, but it had a sweetish, minty flavor.

When she told Butterfly how much she liked it, the Indian woman smiled, finished her own tea, then turned to Taylor. "You can now speak of this trouble you have, Taylor."

Taylor took Laura's hand and gently held it as he related to Butterfly what had happened to his daughter. He explained that she refused to name the bastard, or to marry him. He ended by asking, "What shall we do, Butterfly? Laura is so young. I hate to think of her spending the rest of her life with such a dark cloud hanging over her, her good name ruined."

Butterfly shook her head sadly. "It is a shame what some men will do to a maiden, whether she be red or white." She reached across Taylor and patted Laura's knee. "I will ponder on your problem a moment." She then bent her head and closed her eyes as though she slept. Laura gazed into the fire, doubting, but hoping that Butterfly would come up with a solution for her.

When the black head was raised a few minutes later and quiet words were spoken, Taylor caught his breath and Laura stared blankly at the woman, sure that she hadn't heard correctly.

What Butterfly had said in confident tones was, "There is only one answer, Taylor. So that Laura will not be shamed, you must marry her."

After a stunned silence, Laura squeaked incredulously, "Marry Pa? You're out of your mind, Butterfly. I can't marry my father."

"Taylor is not your father by blood," the Indian woman pointed out. "In fact, he is not related to you at all. There would be no sin in marrying him."

"Good Lord, Butterfly, do you realize how everybody would talk?" Taylor said, adding his objections. "They'd be scandalized."

Butterfly shrugged her shoulders. "They will probably talk some at first, but only for a short time. As soon as something new happens that they can get their teeth into, they will forget your spring-and-winter marriage. In the meantime you have taken the step that will protect Laura's good name. That is more important than anything else. Is it not?"

Her mind in total confusion, Laura gazed unseeing at the dancing flames in the fire pit. Was her good name important enough for her to marry the man who had raised her, had been a father to her in nearly every sense of the word? Then again, what about her unborn child? It deserved to have a father even if that man in actual fact was his grandfather.

Taylor, who had also been thinking over his

lover's advice, looked at Laura finally and said gruffly, "It would be in name only, of course."

When Butterfly answered that he would only be giving Laura and her child his name, he grinned crookedly and said, "I've always dreaded losing Laura to some young man. If I marry her myself I can put that fear to rest."

Butterfly laid a hand on his knee and cautioned, "Laura will fall in love again someday, Taylor, and you will have to set her free. It would be selfish of you to keep her tied to your side, wasting her youth."

"You are right, of course." Taylor nodded, then looked at Laura's downcast face. "You haven't said anything, honey. What are your thoughts on Butterfly's advice? It's your future, after all, and what you decide will be the way it is."

Laura heaved a weary sigh and looked up at Taylor, defeat in her dark gray eyes. "I can't think of anything else, Pa, unless I leave Big Pine. I know that is out of the question. I have no idea where I'd go or what I'd do when I got there."

"Don't ever think of leaving your home," Taylor ordered, half in anger. "We'll get married and carry on as usual. If people want to talk, let them. We'll just grow tough hides and let their words bounce right off us." He gave a tickled laugh. "Won't Fletch be surprised when he comes home and finds he has a new mother."

Laura smiled weakly. Surprised wouldn't be

the word. Furious would more aptly describe what his reaction would be.

Two days later, on a Sunday, the small church was filled to capacity as Laura and Taylor stood before Reverend Stiles and spoke their marriage vows. All through the service there was a constant hum of whispering voices.

Justine Fraser, Laura's maid of honor and her best friend, stood up with her, full of curiosity, Laura knew, but she also knew the young woman would never question her. Elisha Imus, Taylor's longtime friend, stood beside him. When the ceremony was over, they accepted their friends' and neighbors' congratulations, best wishes that they knew were mouthed only because it was considered the right thing to do regardless of what they might think of the surprising marriage.

One woman didn't wish them well. She wasn't there. The widow Martha Louden. That one had had her sights on Taylor ever since her husband had been killed in a hunting accident three years ago. The plump, 54-year-old widow had been so determined to have him she hadn't even noticed that he paid no attention to her flirtatious smiles when she made unnecessary trips to the store almost every day. When she heard the news that Laura and Taylor would wed, she had been so outraged she had taken to her bed.

Before the newlyweds could escape they had

to parry questions for several minutes, giving away nothing, saying only that they had been thinking of marrying for some time.

And since none of their answers had been satisfying, gossip ran rampant, each person expressing his own view on why a beautiful young girl would marry an old codger like Taylor, and him being like a father to her all these years. Some wondered out loud if Fletch had known about their intention and that was why he had gone off to Canada. And if he didn't, what attitude would he take when he returned home?

As Taylor had said would happen, life went on as usual in the Thomas household. There was one exception. Laura took over Fletch's bedroom. It would be more handy than the loft room when the baby came.

And as Butterfly had predicted, Laura and Taylor, after a while, ceased being the main topic discussed whenever two townspeople met. Even when it became apparent that Laura was expecting, it was accepted as the natural result of any marriage.

That was until on a hot August night, after a long, hard labor, Butterfly delivered Laura of a baby girl who she named Jolie. Since the baby was tiny and delicate boned, everyone believed Taylor when he said that Laura had fallen in the barn and brought on an early birth.

However, after the neighbor women had come visiting to see the new baby, and to congratulate the parents, the gossip had started all over again. For Jolie, blond-headed and fair-skinned, looked glaringly out of place in the household of dark-skinned, black-haired Thomases.

Widow Louden was quick to remind everyone that before Laura married Taylor she'd had many young men come courting. "She always seemed to favor that blond-haired, blue-eyed Adam Beltran."

Someone else then pointed out that though he was handsome enough, Adam was built on the small side and was only a couple inches taller than Laura.

And Adam, somewhat lacking in good moral fiber, liked what was being whispered about him and Laura. Consequently, although he never claimed that the baby was his, he didn't deny the rumors either. He left it up to the community to believe what they pleased.

Laura noticed that he was always careful not to come around her with his self-satisfied smirks. She would have set him straight before long. But there wasn't much she could do to combat gossip that went on behind her back.

With a sigh, Laura rolled over and settled herself to sleep. Her last conscious thought was to wonder where Fletch was tonight.

Chapter Three

The day was drawing to an end as Fletcher watched the woman light two candles that sat on a rough-hewn table, then move to the fireplace to light the one on the mantel.

From his bed in the log-walled cabin he had watched Maida do this for three weeks. He lifted his gaze to the smoke-stained raftered ceiling. Maida and her common-law husband, Daniel, had saved his life. Daniel had found him while running his traps and had brought him here. Maida had then dug the bullet out of his shoulder and stopped the flow of blood that was draining the life out of him.

He had fainted in the middle of her probing for the piece of lead, and had remained unconscious as she closed the wound with 13 stitches.

Fever had gripped him then, and it had been Maida's knowledge of herbs and roots that had gradually cooled his burning skin and finally healed him. As Maida moved about preparing their evening meal, stirring a pot of venison stew that hung from a crane over the fire, then mixed up a batch of skillet bread, his mind lingered on the events that had brought him to this place and time.

It had been with mixed emotions he had left Laura and Big Pine that cool autumn morning. Laura had looked hurt and bewildered, and well she might. He had felt lower than a snake's belly for treating her so coolly on his leave-taking. But it wouldn't have been fair to her to do what he wanted to—take her in his arms and ask her to wait for him.

When he was first approached by the fur company he had thought the trip might provide just the breather he and Laura needed. The only reason he had agreed to their request was to get out of Laura's life for a while, give her the time to discover what her real feelings for him were. She was only 16, too young to really know her own mind. He could only pray that when he returned she would still be single and would want to marry him. She could do a lot of growing up in a year. She could change her mind about many things.

And so he had set out with his four companions, certain he was doing the right thing. Strapped on their backs were their bedrolls, a gear of tin cup, fork, and spoon, and the trail supplies they had divided between them. They also carried little bags of tobacco and rock candy in case they ran into Indians, of which there were many tribes between the Upper Peninsula and Canada.

Fair weather stayed with them through the balance of September and most of October with sunny days and cool nights. As they trekked through a forest so thick there were only narrow paths made by deer and moose that wandered aimlessly, they became aware of Indians slipping silently through the woods, keeping pace with them.

"What tribe do you think they're from?" Hank Manners, the leader of the group, asked Fletch.

"I'm not sure but I think they may be Fox or Sac," Fletch answered quietly.

"Do you think they mean us harm?"

"You never know with them. Some tribes are friendlier than others, and some hate the white man, will kill him every chance he gets."

"What do you reckon we ought to do tonight when he make camp?"

"For one thing, keep a fire burning all night and stay close to it. We could try putting out some tobacco and candy for them. Maybe they'd take it and move on. And of course a couple of us should stand guard over the camp all night."

Pretending that they weren't aware of the ghostlike figures dogging their footsteps,

Fletch and the men walked on, their hands close to the butts of their pistols. When they stopped to make night camp, the men went in pairs to gather firewood and to chop pine branches to lay their bedrolls on.

All five set to work clearing a wide area of pine needles, then building a good-sized fire in the center of it. While Dole prepared a supper of salt pork, beans, and hardtack, the others sat close to the fire, surreptitiously keeping an eye on the forest crowding in on them.

Fletch took the first watch after the others had turned in. He selected two pouches each of candy and tobacco and laid them down at the edge of the forest, then secreted himself behind a large boulder a yard or so from camp. From his hiding spot his eyes moved continually, watchful and alert. The Indians might not intend to harm them, but they were known to steal anything they could get their hands on, and the men needed everything they had.

It was nearly midnight and Fletch felt chilled to the bone when an Indian, with stealthy grace, suddenly appeared. By the light of the full moon Fletch watched him walk over to the gifts he had put out, stoop over, pick them up, then fade back among the trees. He waited ten minutes, then shook Hank awake. After a whispered conversation, Hank rolled out of his blankets and took up the watch.

As they moved on during the next several days, never sighting the Indians anymore, the days became cooler and the nights definitely cold. They had been on the trail six weeks when they came to Lake Huron, the separation between Michigan and Canada.

Now they were faced with the problem of getting across the large body of water. That was when they met Gray Owl.

They heard the slap of a paddle hitting the water before they saw the canoe appear from a bend in the lake. An old gray-haired Indian sat in the center of the birch vessel, a fishing line dragging behind him as he fished the edges of the water. When Fletcher hailed him, he nosed onto the shore and sat waiting for him to speak. His wizened face and snaggled teeth suggested that he was as old as the hills surrounding them.

"What is your name, old brave?" Fletcher asked, walking toward him.

"I am called Gray Owl."

Fletch gave his name, then asked, "Do you know where we could buy a craft like yours?"

After a thoughtful pause, Gray Owl answered, "I might let you buy this one, but not with money. Here in the wilderness an Indian has no use for the white man's green pieces of paper."

"What would you want, then?" Fletch wondered if he was going to ask for one of their rifles, and if so, should they give it to him and take the chance of him turning it on them.

"Gray Owl wants firewater. Bad weather is coming on and it will warm my blood."

Fletch shook his head. "We don't have any whiskey. Could we offer you some tobacco?" He felt encouraged by the glimmer of interest that shot into the black eyes that they would strike a deal.

The old fellow had been a wise trader, however, and before he turned the canoe over to them, all the rock candy had been handed over to him as well as half their tobacco.

When Gray Owl clambered out of the canoe and stood beside him, Fletch looked across the long stretch of water and sighed. "It's going to take us forever to paddle across this lake."

The owner of their candy and most of their tobacco pointed down the shore. "Three miles down you come to the narrowest strip of water. You can be across before sunset."

As the old Indian had said, they landed on the opposite shore with an hour to spare before darkness set in. While the others hurried to set up camp, Hank walked along the huge lake's shore. When he returned to a cheerfully burning campfire, he announced that this was the perfect spot for the fur post.

"Here, the Indians and the trappers can bring their furs by water as well as by land."

Everyone was ready to settle in one spot, and the next morning they set to work hacking out a clearing and building a long, sturdy cabin that would serve as the post, and also as their living quarters. All the while they worked, they kept a wary eye on the forest that bounded them on three sides. They knew that in the woods there was game—deer, moose, and rabbit to be shot for fresh meat—but also there were bears, cougars, and wolves. And they mustn't forget that there could very well be Indians slipping in and out between the trees, silent as ghosts. They kept their pistols strapped to their waists and their rifles always handy.

After the roof had gone on, they knocked together a table and two benches from hand-hewn boards. Then from small saplings a couple inches thick they built for each man a bunk bed. After they had moved into the building they would call home for some time, the days were spent felling trees and chopping them into lengths that would fit in the wide fireplace built from fieldstone.

When they felt they had sufficient fuel to last them through the winter, yards and yards of corded wood were stacked behind the post. It took Hank two evenings to burn out the name of the new post on a rough board about a yard long and two feet wide:

CANADIAN FUR COMPANY
TRADER AND BUYER OF FURS

When Hank fastened the sign over the door to their surprise, before they could build a counter in the business end of the building, two customers came in. First was a rough-looking white trapper; then later an Indian brought in some fine mink pelts.

Two mornings later when the men threw back their blankets and stepped outside to relieve themselves, there was a dusting of snow on the ground; an hour later the earth wore an eight-inch white blanket. By sunset the snow was up to the top of their boots. That night, riding out of the north on winds of gale force, roared a blizzard that rattled the windows and drove against the door.

Winter had come to stay.

The next morning they found snow drifted two feet against the cabin door. It took two men to push it open. Stepping outside, the men found that the wind had died down and the snow had stopped falling. However, the white stuff was up to their waists in some spots.

Business was brisk all winter as white trappers and Indians, snowshoes strapped to their feet, brought in fine furs. As word spread that Hank was an honest trader, never cheating any trapper regardless of his color, he had almost more furs than he could handle in the small quarters of the post.

They had been operating a month when one day Dole came in from hunting, bringing with him a young Indian woman. Hank frowned and said, "There's gonna be trouble over her. The rest of us are gonna be jealous, watching you tumble her every night."

Dole laughed good-naturedly. "I'm not gonna hog her. We'll share her equally."

The woman's Indian name was too hard for

the men to pronounce, so they called her Pansy.

Luckily for Pansy she enjoyed coupling as much as the men did, for she got a good workout every night, and sometimes during the day. Fletch received a lot of ribbing because he never took his turn with the willing Indian whore. He was asked if he was a priest in disguise, or if the severe winters in the Upper Peninsula had frozen his pecker off.

It had surprised him too that his manhood hadn't sprung to attention when he watched what went on between Pansy and his friends, especially when she sometimes serviced two men at the same time.

Since Fletch showed no interest in Pansy, she was determined that he would. She paraded around him buck-naked, her black eyes flashing him an invitation. One night, after the men had sated themselves and gone to sleep, Fletch was startled awake by warm lips moving on his rock-hard arousal, which had been brought on by dreams of Laura. It had been months since he'd had a woman, and before he could push Pansy away his body was jerking in a powerful release.

When she lifted her head and gave him a sly smile, he pushed her out of bed, grating, "Don't ever try that again, woman."

Everything went smoothly through the winter and on into the spring when the snow began a slow melting. It was late May with only patches of snow left in deeply shaded spots when visitors came from across the lake.

There were five of them, dirty and unkempt, all with tobacco-stained beards. They had pistols and skinning knives stuck in the waistbands of their greasy buckskins, and their sullen faces said they were looking for trouble.

As they clumped noisily across the wooden floor, heading toward Hank behind the counter, Fletch and the others quickly positioned themselves in places that gave them a clear view of each stranger's hands. If a move was made toward a weapon by any of them, they would know it and would take like action immediately.

Their action didn't go unnoticed by the strangers, and the spokesman said, "We're not here to fight . . . today. We've come to give you warning to clear out." He jerked a thumb over his shoulder. "Me and my men work for Hudson Bay Fur Company and our boss don't want any competition. We don't want to see you around here the next trapping season."

His hand firmly on the wicked-looking skinning knife at his waist, Hank came from behind the counter and stood in front of the belligerent speaker.

A slumbering threat of violence on his face, Hank rasped out, "Go back to where you came from and tell your boss that Hank Manners said he can go straight to hell. We ain't budgin' from here."

With angry, disgruntled noises the man's

companions started forward, then came to an abrupt halt when they saw four hands dart to long-barreled pistols.

It was a standoff as both sides waited to follow their bosses' lead. In the threatening silence that hung in the air, the trapper from across the lake finally grated out, "If you're still here next season you'll be the one who'll go to hell." He wheeled around and stalked out of the post, his muttering men following him.

Fletcher eased his body into a more comfortable position, favoring his wounded shoulder. He had planned to start for home shortly before their unwelcome visitors had arrived. The pain that had been in Laura's eyes when he left had haunted him ever since.

He wondered now, as he often did, if he had done the right thing in going off to give her time to discover if she loved him as a man she would want to marry. Or was it merely brotherly love compounded by infatuation with an older man?

After a month into the wilderness trip, his inner voice had begun to nag him, telling him that Laura wasn't flighty like the other girls in Big Pine who constantly changed their minds about everything.

Even as a little girl, she had been on the serious side. She always knew what she wanted and would stick to it like a dog worrying a bone.

Fletcher reminded himself that Laura was also very proud. His rudeness to her the morning he left might have cut her so deeply she decided to have nothing more to do with him.

He closed his eyes at that painful thought, telling himself it would serve him right if while he was gone Laura became interested in one of the many young men who were always hanging about. Like blond-headed Adam Beltran.

The trouble brewing between the two fur companies had made him stay on in Canada. He felt a sense of loyalty to Hank and the others. When you spent a long winter in one room with a bunch of men, you either became close friends or fierce enemies. In this case they had all developed a strong liking for each other.

The days passed in pleasant idleness, with no more visits from across the lake. In mid-September Fletch made plans to head for home, hopefully to arrive before the first snowfall. Dole, Jones, and Nick talked him into delaying his departure to go hunting with them one last time.

They left early in the morning, leaving Hank and Pansy alone at the post. When they returned in midafternoon, each carrying a young doe over his shoulder, they were met by utter devastation. Only the charred framework and a clutter of partially burned logs and the fireplace remained of the post they had worked so hard to build.

As he stared at the ravaged building, wondering where Hank and Pansy were, Dole shouted, "Over here, men!"

Fletch and Nick ran over to Dole who stood looking down at the ground. At the edge of the forest Hank lay sprawled on his stomach, a bullet hole in his back. Fletch knelt down and placed his fingers on one wrist, feeling for a pulse.

There was none. He stood up, shaking his head. "I'm afraid . . ." he began, then stopped short. The four men who had visited them in the spring stepped out of the forest, rifles held to their shoulders. Dropping their kills, Fletch, Nick, and Dole dodged for cover in the trees back of where the post used to stand. Shots rang out behind them, slicing leaves off the trees. Fletch saw his friends crumple to the ground as he dove into the deeper darkness of the forest. As he raced on, dodging trees and brush, he could hear the thunder of feet following him.

Had they shot and killed Pansy? he wondered, racing on, then thought that they hadn't. They would keep her for the winter and use her.

Run faster, his mind urged, *or you'll never see Laura again.*

It was near sundown, and Fletch was exhausted when he came to a small clearing, and hope rose inside him. Cleared land meant someone lived nearby. Maybe help lay ahead.

He was midway across the stump-scattered field when something caught the sunlight a moment. He saw a puff of smoke, and at the same time felt a bullet slam into his shoulder. As he looked wildly around for a place to hide, and to return the shot, a fierce-looking Indian seemed to come out of nowhere. With a bloodcurdling scream, he launched himself at Fletcher and grabbed him in a bear hug.

Fletch knew that the savage's intent was to squeeze the life out of him and he fumbled for the knife stuck in its sheath. With the last of his strength he withdrew the long blade and with a short, hard jab plunged it under the brave's ribs.

The Indian stiffened, gave a deep sigh, and wilted to the ground, a thin line of blood trickling from the corner of his mouth. The knife dropped from Fletch's nerveless fingers, and he fell to the ground, the back of his shirt soaked with blood.

Lantern-light shining in his eyes brought him back to awareness. It hurt him to breathe, to even move. After one effort to turn over on his side, he lay still. He slowly realized that his upper body was bare and that his shoulder was tightly bandaged. He recalled his encounter with the Indian and wondered who had found him and doctored him.

His slight movement was heard by the shaggy-haired, black-bearded man sitting before a brightly burning fireplace. He raised his stocky body from a roughly constructed chair and walked across the hard-packed dirt floor to stand over Fletch.

"Well, feller," he said in a deep, rumbling voice, "I see you've decided to come back to the livin'. For a couple days there I wasn't sure you was gonna make it."

"How long have I been here?" Fletch's voice was rusty from disuse as he fingered his whiskered face.

"Three days. Ravin' with a fever two of them days."

"Three days!" Fletch stared in disbelief. When he got over his shock he stuck out his right hand. "I sure thank you for savin' my bacon—"

"Call me Daniel. Last names ain't important here in the wilderness," the big man said gruffly as he shook hands.

"Well, then, you can call me Fletch. How did you come to find me?"

"I was out settin' traps along the lake when I heard a shot. I figured it come from the Injun I'd seen earlier skulking through the woods. I thought he must have seen a deer and took a shot at it. Then I heard his bloody screech and I knew he was jumpin' a white man.

"He was dead when I come upon the two of you." A grin stirred Daniel's beard. "You was nearly at the pearly gates, you was bleedin' so bad. I managed to get you on my back and bring you here to my cabin. It took Maida a long while to get the bullet out of you. The dad-burned thing was lodged beneath your shoulder blade."

Fletch eased his wounded shoulder into a more comfortable position. "I was one lucky man that you came along, Daniel." He looked solemnly at the big man. "I won't be forgetting that you saved my life, Daniel."

"Weren't nothin'." Daniel waved a dismissive hand. "I expect you'd do the same for me. Anyhow it was Maida who actually saved your life. It was her who got the bullet out, then sewed you up."

When Fletch glanced around the room looking for Maida, Daniel said, "She's out in the barn milkin' the cow. We ain't got around to marryin' yet. Ain't no preachers in these parts. We been meanin' to get back to civilization long enough to tie the knot. We want children, but Maida says not until we are hitched, that she won't bring a bastard into the world. You see, she's a bastard. Her stepfather was a mean son of a bitch. One night, a week after her mother had died from pneumony he tried to force himself on Maida. She managed to get away from him and run into the woods. That's where I found her, shivering and half scared to death. When she finally managed to tell me why she was out alone at night in the forest, I knew there was only one thing to do. Take her home with me."

Daniel rose and laid another log on the fire. When he sat back down he continued. "She was only fourteen, skinny, and not real purty. But she was awfully sweet. That sweetness of hers kept me from beddin' her until she was sixteen. I let her get to know me first, to know that, unlike her stepfather, I would never lay a hand on her in anger."

Fletcher thought of all his men friends, wondering if any of them would be as thoughtful as Daniel. He was pretty sure none would. He knew one thing, though. Daniel was one fine man.

Knowing that the bearded one wouldn't want his praises sung, Fletch said, "I hope my killing the Indian doesn't start an uprising against the whites in the area."

Daniel gave a short laugh. "His people will never know what happened to him. After I turned you over to Maida, I went back and buried him: scooped out a deep hole under a big rotten log. He won't be found in a hundred years. When he don't show up in his village and his people can't find him, they'll think a bear dragged him off to his den."

Before Daniel could say more the door opened and a young woman stepped inside, a pail hanging from her hand. "Your patient is finally awake, Maida." Daniel grinned at the bright-faced young girl.

"About time," she said, and Fletch received a wide, white smile. "I was beginning to think you were going to sleep your life away." Maida set the pail of milk on the table and walked over to the bed.

As Daniel had said, she wasn't pretty, Fletch thought, but she was comely enough with her brown eyes and shiny brown hair. Her voice was soft as she asked, "How are you feeling?"

Fletch's lips twisted wryly. "Pretty fuzzy-headed, but otherwise I feel all right."

"I expect you're hungry. I've got a pot of rabbit stew keeping warm on the hearth."

"I could eat that bear Daniel was talking about, fur and all." Fletch grinned. "My stomach hasn't known food for close to a week. I'm surprised I'm as strong as I am."

"It's not true that you haven't had any substance in your belly," Daniel spoke up. "Maida spooned a lot of venison broth down you while you was out of your head with fever."

"You did?" Fletch looked his surprise at Maida. "I guess that's why I don't feel so weak."

"Yeah," Daniel said. "Ain't nothin' like venison broth to build up a man's blood and strength."

As Maida began ladling stew into a wooden bowl from a black cast-iron pot, then sliced up half a loaf of sourdough bread, Fletch let his gaze travel over the room.

It was good-sized, caulked tightly between the logs. He felt no drafts in the corner where double bunk beds had been constructed. Opposite the fireplace was a table, a bench on either side of it. The two chairs flanking the fireplace completed the furnishings. And though the room was sparsely furnished, it was neat and clean.

Daniel was placing another pillow behind Fletch, then helping him to sit up. When Maida placed his meal in his lap, he tore into it like a hungry animal. When he had scraped the bowl clean and asked for more, Daniel shook his head.

"Your stomach will cramp if you eat any more. It's not used to solid food."

Daniel took a smoked-up coffeepot off the hearth. "How about a cup of coffee?"

Fletch grinned. "Sounds good. "Maybe it'll help fill the empty hole in my belly." Fletch was allowed a second cup of coffee, and while he drank it slowly, savoring its strong flavor, he asked, "When do you think I can travel?"

"Not for a while." Daniel poked up the dying fire and laid another log on it. "I'd say in about three weeks."

"Three weeks! I want to get home before winter sets in."

"You've got a nasty wound there, friend," Daniel said. "If it should start bleedin' again and you're on the trail alone, you'd most likely bleed to death."

"Where are you from, Fletch?" Maida settled herself on Daniel's lap. "I know you're not a native."

"I'm from Big Pine. It's in the Upper Peninsula in northern Michigan."

"I've heard of that settlement," Daniel said. "It's a right far piece from here." He stared thoughtfully into the crackling flames and after a couple minutes spoke again.

"You could probably strike out in a couple weeks if you had someone with you."

"Do you have someone in mind?"

"Maybe." Daniel tugged Maida's hair to make her look at him. "You still want to get married, gal?"

"You know I do, Daniel. I ache to hold your baby in my arms."

"All right then, we'll go with Fletch to Big Pine and stand before a preacher." He looked at a surprised Fletcher. "You've got one in Big Pine, don't you?"

"Hell, yes." Fletcher's teeth flashed in a wide smile. "I plan on using his services myself when I get back. We'll make it a double wedding."

"Is your intended named Laura?" Maida gave him a teasing grin.

Fletch smiled sheepishly. "I guess I talked a lot during my fever."

Daniel let loose a loud guffaw. "Talk? You never shut up talkin' about Laura. We know everything there is to know about her. You also raved a lot about some friends bein' killed. Do you mind tellin' us about that?"

With a long sigh Fletch told his story. After a few moments of silence, Daniel said, "You sure acted the fool when you went off and left your woman like that. Don't be surprised if she's not waitin' for you when you get back."

"I know it, man. I have nightmares about her marrying someone else."

"Well, let's hope for the best and in the meantime work at gettin' your strength back." Daniel gave Maida a light slap on the rear. "Bedtime, gal."

While the big man shoveled ashes over the fire, Fletch turned his head to the wall as Maida undressed and pulled on a nightgown. Minutes later, in the dark room, the bunk above him began to rock and creak as Daniel made love to his gal. Fletch hoped with a wry smile that the bed wouldn't fall on top of him.

Chapter Four

The valley below was veiled in a thin gray mist when Laura walked out onto the kitchen porch and sat down on the top step. With her knees drawn up and her chin cupped in the hand whose elbow rested on one knee, her gaze drifted over the wide yard that separated the cabin from the post. The flowers in their beds had long since bloomed, with nothing left but dried stalks and brittle leaves that had been driven into the mud by the cold rain last week.

She had saved their seeds, however, and would scatter them over the rich soil next spring. She narrowed her eyes at a movement at the edge of the forest. Animal or renegade Indian?

Laura relaxed when a bear, weighing close to

a thousand pounds, she judged, lumbered across the clearing, then disappeared in the forest.

"You'd better get yourself into a cave or hollow log pretty soon, fatso," she muttered. "Snow will be falling any day now."

And I'll be glad, she thought, leaning her head on a supporting post. Big Pine's women would be mostly shut in then and she wouldn't have to see their sly looks, or hear the snide remarks and whispered words that went on behind her back.

There had been some talk and raised eyebrows when she and Pa got married, but that was nothing compared to what was being said after they saw Jolie's fair skin and light blond hair. She had seen the shocked looks on their faces, the knowing smiles that had been exchanged.

No one in the village believed that Taylor Thomas had sired the little one.

Laura knew they were convinced that Adam Beltran had fathered her child. If she and Adam happened to be in the post at the same time, knowing looks and smirks appeared on the faces of others in the post.

A long sigh escaped Laura's lips. No one had been more surprised than she when she had her first look at the almost white hair on her little daughter's head. And later when the soft blue eyes remained blue she was doubly bewildered. The Thomases, as well as the Morrises, were dark of hair, skin, and eyes.

She had come to the conclusion that there could be only one explanation. Generations back there must have been a fair man or woman on one side of the family. An aunt or an uncle or maybe a grandparent.

She wondered what Fletch would think of Jolie if, and when, he ever saw her. And what would be his reaction to her marrying Pa? It would be awkward all the way around. Pa would probably be embarrassed a little, and Fletch was sure to feel shame that he had made love to his father's wife.

Laura hoped that the son would feel a lot of shame. It wouldn't be fair if he got off scot-free from their one time of lovemaking. So far she had borne the brunt of that event.

When would Fletch get home? she wondered. It was the last of October with winter nipping at their heels. If he didn't make it in soon, it would be many more months before the snow-choked passes melted, enabling him to get through.

But he'd return sooner or later, she knew. He and Pa were very close, and Fletch wouldn't stay away any longer than necessary. And there was Milly Howard, whom he'd been courting, the woman whom, according to gossip, he would marry.

Laura snorted her disdain for the woman. Milly certainly wasn't sitting home waiting for Fletch's return. Nightly she entertained some man or other. Laura shook her head. Why was Fletch so blind when it came to that slut?

The sun was beginning to sink and the air to grow colder, and Laura was thinking of going in when her friend Justine Fraser, the only one who had stood by her, called out a greeting. Laura looked up to see the pretty, bright-faced young woman walking briskly down the path that led from her parents' home a quarter mile away.

"You look mighty pleased with yourself." Laura smiled when her friend plopped down beside her.

"Oh, I am pleased. You'll never guess why."

"Old Eli at the mill asked you to marry him?" Laura teased. Eli was 75 years old and did odd jobs around the grain mill.

"You are so funny today, Laura." Justine slapped playfully at Laura's hands. "But someone did ask me to marry him."

"Justine! Who?" Laura exclaimed.

"Tommy Weatherford. Besides my parents you are the first to know."

Laura clasped Justine's hands between her own. "I can't tell you how happy I am for you, Justine. You've loved him for so long."

Justine smiled, her eyes twinkling. "I guess when you married Taylor, Tommy gave up his hope of getting you and turned to me."

"That's not true," Laura protested. "Tommy was never seriously interested in me. We were only good friends."

"He was interested in you, Laura, but I never held it against you. Every single fellow in the village had dreams of marrying you. Haven't you noticed that there have been two other weddings since yours? When you were suddenly out of their reach, the men started looking at the rest of us girls."

"You're mistaken, but I'm not going to argue with you. Now, when is the wedding taking place?"

"We hope before it snows." Justine blushed. "Tommy doesn't want to wait too long."

"I wonder why," Laura said, tongue in cheek, and Justine blushed all the redder.

Laura laughed softly, then asked, "Will you have your own home or will you live with his mother?"

"We'll have our own place," Justine said proudly. "Tommy felled the trees for the cabin a couple weeks ago and started framing it out yesterday. He waited until then to ask me to marry him."

"He's a smart young man to know that there is no roof big enough for two mistresses."

"Of which I'm thankful," Justine said. "His mother is very domineering. I'd hate living with her. The first thing Ma asked me was 'Do you have to live with that woman?' "

Justine looked at Laura and changed the subject. "I want you to stand up with me on my big day."

"Oh, but, Justine, are you sure?" Laura looked

alarmed. "You know the bad name I have now. Everyone will be scandalized."

"I don't care if they are or not. We've been close friends since we were little girls. It's my wedding and I'll ask whom I please to stand up with me. Those who take offense can just stay away."

"If you're sure, I'd be honored to stand beside you," Laura said, tears glimmering in her eyes.

Pretending not to see that Laura was ready to cry, Justine stood up and said, "Good, that's settled." Then she walked away, her head in the clouds.

Laura watched Justine disappear in the gathering twilight and felt a pang of envy. Lucky little friend, she thought, getting to marry the man you love. She stood up after a while and walked back into the cabin. Maybe she'd never know that joy, but her baby had a name, and that was more important than anything else.

It was a raw and wet day when Fletcher, Daniel, and Maida set out. A misty freezing rain glazed the surface of the deer trail they followed, making it almost impossible for Maida to stay on her feet. When she slipped and fell the second time, Daniel laughed, and after he helped her to her feet he hung on to her arm as they moved on.

Fletch, being a healthy specimen of manhood, had healed rapidly. Within a week he was able to go hunting while Daniel spent the time gathering up the traps he had laid down. He would reset them when he and Maida returned, weather permitting.

Fletch had shot three deer in as many days, and with Maida's help he had cut them into serving pieces to be cooked on the trail when they made night camp. He also cut thin strips of the venison which Maida roasted slowly over a low-burning fire. These strips of jerky could be chewed as they walked along, making it unnecessary to waste time by stopping to cook a noon meal.

All three were in high spirits. Fletch was looking forward to seeing Laura, to ask her to marry him, and Maida couldn't wait to get married and start her family. As for Daniel, he was always happy when his Maida was happy.

The rain stopped shortly before they made their first night camp, but it remained bitterly cold. As Fletch and Daniel erected a three-sided windbreak from pine boughs and Maida built a fire that would be their fourth wall, the men glanced up at the sky often, silently praying that snow wouldn't follow the rain.

Their prayers were answered. The skies remained clear and the air dry and cold.

The three travelers had passed into Michigan when they narrowly missed walking into a group of Chippewa Indians with war paint smeared on their faces. They barely had time to drop down in a thick patch of brush and hold their breath as they counted the braves passing within five feet of them.

There were 23 Indians. Fletch shivered when the last one disappeared out of sight. He and Daniel wouldn't have had a chance in hell trying to fight them off.

After that scare, for the next four days they holed up in the daylight hours and worked their way toward Big Pine under the cover of darkness.

One early afternoon under gray lowering skies the three finally stepped out of the forest and looked down on Big Pine. Maida was exhausted and needed a long rest. Both men had thinned down considerably, and Fletch's beard was as full as Daniel's. The surprising thing was there were streaks of blond in his mustache and facial hair.

Fletch's heart set up a wild beating as he paused to gaze down on the village. His eyes went straight to the post and the home place. No one stirred around the cabin, but the four horses tied up outside the post told him there was activity going on inside.

He looked at Daniel and Maida, the girl leaning tiredly against the big man, and said, "We'll drop in at the post first so you can meet my pa. While you gab with him a bit I'll look in on Laura." A flash of white teeth stirred his beard. "I'd like to see her alone at first."

"I don't blame you, friend." Daniel nodded. "You've got a lot of fence mendin' to do there."

A hush fell over the big room when Fletch pushed open the door of the post and stepped inside, Daniel and Maida behind him. None of the five men there recognized the bearded man at first, and suspicion flared in their eyes. Strangers weren't overly welcome in Big Pine.

"Hey, you wild timber wolves, it's me, Fletch," he laughed, his eyes going to the counter expecting to see his father standing there. Elisha Imus stood there instead, an uncertain smile on his weathered face.

Laughing and swearing good-naturedly, the men gathered round Fletch, slapping him on the back and shaking his hand. "We'd just about given up on seein' you make it in before bad weather," a trapper friend said. "How did you like Canadian land? Did you get them fellers settled in all right?"

Fletch's face grew sober. "I did. It's a long story, though, that I'll tell you about later. In the meantime I want you to meet my friends, Daniel and Maida. They came out with me to visit Reverend Stiles. They want to get married, and there aren't any preachers in the wild country where Daniel traps."

The men shook hands with Daniel and nodded to Maida. Then the door opened and Milly Howard came rushing in. She ran over to Fletch, crying, "I knew I recognized that big body of yours come in here." Grasping his arm, she smiled up at Fletch and said softly, "I'm so glad you're back. I've missed you so much."

Snorts of low-toned laughter said that Milly had been too busy with other men to miss Fletch Thomas. Every man there with the exception of old Elisha had slept with Milly while Fletch was gone.

Fletch gave his own amused laugh at the phony claim. He shook off her hands and asked, "Where's Pa?" When no one answered, concern etched Fletch's face. "He's all right, isn't he? Nothing has happened to him while I was gone?"

After several moments in the suddenly tense room, Elisha said evasively, "I take it you ain't been home yet."

"No, I haven't. We just got in. I figured to say hello to Pa before going up to the cabin."

"You're gonna have a big surprise when you get home," Milly spoke up slyly.

"Oh? What's that?" Fletch frowned at Milly, her tone telling him that he wouldn't like hearing her answer.

"You've got yourself a new mama."

"The hell you say?" Fletch laughed his surprise. "You don't mean to tell me that Pa finally got up the nerve to marry—"

"Laura," Milly said, finishing his sentence. "They got married shortly after you left for Canada."

While Fletcher stared at the smirking Milly, she added, "You'll get another surprise when you get home. You've got a new baby sister."

Their shoulders touching, Daniel felt Fletch

stiffen, so he said from the corners of his lips, "Steady, friend. Don't let your hurt show."

Fletch forced the rigidness out of his body, but as he fought to control his features, to pretend that he accepted the unacceptable, a black anger was coursing through his blood. How long had his father had his eye on Laura? Or had it been the other way around? How long had she planned on marrying the old fool? Did she hope to secure a permanent home for herself, to one day be a well-off widow?

Well, he thought with a rage that defied reason, his sire had slipped up. He should have taken the little bitch to bed a long time ago instead of treating her like a little princess, waiting until they spoke their wedding vows. His son had taken her virginity.

Fletch got another jolt when Milly volunteered, "We don't think the baby is Taylor's. It's fair and very blond . . . like Adam Beltran."

His fingers clenched into fists. She had put the horns on Pa right away. He hadn't been able to satisfy her, and she had turned to Beltran, the one she had always seemed to favor among the men who came courting her.

He turned his back to Milly. He didn't want to hear any more from her. He didn't think he could bear hearing one more word about Pa and his wife.

His tortured mind became aware that Daniel still stood beside him. What was he to do with him and Maida? It was out of the question to take them to the Thomas cabin as he had planned. It was his intention never to set foot in his old home again. He wished that he'd never have to lay eyes on the pair again. Maybe he would return to Canada with Daniel and Maida.

After thinking a minute, he looked at Elisha and asked, "Is that old place of Sam Crock's still empty?"

Elisha scratched his gray head. "I think so. It was last week. Why do you want to know?"

"Me and Daniel and his woman need a place to live for a few days. And we'll need some grub. When you get it together, send some kid over with it."

"What do you want, Fletch? Just regular staples?"

"Right," Fletch said, hurrying Daniel and Maida toward the door. If Pa should enter the store now he might hit him.

The sun had a couple hours left before setting as a brisk ten-minute walk took Fletch and his friends to the old forlorn cabin sitting in a clearing of about three acres. It had been vacant for over four years, ever since old man Crock had died from the flu one winter.

Weeds had taken over the place, even choking out the path that led to the sturdy building. Fletch ran a swift glance over the cabin. Its shutters were in fair condition, although one hung by one hinge and the second one had fallen off and lay on the ground. He noticed that some of the chinking between the logs needed to be replaced, but other than that the place was sound.

A good place for a man to live, he thought. *A place for a man such as you*, his inner voice suggested, making him ask why he should leave the community he'd lived in for 16 years, leave behind friends he'd known since he was a teenager. He had done nothing to be ashamed of, and damned if he would run away.

When Fletch pushed open the door, hung with leather hinges, there came the scampering of tiny feet as he stepped inside and field mice scattered in all directions. "Well, Maida, what do you think?" he asked as they stood amid an accumulation of four years' rubble.

She became ecstatic when she discovered there were two other rooms that led off the combination kitchen and family room. To one who had spent her entire life in a one-room cabin, first with her parents and then with Daniel, this cabin seemed like a palace, and she wished she could stay here forever.

When she walked back into the living quarters, she exclaimed in awe, "They have regular beds and chests in the bedrooms."

Daniel grinned at her enthusiasm and hugged her. Then Fletch asked with a crooked smile, "Do you think I could use one of the bedrooms? Or would I be in your and Daniel's way?"

"Oh, Fletch, do you need to ask?" Maida

scolded. "Me and Daniel wouldn't have it any other way."

With a rumbling laugh and a slap on Fletch's back that almost brought him to his knees, Daniel said, "Our castle is your castle, friend."

"Well, let's get busy and get this castle cleaned up," Maida said.

While Daniel made a fire in the rusty stove, and Maida grabbed up the broom leaning in a corner and began sweeping down cobwebs, starting with the ceiling corners, Fletch picked up a dented pail and walked to the back of the cabin where he knew there was a springhouse.

When the sun was about to set, and a curious youth had delivered their provisions, the kitchen and family room had been scrubbed clean. And though Maida looked ready to drop in her tracks, she hummed a little song as she bustled about preparing supper.

That night, early, all three completely worn out, they spread their bedrolls on the clean floor before the fireplace and fell asleep as soon as their heads hit their pillows.

Chapter Five

Laura had just bathed Jolie, dressed her, and laid her back in the cradle when she glanced out the window and saw Taylor hurrying toward the cabin. I wonder what he's forgotten this time? she thought, smiling to herself. Pa was always forgetting something.

"What did you forget this—" she said, starting to tease when Taylor stepped inside, then stopping at the look of bewilderment on the handsome middle-aged man's face. "What's wrong, Pa?" she asked with concern. "You look upset."

"I am upset." Taylor pulled a chair away from the table and sat down heavily. "Elisha just told me that Fletch came back to Big Pine yesterday afternoon. He had a man and woman with him, and instead of bringing them here, the three of them moved into that old cabin of Sam Crock's. He said that, although Fletch didn't say anything, he could tell that he was upset at the news of me and you getting married."

At first the news that Fletch had returned was all that stuck in Laura's mind. Then her pulse settled down and she could take in the rest of what Taylor had said. She wasn't too surprised at Fletch's reaction. Not that she thought he would be all that angry with Taylor, but she had figured all along that he would be incensed at her for marrying his father after letting him make love to her.

She sat down across from Taylor. "It was a big shock to him, Pa. Give him time to get used to the idea and he'll come around," she said, not believing a word she spoke. Fletch would never come home as long as she was here.

"Do you think so, Laura?" Taylor looked anxiously at her. "Me and Fletch have never had any harsh words all these years."

Laura reached across the table and gripped his hands in silent sympathy, heartsick that she had caused the rift between him and his son.

After a moment Taylor stood up. "I'm going over there to explain the whole thing to Fletch." He looked at Laura earnestly. "Don't be afraid that he'll tell anyone what I say to him."

Laura nodded. "I know that, Pa, but I still think you should give him a couple days to think things over."

Taylor shook his head. "I couldn't stand the

suspense of not knowing how he feels."

Laura went to the window to watch him strike off toward the old Crock place. After Pa told Fletch everything, would he suspect that Jolie was his, or would he believe, like everyone else, that she was no Thomas? Would he, too, think that Adam Beltran was her father?

Laura moved away from the window thinking that at least Fletch would feel better knowing that she and Pa didn't sleep together.

Taylor heard the ring of axes as he neared the old cabin and knew what it meant. Fletch and the man from Canada were cutting firewood. If they had an extra ax he'd give them a hand. When he was a few yards away from the sweating men, he called out, "Howdy. Laying in a wood supply, I see."

From the corners of his eyes he saw the stranger stop and lean his ax against a tree stump. But Fletch, after one glance at him, continued to swing his ax, sending wood chips flying. When it was evident that he had no intention of stopping and introducing his companion, Taylor walked up to the big man and with a friendly smile held out his hand.

"I'm Taylor Thomas. Fletch's pa."

Daniel looked at the weathered, open face, the warm glint in the eyes, and liked what he saw. Here was a good and honorable man. He grasped the offered hand and said as he shook it, "I'm right glad to meet you, Taylor Thomas.

Fletch has spoke of you often. Call me Daniel."

Taylor looked at his son, who still refused to look at him. "I don't suppose he's said anything good about me recently, has he?"

"Well, come to think about it, he ain't said anything, good or bad." Daniel grinned. "We've been busy cleanin' out the place a little. Although me and my Maida are only gonna be here long enough to get married, she wants the place shaped up a tad."

"Yes, women are like that." Taylor grinned. "They're great ones for neatin' things." He hesitated a couple seconds, then asked, "Is my son planning on going back to Canada with you?"

"Not that I know of."

"Daniel, I'd like a few words alone with Fletch."

Daniel nodded his understanding, then called to Fletch, "I'm gonna take a break and have a cup of coffee."

When Fletch continued to send the ax blade into a felled tree, Taylor walked up to him and grasped his wrist before he could raise the tool for another heavy whack at the birch timber.

"We've got to talk," he said when Fletch turned impatient eyes on him. "I know it must have been a shock to you, learning that me and Laura are married. But there was a good reason for us to wed. You see, I wanted to—"

"You wanted to bed her," Fletch said callously, angrily. He looked at Taylor with contemptuous eyes. "Wasn't Butterfly woman enough for you, you randy old goat?"

The blood drained from Taylor's face. He couldn't believe that his son had spoken so coarsely to him, thought so poorly of him. While he debated whether or not to go ahead and try to make Fletch listen to him, Fletch spoke again.

"I guess you know the little bitch cuckolded you into a laughingstock right off: birthing a fair white-haired baby."

Taylor stared at his son who had become an ugly stranger. He did not know this man, did not want to know him. After a moment he said with icy control, "If that's what you want to think, so be it." He turned and walked away, almost bumping into Daniel who was bringing him a cup of coffee.

"You were pretty hard on him, friend," Daniel said quietly. "He probably had no idea that you wanted the girl for yourself." He shoved the cup of coffee at Fletch. "Here, drink his coffee."

Fletch knew Daniel spoke the truth. He had never, by word or action, let anyone know how he felt about Laura. Hell, she hadn't even known until that night in the barn, and even then he hadn't told her that he loved her. He had acted like an ass by going off and leaving her, giving her time to know her own mind.

"He's still too damned old for her," was the only rebuttal he could come up with. "Look what she's done to him already, making his friends snicker behind his back."

Daniel nodded. "So it would seem. But if you had listened to Taylor you might have got a different story. The true one, I believe."

"I don't want to talk about it," Fletch growled and swung the ax into the log as though it were an enemy he was intent on killing. However, he was more angry at himself now. He was also ashamed of how he had struck out at the kindly man with such hurtful words.

But he hadn't wanted to hear that Taylor and Laura loved each other. There was no telling what he might have done. He might have struck Pa, and that would have been unforgivable.

Fletch continued to swing the ax for close to an hour, split logs piling up all around him. Daniel kept pace with him, wondering when Fletch was going to work the anger and bitterness from his mind.

When Fletch at last stopped to wipe the sweat off his face, Daniel leaned on his ax handle and asked, "You feelin' better now?"

"A little." Fletch shrugged and brought his ax down to bury its blade in one of the new half-dozen tree stumps. "I guess we ought to cord awhile," he said, clearly sending a message that he didn't want to discuss his run-in with his father any further. He bent over and started lining up the cut pieces of wood, separating the short stove pieces from the longer, larger pieces meant for the fireplace.

Daniel pitched in, and they had almost a cord finished when a feminine voice called, "My, but you fellows have been busy."

Both men turned around to look at Milly Howard coming toward them. Daniel's eyes narrowed on the overblown figure; the ripe breasts that bobbled as she walked, the wide hips that swung with each step she took. He knew women, and this one was man-crazy. It was almost embarrassing the way her eyes licked over Fletch, fastening on his crotch. He knew that she had known Fletch in the biblical sense and would like to again.

He looked at his friend to see if he was responding to the scarcely hidden invitation in the pale brown eyes. If Fletch wanted to, he could take the bitch behind a tree and hump her right now.

To Daniel's surprise, but satisfaction, Fletch didn't seem to be in the least interested in what Milly was offering. That was good. He didn't want his friend to become involved with this one.

Daniel didn't know that Fletch knew women even better than he did. Fletch was very much aware that he could take Milly right under the big man's nose if he had a mind to. But he had no desire to do so.

However, an idea struck him. He could use Milly to hit back at Pa and Laura. Pa had no use for the village tramp and had been upset last year when rumor had it that his son was thinking of marrying the woman who had known so many men. Fletch hadn't bothered to squelch the gossip, for he was using the older woman to hide his attraction for the younger one.

And Laura and Milly didn't like each other, so if he pretended to take up with Milly again, Laura wouldn't like that one bit. She'd be afraid he might marry her enemy and move her into the Thomas cabin.

He made himself smile at the woman clinging to his arm and say, "How've you been, Milly? Have you missed me?"

"Oh, I surely have, Fletch." Milly crushed his arm against her full, soft breast. "Shame on you for going off and leaving me for such a long time."

Fletch flicked a playful finger across the tip of her nose. "Were you true to me all that time?"

Daniel snorted his disgust when Milly answered sweetly, "You know I was, Fletch." He hoped that Fletch hadn't swallowed that lie.

All three looked at the cabin when Maida called from the door, "You men come wash up. I'm putting lunch on the table."

Damn, Fletch thought, Milly will expect to eat with us, and I don't think Daniel will want her around Maida. When Maida added with a smile, "Bring your company in with you," he looked at Daniel, and his big friend lifted a helpless shoulder as if to say, "What could I do?"

A short time later Daniel was sorry he hadn't done something.

Everything had gone well enough at first even though Milly had adopted a condescending attitude toward Maida within minutes. "I'll come over and show you how to pretty up the place," she said, gazing around the room. "And we must get you some nice dresses and put some curls in your hair; get you fancied up a little."

While Fletch held his breath at Milly's rudeness, Daniel grew stiff with indignation. "I don't want her fancied up like some whore," he said in a voice that Fletch and Maida knew came from a building anger. "I like her just the way she is."

Milly was smart enough to drop the subject of Maida's looks and switched to another topic. "I notice you don't have any young'uns runnin' around." She slid belittling eyes over Maida's slender, boyish figure. "Ain't you able to get bigged?"

"Oh, I'm sure I can." Maida laughed. Nobody knew better than she that her breasts were almost nonexistent and that she didn't have any curves to speak of. But Daniel didn't care, so she didn't either.

She looked at Milly and answered innocently, "As soon as me and Daniel get married we plan to have a large family." She laid an affectionate hand on her man's arm. "What with Daniel being so much older than me, he wants a son who will take care of me after he's gone."

"You mean you ain't married?" Milly pretended to be scandalized. "How long have you been livin' together? He can't have much respect for you." She nodded toward Daniel.

"Don't be too surprised if some mornin' you wake up and he's gone."

Daniel put an arm around Maida's shoulders when her face turned pale at Milly's harsh words. His black brows drawn together and his voice as cold as ice, he bit out, "You bitch. Don't you look down your nose at my little gal. She's only ever known one man. Can you say the same?"

When Milly only gazed at Daniel, knowing she had gone too far, he said through tight lips, "I want you out of our home right now. You're not fit to sit at the same table with this little lady."

Milly's face took on an angry red and she looked at Fletch for support. He was occupied with washing his face and hands. When he reached for a towel, completely ignoring her, she wheeled and stormed out of the cabin, a wide hip bumping into the table in her haste, making the plates and flatware jiggle.

"I'm sorry if I've offended you, Fletch, by ordering that woman away," Daniel said when the door slammed. "But I couldn't let the likes of her insult my little gal."

"Think nothing of it," Fletch said, pulling a chair away from the table and sitting down. "You beat me by a heartbeat telling her the same thing."

Daniel breathed a relieved sigh. "I'm sure grateful you feel that way. For however long me and Maida stay, this is your home. I'd sure hate for our friendship to break up over a slut like that one."

Fletch nodded that he had the same sentiments. Then, reaching for a hot biscuit, he said, "I don't want you and Maida upset, however, when I pretend to court the bitch."

Daniel studied his friend's face a minute, noted the bitterness on it, and said soberly, "Revenge is no good, Fletch. It can turn to ashes in your mouth."

"Not in this case, Daniel. It will taste as sweet as honey."

Maida nudged Daniel, cautioning him to let the matter drop. She changed the subject by saying, "I'd like to visit your preacher today, Fletch, and make arrangements for me and Daniel to get married as soon as possible. We can't waste much time if we're to get back home before all the passes are blocked with snow. I'm sure Canada has had some snow already."

"We'll go see him as soon as we're finished eating." Fletch smiled at her. "His place is only a scant mile from here."

Laura laid out everything she'd need for Jolie's bath on the kitchen table. When she finished bathing her daughter, she intended to take her outside for their daily walk. Once winter set in, the little one would seldom leave the cabin.

When she gently lowered the plump little body into the warm water, Laura was rewarded with a wide, toothless smile. Jolie loved her bath. Laura talked softly to her daughter as she lathered the soft skin and the blond hair that had grown long enough to twist into tight little curls.

When she had rinsed all the soap off the tiny body and curly hair, she lifted Jolie onto a towel that had been warmed and began to pat her dry. She had just powdered and dressed the little one when Taylor entered the room. "I forgot to take that loaf of bread you promised Elisha," he said. "He's waiting for it. Hunter hinted that he'd like a loaf too, if you can spare it."

Laura smiled. She liked Hunter, Pa's bartender. He was a quiet, handsome man who went about minding his own business. "The bread is over there." She nodded at the work bench next to the stove. "Take a loaf for Hunter too. But before you leave, will you hold Jolie while I get my jacket on?"

"Going for your morning walk, are you?" Taylor held out his arms for the baby.

Laura nodded, then smiled to herself as he started talking baby gibberish to the little one. When she had drawn on her jacket and taken Jolie from him, Taylor said musingly, "This little scutter reminds me of someone and I can't figure out who. It's the expression in her eyes and the way her lips curl up when she smiles."

Laura made no response. Little Miss Thomas didn't look like anyone she knew.

It was decidedly cool when Laura opened the

door and walked outside. An upward glance showed her a gray, threatening sky. Bad weather was on the way. When the baby caught her breath from the sharp air, Laura covered the small face with the end of her shawl.

Laura had no destination in mind when she started out and she was at first surprised, and then disgusted when she found herself walking along the path that led to the old Crock place. She never walked this way because it was a lonely stretch through the woods. She asked herself crossly if she had unconsciously hoped to run into Fletch.

Her lips firmed tightly. Surely that wasn't so. Not after the cruel and uncaring way he had treated her. She was about to turn around and retrace her steps when she heard the deep laughter of a man mingled with that of a woman. Almost at the same time two men and a woman appeared from around a bend in the path.

Her feet felt as if they were frozen to the ground as Fletch and his friends came toward her. When they were abreast, her eyes looked straight into Fletch's, and everything and everybody faded away.

He looks different, she thought, and not because of the beard he now wears. There's a hardness on his face that wasn't there before, and threads of gray at his temples. She shivered at the cold contempt that looked out of his eyes.

She forced her gaze away from him and

looked at his companions. They both smiled at her and she was quick to smile back. She needed these strangers' warmth to take away the chill of Fletch's stare boring into her.

She knew that he wouldn't introduce her, so she said, holding out her hand to Daniel, "I'm Laura Thomas and this is my daughter, Jolie."

Startled surprise darted across Daniel's and Maida's faces for a split second and then was gone. "I'm Daniel, ma'am," Daniel said, shaking hands. "I'm right pleased to meet you." He pulled Maida to his side. "This is Maida, the little gal I'm fixin' to marry." There was so much love for the young girl in the big man's voice that Laura knew a moment of envy. She would never receive that from a man, thanks to the one who had now averted his face from her.

Not allowing her bitterness to show on her face, Laura held out her hand to Maida. "Congratulations to both of you. I'm sure you'll be very happy."

"Thank you," Maida said, then asked, "May I see your baby? I can't wait to have one of my own."

Always eager to have Jolie admired, Laura lifted the shawl off the little face which immediately broke into a sunny smile.

"Oh, Daniel, look!" Maida exclaimed delightedly. "Did you ever see such a beautiful little thing?"

"She looks like one of them porcelain dolls," Daniel said, tickling Jolie under the chin, making her gurgle with laughter and wave her little arms around.

"May I hold her?" Maida looked hopefully at Laura.

"Certainly." Laura smiled and handed Jolie over into Maida's arms.

As the transfer was made, curiosity got the better of Fletch and his eyes were drawn to the infant. It was only a fast glance, one that the others didn't see. A strange feeling gripped his heart. It was almost as if this little one belonged to him. He felt a sense of pride toward her.

He knew a stab of hatred for Laura. Why couldn't she have waited until he returned home and let him give her a baby? He ignored the fact that he had never given her any indication of his feelings for her.

All he thought of now was to lash out at her, to hurt her the way he was hurting. "What does Pa think of this fair-haired baby you've presented him with?" he sneered. "The old fool can't possibly think it is his."

Maida gasped at his harsh words, and Daniel growled a low protest. But Fletch continued to flare at Laura with cold, contemptous words.

"You must have discovered right away that Pa wasn't man enough for you in bed, so you didn't waste any time picking up with that white-haired Beltran. That innocent baby is proof of your cheating."

When Laura only stood staring at Fletch, tears welling up in her beautiful gray eyes, Daniel growled, sharply and decisively, "That's enough, Fletch."

Turning his glaring eyes on Daniel a moment, Fletch struck off on the path that would branch off a few yards away to the preacher's cabin.

While Daniel stood helpless against Laura's tears, Maida asked her gently, "Are you all right, Laura? Should Daniel and I walk you home?"

"I'm fine, Maida." Laura scrubbed her eyes with her fists. "Fletch only said what everyone else is saying behind my back." With bitter resentment flashing in her eyes, Laura said through trembling lips, "They are all wrong. I swear before God that my baby is a Thomas. I don't know where my baby got her blue eyes and blond hair, but she certainly didn't get it from Adam Beltran. I've known only one man in my entire life."

Maida believed her and said so as she laid Jolie back in Laura's arms. "Someday, somehow, everyone is going to realize that, and there's going to be a lot of crow eatin' in Big Pine."

"And nobody will eat as much as Fletcher Thomas," Daniel predicted.

"Isn't it ironic that two strangers believe me when the people I've known all my life don't?" Laura heaved a ragged sigh and said lifelessly, "I usually don't care about what is whispered behind my back. I've grown a hard shell, and usually people's cruelty doesn't reach me. But

Fletch's words cut too deep. I felt the sting of his every word."

She smiled weakly. "He's had his crack at me now, and I don't think there's anyone else left that hasn't taken a swipe at me one way or the other—except for my friend, Justine." She pulled the shawl back over Jolie's face, as the air had grown colder, and said, "I'd better get back home. It's near Jolie's feeding time."

She looked at Maida. "It would please me if you'd come visit me once in a while. Of course if you're afraid of angering Fletch by doing so, I'll understand."

"Fletch doesn't pick our friends, little lady," Daniel spoke up. "But the thing is, we'll be pullin' out as soon as we get hitched. That's why we come home with Fletch. We're from Canada and it's a far piece from here."

"Oh." Disappointment showed in Laura's eyes. "I'm sorry to hear that, but I wish you both happiness in your marriage and I hope you have lots of babies."

"Me and Daniel wish you happiness, too, Laura, and we hope that Jolie will have a lot of little sisters and brothers to play with."

Laura shook her head. "Jolie will be an only child, I'm afraid." She shook hands again, wishing them good luck on their trip back home, then turned and walked away.

"I wish I knew the whole story there," Maida said when the slim figure moved out of sight and they walked on. "There's some kind of mystery there."

Chapter Six

Daniel and Maida came within sight of Fletch a short distance along the path to Reverend Stiles's cabin, but lagged behind him. They knew by the stiff carriage of his body that his mind was still on his meeting with Laura, and that his mood was dark.

Fletch's mood was actually a brooding one. Why, he wondered, did he still care for this woman who had come between him and his father, had had a child by another man, and then had the gall to pass it off as a Thomas? Why was it that even as he lashed her with insulting words, all he could think of was how soft her inner thighs were when he lay between them?

By the time the preacher's cabin came in sight, Fletch had firmly made up his mind that he would accompany Daniel and Maida back to Canada. He knew beyond a doubt that if he stayed in the vicinity he would do the unforgivable. He would seduce his father's wife.

He pulled his features into a semblance of calm and waited for his companions to catch up with him. As though nothing upsetting had happened, he said, "You're gonna like Preacher Stiles and his wife Ina." He led off down the path, and Maida and Daniel followed him.

A case of nerves gripped Daniel and Maida as Fletch knocked on the wide plank door. Other than having a baby, getting married was the biggest step either would ever take. Even so, they hoped they could say their vows within the next couple days.

They felt at ease immediately when a short, rotund man opened the door and greeted Fletch with a warm, welcoming smile. "Fletch!" he exclaimed. "It's good to see you again. We've all missed you, especially your pa." His gaze drifted to Maida. "Have you stopped by for a visit, or are you on official business?" His eyes twinkled.

"I guess you could say both," Fletch answered, stepping inside when the door was opened wider. "I want you to meet my friends Daniel and Maida. They've come down from Canada to get married."

Before he could control it, a brief flicker of surprise showed in Stiles's eyes. The man Daniel was old enough to be the girl's father. But, he thought, they seemed contented with each other and he shook hands with Daniel, and then with Maida.

"They'd like to get married as soon as possible and get started for home before the heavy snow blows in," Fletch explained as they took seats.

Stiles looked thoughtfully at the floor a moment, then looked up and said, "Why don't we do it now? Unless, of course, you're planning on something fancy, all dressed up with a party afterwards."

"No, we ain't got nothin' like that in mind," Daniel denied in a hurry. "We just want to get hitched all legal like so Maida can have her babies she's always yammerin' about."

Stiles smiled at Maida and said, "Then we'll do it now. I'll call my wife Ina in to be the other witness."

A short, plump woman with smiling eyes and gray hair pulled into a bun on top of her head bustled into the room and, after a short pause, threw herself at Fletch. "I didn't recognize you at first, Fletch." She hugged him. "Why are you hiding that handsome face behind all that brush?"

"I guess I just got too lazy to shave." Fletch grinned down at her. "I'm gonna get rid of it, though. It's scratchy as h . . . the dickens," he caught himself.

"Ina," her husband interrupted, "this is Daniel and Maida. They're going to get married now and we need you to witness the ceremony."

After introductions had been made, everyone took their places and the reverend opened his worn Bible.

It was a solemn ceremony, the man of the cloth giving it the same careful attention he would to someone of more importance than the rugged trapper and the thin, young girl. He recognized true love when he saw it. Ina loaned Maida her wedding ring, and it was done.

Fletch shook Daniel's hand and kissed Maida's cheek. When Daniel and Stiles bent over the marriage certificate, the preacher writing down the year and date, taking the newlyweds' names, Fletch thought with a wry grin that he still didn't know his friend's last name.

Maida returned the ring to Ina, and Daniel slipped a bill into her husband's hand. Then, with the preacher's blessing following them, the three left the cozy little cabin.

Maida and Daniel, moving in a happy glow, didn't notice that the air had grown colder and that the sky was darker. But Fletch noticed and spoke about it.

"We'd better move out early tomorrow morning. There's a blizzard building up, and when it hits it's gonna be a bastard."

Daniel pulled Maida to a halt in the middle of the path. "Did I hear you right, Fletch? You intend going back with us to Canada?"

Fletch nodded soberly. "I think it's best I get away from here for a while. There's no telling what I might do if I stay on in Big Pine."

Daniel studied his drawn face a moment, then with a knowing look in his eyes nodded and said, "You're probably right, friend. Me and my missus"—he paused and grinned down at Maida—"will be glad of your company. We'll move out tomorrow mornin' at daybreak."

That evening, after Maida and Daniel had gone to bed, Fletch stepped out on the small porch and leaned against a post. A full moon drifted in and out of dark clouds, lighting up the area, then throwing it into darkness. When one of its illuminations revealed a man slipping through the forest, Fletch jerked erect, swearing under his breath.

That shadowy figure was his father. Surely Pa wasn't still going to visit Butterfly! I'll soon find out, he thought, and stepped off the porch.

He kept a safe distance behind Taylor, stepping quietly. When Taylor turned onto the path leading to the Indian village, Fletch feared his suspicions were right. Then, at the edge of the village, Butterfly stepped out of the forest and Taylor took her into his arms.

Fletch clenched his fists, wanting to go after his father and do him harm. How could he continue to see his Indian lover when he had a young, beautiful wife like Laura waiting for him at home?

The thought came to him that it was Taylor's fault that Laura had gone to another man to get what her husband wasn't giving her.

In the end he told himself it was none of his

business and turned around and walked back to the cabin. He was more sure than ever that he had made the right decision to leave Big Pine.

After Laura had laid the sleeping Jolie in her cradle, the snow began to fall. It fell silently and straight down, a white curtain that Laura couldn't see a foot beyond. Winter has arrived, she thought as she took up her knitting needles and sat down before the fire. As the needles clicked against each other she worried about Taylor getting home. Surely he wouldn't try to return tonight. He could very easily get lost in the forest. She felt he'd be wise enough to stay with Butterfly until daylight.

Laura refused to let her mind stray to Fletch the way it wanted to. After the things he said to her today she'd be a fool to give him another thought.

When she went to bed, a peek out the window showed that at least a foot of snow had fallen, and more was still falling. She looked around the area and saw only one light burning. The lamps were still lit in the pleasure house. There would be some surprised people when they looked out the window in the morning.

When Fletch awoke, he knew by the silence that it had snowed last night. "Damn," he swore, rolling out of bed. "I hope it was only a light squall." When he opened the door he couldn't believe his eyes. A carpet of snow on the ground reached to the thighs of an average man. Smoke lifted from cabin chimneys, but he saw no one stirring outside.

His first thought, like it or not, was that he and Daniel and the new wife were stuck here until spring.

As he got dressed, preparing to find a shovel and start clearing a path to the post, he told himself that if he was careful he shouldn't run into Laura very often. The weather would keep her inside.

He was debating whether to wake Daniel and give him the bad news when the big man walked out of his bedroom, clad in longjohns and scratching his beard.

"Take a look outside," Fletch said by way of greeting.

Daniel swore long and loud when he saw the snow that reached past the porch floor. "Dammit, Fletch," he raged, "we're stuck here for the winter. How am I supposed to provide for Maida?"

"You're not thinking straight, man," Fletch said. "You'll take care of her the same way you did in Canada. Do you think that's the only place a man can lay his trapline? There's real good trapping around here. The men mostly catch wolverines, but there's otter and mink and silver fox and beaver.

"And another thing. Maida might like spending a long winter where she can have female company for a change. She's got to have been awfully lonesome while you were out running your traps all day. And the cabin will be weather tight once we do some caulk patching and tightening the window sashes and mending the shutters. You've got to admit it's a hell of a lot bigger than your place in Canada."

"All right!" Daniel held up his hands in surrender. "I get your meanin'. You reckon I can buy traps and a pair of snowshoes at your pa's store?"

"Yes, you can, but I wouldn't be surprised if you can't find all you'll want in that shed back there in that stand of birch. Sam Crock was a trapper."

Daniel rubbed his hands together, excitement building in his eyes. He'd be able to do what he most loved doing. The only difference was that he'd be doing it in a new locale. "Maybe we'll find some shovels in there too so we can start digging out of here."

"I expect so. Every cabin has two or three shovels. The snow is powdery soft, so it won't be too difficult to wade through it."

"I'll get some clothes on and be right with you," Daniel said, rubbing his arms, beginning to feel the chill of the room. "But first I'll roust up the fire in the fireplace and build a fire in the stove. I want it to be warm when Maida gets up."

Fletch's lips twisted in an amused smile as he

left the cabin. Daniel sure took good care of his gal.

They found two shovels in the shed and noted the many traps hanging on the walls. Daniel would have to grease them up, but they all seemed in good condition. Three pairs of snowshoes were hanging with the traps. Daniel grinned. He was in business.

Fletch and Daniel had been shoveling but a few minutes when other men and their sons were out doing the same thing. The younger boys were making a game of it, whipping snowballs at each other, wrestling around in the snow.

Greetings were called to each other as shovelsful of snow flew in the air. Fletch kept looking toward the post and the Thomas cabin. Smoke curled from the home place chimney but none showed from the post. Nor was his father out shoveling. Was he still with Butterfly? He wondered then if Taylor had tried to make it home last night and couldn't make it. What if he'd become lost in the storm and lay exhausted and freezing somewhere?

Fletch had made up his mind to make his way to the cabin and find out if everything was all right when through the snow-laden pines back of the post he saw Taylor approaching the post. The snow was only half as deep on the forest floor, and Taylor was moving at a fast clip.

"You'd better hurry, you stupid old man," Fletch muttered. "Someone is going to spot you sneaking along any minute and start asking a lot of embarrassing questions. Like how did you get to the post without leaving any tracks in the snow from the cabin."

He watched Taylor push his way through the deeper snow of the clearing, and he was reaching for the post's doorknob when suddenly he was slipping and falling awkwardly into the snow. Fletch saw his father clutch his right leg, his face contorted with pain.

Concern in his voice, he called out to Daniel who was shoveling a path to the privy. "Pa just fell—I think he's hurt. Let's go take a look."

Taylor's face was pinched and white when Fletch and Daniel reached him. He looked up at Fletch through pain-clouded eyes. "I think my leg is broken, son," he said, his voice ragged.

"Let me take a look." Fletch knelt down beside him and ran his hands over the twisted leg. After a couple minutes he looked at Taylor and said, "It's fractured just above the knee. There's no bone sticking through the skin, so I think it's a clean break."

"Damn." Taylor grimaced. "Just when I'll be busiest at the post."

The other men who had been shoveling had waded through the snow and now stood looking down at Taylor. In their concern for him they hadn't noticed that the snow was untouched between the post and the cabin.

"Shall we carry you into the back room of the store or get you up to the cabin?" Fletch asked.

"Best put me on the cot in the storage room. I can at least keep an eye on what goes on in the store."

Fletch nodded and lifted Taylor's broad shoulders while Daniel carefully took hold of his legs. One of the watching men jumped forward and supported his back and waist, and Elisha opened the post door. Taylor was carried inside and carefully laid on the narrow cot.

When Fletch straightened up he asked Daniel, "Do you know anything about bone setting?"

"I've set a few." Daniel nodded. "A man has to be able to do a lot of things when he's living in a Canada wilderness. If it's a clean break like you think, there won't be nothin' to it. I'll need two flat boards about fourteen inches long and about five inches wide. And several strips of cloth around four inches wide."

"Fletch," Taylor said, pain evident in his voice, "try to make it to the cabin and tell Laura what's happened. She'll be worried. She'll also tear a sheet into strips for you to bring back."

The last thing Fletch wanted to do was see Laura, especially alone. He knew, however, that he had no other alternative. Their neighbors would flap their tongues if he refused.

Drawing a long breath, he left the post and started battling his way through the snow toward the cabin.

Gray morning had arrived by the time Laura awakened and found the snow up to her windowsill. She hadn't rested well last night, half awake, listening for Taylor to come home. For though she had told herself he was sure to stay with Butterfly until the weather cleared, she couldn't help worrying that he was out there somewhere in the storm, maybe in need of help.

She had toyed with the idea of going to Fletch and asking him to go look for his father. Two things warned her not to. One, he'd probably refuse to and they would get into a heated argument, and two, she didn't want him to know that Pa still made his trips to visit Butterfly. He'd really chew on that piece of information. As would everyone else if they learned of Pa's long association with the Indian woman and that it still continued.

The second time Laura went to the window to gaze in the direction of the post, hoping to see smoke rising from the chimney, the village men were out shoveling paths, Fletch and his friend among them. She wondered if Daniel and Maida had fulfilled their arrangement with Reverend Stiles to marry them. It occurred to her that the couple wouldn't be able to leave Big Pine now. She hoped that they wouldn't mind, because she would like to know the young girl better.

Jolie fussed, and Laura picked the little one up and sat down in the rocking chair before the fire, talking nonsense to her as she laid back the lapel of her robe and undid the ties to her gown.

By the time the baby had finished nursing

and had been changed and laid back in the cradle, close to an hour had passed before Laura went to the window again and gave a startled, "Oh, my God."

She saw Taylor being carried into the post. Her mind raced with questions. Had Pa suffered a heart attack from fighting his way through the snow? Had he reached the post sometime last night only to fall exhausted outside its door? God forbid that he had frozen to death. She desperately wanted to go to him but knew it would be next to impossible to get through the snow that would reach her waist. Besides, she couldn't leave Jolie alone.

So she stayed glued to the window willing someone to come and tell her what had happened to Taylor. When the post door opened and Fletch stepped outside, she leaned forward, peering intently. He spoke a moment to the men standing around, then started plowing his way through the snow toward the cabin.

It seemed to Laura that it was taking forever for Fletch to close the distance between the cabin and the post. When he finally pushed his way onto the porch, she swung the door open, demanding in a shaky voice, "What's happened to Pa?"

Fletch stood a moment, catching his breath, then said derisively, "Pa? You call your husband Pa?"

Laura wished she had the strength to grab his wide shoulders and shake them until his head wobbled. "I said Pa out of habit," she said impatiently. "Is he all right? What's happened to him?"

Brushing the snow off his legs and stamping it off his feet, Fletch answered, "Let me inside and I'll tell you."

Laura stepped back, giving him ample room to enter. Still, he managed to brush against her, his elbow sliding against her breasts. She shot an angry look at his handsome, bland face. Had it been an accidental touching, or had it been meant as a deliberate action that a man would do to a loose woman?

However it had happened, she let it pass. She had more important things to wonder about. "All right, Fletch," she said impatiently, closing the door behind him, "you're inside now. What's happened to P . . . Taylor?"

Fletch deliberately took his time unbuttoning his heavy fur-lined jacket before finally saying, "Pa slipped in the snow and broke his leg."

"Oh dear!" Laura's face paled. "Is it a bad break? Is he suffering a lot?"

"He's in pain, of course, but it's a clean break according to Daniel and should heal all right. Daniel is going to set it, and he needs some strips of cloth to bind the splints with. Pa said you'd give them to me."

"Of course. Is there anything else you need?"

Fletch looked at her slender form, the curves revealed by the robe wrapped tightly around her, and wanted to say, *I need you. I need to bury myself inside you to take away my ever present ache for you.*

He looked away and said, "He'll need bedding. That old cot in the back room only has a straw tick on it."

"Won't he be coming home?" Laura asked, a tiny frown forming between her eyes.

"He says he's gonna stay there, keep an eye on things."

"How's he going to do that, flat on his back?"

"I guess he'll keep the door open between the two rooms. The cot sits right across from it, so he can see what's going on, keep an eye on whoever is gonna run the place."

"He'll probably ask Elisha to run it."

"Probably," Fletch said, then asked abruptly, "How come Pa is still seeing Butterfly? Don't you give him what he wants?"

Fire flashed in Laura's eyes. "I can't believe your gall, your crudeness." She glared at him. "First off, it is none of your business what goes on between me and Taylor. And as you know, he and Butterfly have been friends for years. It's only natural that he would like to see her once in a while."

"And sleep with her too?"

"You don't know that," Laura snapped and wheeled around, heading out of the kitchen. "I'm going to get dressed now and gather the strips and bedding."

Fletch made no response as he watched the angry twist of her hips as she passed into what used to be his bedroom. A puzzled look came over his face. Didn't she and Pa share the same bed? What in hell went on here?

Laura had barely closed the door behind her when Jolie began to fuss. Against his will Fletch was drawn to the cradle. When he gazed down at the tiny mite he received the same sensation he'd experienced the first time he'd seen the baby. What was it about this little one that gave him such a warm feeling?

He bent over and held out a finger to Jolie, who watched him with wide blue eyes. She grasped it and held on tightly. He was startled at the tenderness that rushed through him. He wanted to pick her up, hold her against his heart to mingle its beat with that of her tiny one.

Fletch forced himself to remember that Adam Beltran had fathered the child, and when Laura returned with an armful of bedding, he was back on the kitchen side of the room, staring moodily out the window. She laid everything on the table, then walked over to the cradle. When Fletch turned around and looked at her, she had taken Jolie up and was wrapping her in a heavy shawl.

"Why are you bundling her up like that? It's plenty warm in here."

"I can't leave her here by herself."

Fletch narrowed his eyes at her. "I hope you're not planning on going to the post."

"I certainly am. Taylor needs me."

"You're crazy, woman. You can't get through that snow."

"Yes, I can," Laura insisted as she shrugged into a heavy jacket and buttoned it up. "I'll walk in your footsteps."

Fletch looked at her small, mutinous face and sighed. Ever since she was a little girl, if she got a thing in her head to do, she was bound to do it.

"All right." He scowled, picking up the folded bedding and walking to the door. "But you're gonna find it hard walking."

"I'll be right behind you, Mister Know It All." Laura gathered Jolie up and followed him outside.

They hadn't gone three yards when Fletch heard Laura puffing as she stretched her legs to step in his tracks. He tried to harden his heart against her struggling but found that he couldn't. He had looked after her too many years to break the habit now.

He stopped and turned around. "Give me the baby before you fall and hurt her," he ordered.

He thought for a moment she was going to refuse, but finally she said, "All right. I'll carry the blankets."

The transfer was made, and holding the little one close to his chest, liking the feel of the little body next to him, Fletch shortened his steps so that Laura could more easily place her feet in his tracks.

"Honey, what are you doing here?" Taylor exclaimed when Laura pushed her way through the group of men gathered outside and burst into the storage room. "How did you get through all that snow, and where is Jolie?"

"Fletch has her," Laura answered, taking off her jacket and kneeling beside the cot.

"Fletch has her?" Taylor said, disbelief in his voice.

Laura nodded with a crooked grin. "He was afraid I'd drop her in the snow." She looked up and smiled a greeting to Daniel and Elisha standing nearby, waiting to set Taylor's leg.

"You about ready to get on with it, Daniel?" Fletch asked gruffly from the doorway, strips of cloth he had torn from the sheet clutched in his hand.

"Where's Jolie?" Laura jumped to her feet.

"I put her in a basket and set her on the counter so she wouldn't get stepped on," Fletch answered indifferently. "She's still asleep."

"You put her in a basket like she was a little puppy?" Laura screeched at him.

"Settle down, she's fine." Fletch busied himself with taking off his jacket and hanging it on the wall. Elisha had built a roaring fire in the potbelly stove in the store and its heat now reached the storage room.

"Go look after her, Laura," Taylor said, "and close the door behind you."

She knew that Taylor didn't want her to see or hear his pain when the bone was set. Still she hesitated. She wanted to hold his hand, to comfort him when Daniel ministered to the break. But when Taylor said firmly, "Go on, Laura," she walked into the store and quietly closed the door, leaning on it, waiting.

Her fingers clenched into fists a few minutes later when Taylor gave a harsh cry of pain. Daniel had set his break. She rushed back into what would be Taylor's bedroom for some time and sat down on the edge of the cot. She took a handkerchief from her sleeve and dried the sweat that had beaded on his forehead.

She watched Daniel and Fletch winding the strips of cloth around the splint that would keep the break together until it knit and healed. She looked back at Taylor's pale face and asked gently, "Can I get you anything, Pa? Maybe a swallow of whiskey?"

Taylor smiled weakly and shook his head about the whiskey. "Believe it or not, it's food I'd like. I'm hungry as sin."

"Fine. How does bacon and eggs sound to you?"

"Sounds real good, but first I'd like a cup of coffee. Haven't had any since last night at supper."

While Laura was wrinkling her brow, wondering how she could fry bacon and eggs and brew a pot of coffee on a 14-inch stove top, Daniel and Elisha left.

Laura remembered the potbelly stove in the tavern part of the post and looked at Fletch, who was pulling on his jacket, preparing to leave. "Would you build a fire in the other stove and put a pot of coffee to brewing before you leave?"

Fletch frowned, but before he could answer, Taylor said anxiously, "Don't leave the post until we've talked, Fletch."

"I can't hang around long," Fletch said coolly, not looking at Taylor as he took his jacket back off. "I have to give Daniel a hand with the shoveling."

There was so much hurt and sadness in Taylor's eyes as he watched his son leave the room that Laura wanted to run after him and beat his broad back with her fists. He had no right to hurt Pa like that.

If only I could tell him the truth about everything, he wouldn't act so high and mighty, she thought, walking into the store area.

But that would never happen, she knew, and she set about taking the utensils she would need from the shelves where they had been placed for sale. She ground a handful of coffee beans and set them aside, along with the old coffeepot Taylor always kept on the stove.

She didn't look up from slicing bacon when Fletcher came to collect the coffee and pot. If she looked at his sullen face she would say something that would start an argument, and Pa didn't need to be any more upset than he was already.

She exclaimed impatiently when Fletch took the pot outside to pack it full of snow and slammed the door behind him. He had awakened Jolie, who had set up a wailing, hungry cry. Without thinking, she put the bacon aside and picked the little one up and sat down on a stool behind the counter. She had bared her breast to the tiny mouth when Fletch returned.

He stopped dead, his eyes fastened on the creamy mound of Laura's breast pressed against her daughter's mouth. He remembered his mouth there and immediately became aroused, his hard length pushing against his buckskins. Laura hadn't seen him yet, all her attention on her nursing baby. He made a scraping sound with his feet and pretended not to see her as he walked into the tavern room.

Jolie finally had her fill, and Laura laid her back on the blanket Fletch had folded and placed in the bottom of the basket. She begrudgingly admitted that it had been thoughtful of him to make her baby as comfortable as possible. At least he wasn't taking his spleen out on her.

When she brought a loaded breakfast tray to Taylor later and placed it on his lap, Fletch leaned against the wall, his arms folded across his chest, watching her fuss over his father.

She doesn't treat him like a husband, he said to himself. *She still treats him like a father.* What in the hell kind of marriage did they have anyhow? They didn't even share the same bed, for heaven's sake.

It came to him like a hard blow to the head.

In the biblical sense they weren't husband and wife. He hadn't really believed it before, but he believed now what was whispered about Laura and Adam Beltran. The bastard had got Laura in a family way, and Pa had married her to save her good name. Everything fell into place, including his father's continued visits to Butterfly.

He looked at his father's pain-etched face and regretted the harsh accusations he had hurled at the kind man. Somehow he must make it up to him. As for Laura, nothing had changed in his regard for her. If anything, it had slipped lower. While he had lain awake nights, longing for her, praying that she would have him when he returned, she had been lying with Beltran, letting him get her with child.

He couldn't bear to look at her as she sat before Pa, talking to him in her low, sweet voice. How could Pa still be so nice to her, knowing what she had done?

When Taylor finished his breakfast and Laura took the empty plate away, Fletch began his atonement by walking over to the bed and saying cheerfully, "Well, Pa, it looks like I'll be running the post while you're laid up."

Taylor looked up at him in startled surprise, then gave him a wide, pleased smile. "I was gonna ask you to do that, son. Reckon you can handle it?" he bantered. "There won't be much time for you to carouse with your friends. You'll be stuck here fourteen hours out of twenty-four, every day, seven days a week."

Fletch's eyes glinted humorously. "I guess if an old codger like you can do it, a young buck like myself will have no problem at all. I'll manage to find time for my friends and women."

Taylor stretched a hand to him. "Shake. It's a deal. You might as well start right now. The place should have been opened for business a half hour ago."

"I've got to go tell Daniel first."

"You've got to help Laura and Jolie home, too. And hire a couple teenagers to shovel a path to the cabin."

He's going to refuse, Laura thought as a dark flush of resentment spread over Fletch's face. After a moment, he turned frosty eyes on her and practically growled, "Are you ready to go?"

"I can make it on my own," Laura answered, her voice as cold as his.

"Get your jacket on and stop acting like the Queen of Sheba," Fletch half snarled. "I haven't got time to put up with your foolishness."

"I'm not being foolish, you . . ." Laura began, then saw that their bickering was upsetting Taylor. She snapped her mouth shut. She'd give the no-good woman chaser a tongue-lashing later on.

Chapter Seven

Laura wasn't to get the chance to give Fletch a piece of her mind. As soon as they pushed their way through the snow to the cabin, Fletch shoved Jolie in her arms as soon as she opened the door. Before she could spit out the heated words she'd been holding back, he turned and walked away. She couldn't very well run after him hindered by the snow and Jolie in her arms, so she slammed the door shut, still biding her time.

Daniel was clearing a path from the post to the house.

"How's it goin' with your pa?" he asked, pausing in his shoveling.

"He's doing all right. He just ate a hearty breakfast." The corners of Fletch's mouth lifted.

"We kind of made up. I'll be running the post for him until his leg mends."

"Well, now, I'm right happy to hear that." Daniel's teeth flashed in a smile. "A son and father should get along with each other. Me and my pa was always close. He's been gone twenty years now, but I still think about him and miss him."

"Daniel," Fletch said soberly, "I hope you and Maida have a whole bunch of sons. You're gonna make one hell of a good father."

"Thank you, friend." Daniel was pleased at the compliment. "I'd like for there to be a couple little girls for Maida, though. You know, little dolls for her to play with, her bein' so young herself."

Girl babies were like little dolls, Fletch thought, thinking of Jolie, remembering how good she had felt in his arms, and how he had resented the fact that she wasn't his.

"Will you be stayin' on with me and Maida, or will you be livin' at home?"

"I'll be staying with you two if it's all right. I don't want to be around Pa's wife any more than I have to."

"Of course we'll be glad to have you with us," Daniel said, then frowned at his stony-faced friend. "I've got the feelin' you've forgiven Taylor, why not the girl, Laura? Why do you still hold this animosity for her? I'm sure she didn't hold a gun to your pa's head and force him to marry her."

"No, she used something more powerful. She used his love for her against him."

Daniel thought that he understood what Fletch was saying but he wasn't too sure. He'd ask Maida later. She was a very wise person.

"Well," Fletch said, "I'd better get on and open the post for business. I see a couple men headed this way. They'll be wanting something."

"What about your breakfast? Have you eaten anything?"

"I can make myself some bacon and eggs on the heating stove."

Daniel nodded. "I'll bring you over a meal around noon."

"That sounds real good, Daniel. As for supper, Pa always closes the store between five and six so he can eat the evening meal."

Daniel nodded again. "Maida will have supper on the table then."

Fletch said, "Thank you," then added as he turned to leave, "I've got to get hold of a teenager to shovel a path to the cabin and to the barn." The low bawl of a cow drifted on the cold air, and he added with a wry grin, "and to milk the cow."

"Look, I'll shovel the snow," Daniel said, "but I don't know nothin' about milkin' a cow."

"That's right thoughtful of you, Daniel, but don't you want to get started laying your trapline today?"

Daniel shook his head. "Not today. I'll do it tomorrow. The snow will form a frozen crust on top of the snow tonight, makin' it easier to walk on."

Fletch was hailed from the post by George Morse, waiting for him to open up. "I'll see you later," he said and walked off on the now well-trodden snow.

As he unlocked the door and stepped inside the store, he answered the questions put to him. Yes, Pa would probably be laid up most of the winter, and yes, he'd be running the place until Pa could take over.

"Reckon you won't be too happy bein' tied down to the post all the time," Morris said in his nasal voice, hitching up the trousers that had slid down past his paunch. "Are you gonna miss raisin' hell with your drinkin' buddies?"

"I'll survive," Fletch answered shortly as he pulled open the door of the stove and chucked some wood into its belly. He didn't like the meddling man any more than he did the man's widowed sister, Martha Louden, the biggest gossip in Big Pine.

"I reckon you'll find time to pleasure all your women, though," George said with a leer. "A man has to keep his rod greased or it gets rusty."

It was on the tip of Fletch's tongue to say *I'll bet yours is greasy as hell,* but then he thought why give the lout the opportunity to brag about his power in bed. He'd heard him brag often enough how he rode his Agnes three or four times a night and once in a while a couple times in the daytime if the mood struck him.

Fletch slid the man a contemptuous look. If George Morse thought his neighbors envied him, he was mistaken. Every time they saw the rail-thin Agnes coming to the post, a dozen children at her heels, they growled to each other that Morse should be castrated like a bull or a stallion. If he'd spend some of that energy working his farm, his family wouldn't be near starvation all the time.

Ignoring the braggart's remarks, Fletch asked coolly, "Did you want to buy something, Morse?"

"Yeah, I need a gallon of kerosene. Ran out a couple days ago and I kept forgettin' to buy some."

You didn't forget, you fat bastard, Fletch said to himself. *You were too damn miserly to buy some.*

While Fletch was filling a gallon container with the clear liquid, the door opened and Tommy Weatherford stepped inside, his face red from the cold.

Fletch liked the young man and felt sorry for him. Tom worked hard from dawn to dusk on the farm where he lived with his widowed mother, Agatha. She watched over her son as though he were a virgin in danger of being raped by one of their neighbors' young ladies. Whenever Tom attended a social event, his mother was with him, glued to his side. If he danced or talked too long with any girl, she developed a headache and insisted she and Tom go home.

Fletch pushed the can of fuel toward Morse, then turned and smiled at the young man. “What can I get for you, Tom?”

“Ma needs some salt. I reckon a pound will do.”

“I hear you're courtin' the Fraser girl,” George said. “You got between her legs yet?”

Fletch and Tom looked at each other in disbelief at the man's crass question. Fletch opened his mouth to order him out of the store, but Tom had wheeled around and aimed his foot at George's crotch with all his strength. “There,” he grated out. “Agnes will get a long rest from you.”

“Damn you, Weatherford.” George howled with pain, tears running down his bewhiskered cheeks. “You've ruined me.”

“I sure as hell hope so,” Tom said. “If you ever so much as speak Justine's name again I'll beat you half to death.” He picked up his salt and left a grinning Fletch as he went out the door.

Taylor called to Fletch from his cot, and Fletch went into the storage room, closing the door behind him, leaving the injured Morse to get home the best way he could.

The cow's continual painful lowing brought a sympathetic sigh from Laura as she sat at the table going over in her mind the happenings of the morning. She knew how painful it was when her own breasts filled up with milk and

Jolie wasn't ready to nurse. Poor Bossy was feeling the same pain.

She had to be milked, Laura knew, but who was to do it? She couldn't wade through the snow carrying Jolie. And she couldn't leave the little one alone for that long a time.

At a scratching sound outside, Laura stood up and went to the window. A wide smile curved her lips. Thin, gawkish Jebbie Morse was shoveling the snow away from the Thomas path.

She watched the teenager, thinking that his well-worn jacket wasn't much protection against the frigid weather, nor were the raggedy gloves he wore. George Morse should be ashamed of himself not to clothe his children in decent clothing. She'd noticed that he always had a heavy jacket when winter set in.

When the path had been cleared to the porch, Laura opened the door. "Come in, Jebbie, and warm up with a cup of hot coffee."

"Thank you, Laura, but Fletch told me to shovel a path to the barn and then milk the cow for you."

"I'd be so pleased if you would. I've been worried about the poor cow. When I see you reach the barn I'll bring the milk pail to you."

Laura closed the door, unable to believe that Fletch had given a thought to her welfare. The shoveling and all had to have been on Pa's orders. She looked at the clock. By the time Jebbie finished shoveling and milked the cow it would be time to take Pa his lunch.

Should she take enough for Fletch? she wondered. It would be just like him to refuse to eat it. He hated her. It shone out of his dark eyes, showed in his actions, and sounded in his voice.

Would he accost Adam Beltran and demand to know why he hadn't married her? And what would Adam's answer be? Adam knew very well that Jolie wasn't his. But he was basking in his peers' belief that he had slept with the aloof Laura Morris. It was the weak man's one claim to glory.

Laura vowed that someday she would face Adam Beltran in front of their neighbors and yank that undeserved fame from under his feet. She would make him tell all of Big Pine that Jolie wasn't his, that he had in fact never touched Laura intimately.

In her rising anger she thought she might even tell all those people who looked down on her now that Fletcher Thomas was her baby's father, that he had used her one night and then gone away for close to a year.

Of course I'd never do that, she rethought her threat. Fletch would never believe her because of Jolie's fairness, and it would crush Pa.

When Laura walked into the post carrying Jolie, with Taylor's lunch basket over her arm, she wanted to turn around and leave. Milly Howard and the widow Martha Louden were standing at one end of the counter, watching Fletch measure sugar into a cloth bag for Reverend Stiles who stood at the other end. It was apparent the women had been there for some time, for they both had their heavy coats open and the shawls pulled off their heads.

A glance at the storeroom door showed it only partially open, just wide enough to let the heat from the stove filter into the storeroom. The corners of her lips twisted wryly. Fletch had had the foresight to put a barrier between Pa and the widow. That one was as determined as Milly to land a Thomas man. No one, it seemed, put any importance on her and Pa's marriage to each other. He was still fair game as far as Martha Louden was concerned.

Wouldn't her fat lips flap open if she knew where Pa's real affection lay?

Her back stiff and her head held high, Laura walked past the two women who had only glanced at her when she entered the store, and walked toward the storeroom door. She received a cold stare from Fletch, but the preacher gave her a friendly smile.

"How are you and that little doll of yours?" he asked, laying back a corner of the blanket that covered Jolie's face.

"We're both fine, thank you, Reverend Stiles. How are you and Ina?"

"Ina's fine, but I'm a little tired right now. Been shoveling snow since sunup." He grinned and jerked a thumb toward the storage room. "Do you suppose Taylor broke his leg on purpose so he wouldn't have to clear paths all winter?"

"I heard that, Stiles," Taylor's voice boomed out. The preacher and Fletch laughed, and Martha tittered. The widow gave a disgruntled snort when Taylor called, "Laura, bring that little scrap in here to me. I've missed her." Laura's fast glance at Fletch saw cold rage in his eyes.

She said good-bye to Stiles, then walked into Taylor's room, closing the door behind her with a sharp click. What she and Pa said to each other wouldn't be heard in the other room.

"Put her right here in my arm." Taylor carefully edged over a few inches to make room for the tiny bundle. "Keep her wrapped up, though, for I want that door closed while that widder is in there. I don't need her fussing over me."

"How are you feeling? Are you in much pain?" Laura asked as she settled Jolie into the crook of his arm, then took the basket holding Taylor's lunch off her arm and set it on the floor.

"I don't have too much pain to speak of, just a dull throbbing." He gave Laura a sheepish look. "Butterfly would boil up some roots and dried berries that would ease my pain and help my leg to mend faster."

Laura arched a teasing brow at him. "Are you hinting that I should go to her village and ask her to do that for you?"

"Well"—Taylor looked away from her—"I would like to get word to her about my accident and that it will be quite a while before I can visit her again."

"Yes, she should know." Laura's face sobered.

"When you don't show up next Thursday, she'll think you've grown tired of her."

Taylor shook his head. "She'd know better than that, but she'd worry a lot."

Laura waited until Taylor finished the thick beef sandwich she had brought him, then checked on Jolie. "She should sleep all the time I'm gone, Pa," she said.

"She'll be fine. You go on along." When Laura straightened up, Taylor grabbed her wrist and said, "Be careful and take my pistol with you. The wolves will be out looking for something to eat. I sure as hell don't want it to be you."

"I'll be careful, Pa, and if need be I'm a pretty good shot with your gun, you know. I'll go get your pistol and strap on my snowshoes."

"You won't need them if you go through the woods. The snow isn't nearly as high there."

When Laura walked back into the store she found that the widow had left, but Milly was still there. She was leaning against the counter, most of her heavy breasts escaping her bodice, her eyes flashing an invitation to Fletch who lounged on the other side of the counter. When he saw Laura enter the room he leaned over and whispered something to Milly that sent her into a fit of giggles.

Laura ignored them and walked on outside. But she had been very aware of their presence, and her heart had twisted, seeing Fletch's dark head so close to Milly's. What had he said to his lover? she wondered as she followed the path through tear-blurred eyes. Had he been telling her that he would visit her tonight after the post was closed? Most likely, for Milly had looked very pleased.

You must accept the fact that someday they will marry and you will have to see them together all the time, she told herself firmly. *You must reconcile yourself to seeing their little black-haired children running around, Jolie's little half brothers and sisters.*

And those dark Thomases would be accepted by the community while her little one would be looked down on as the bastard child of Adam Beltran.

"Oh, Jolie," she half cried, "where did you get those blue eyes and pale hair?"

Laura searched the cabin for half an hour looking for Taylor's pistol. She finally gave up. The gun wasn't there. It had to be in the store. She put her jacket back on and hurried back to the post.

She was hardly aware of opening the post door and closing it behind her, she was so stunned when she walked inside. Fletch and a couple of his rowdy friends were gathered around a familiar-looking basket that had been placed on the counter. She took a step closer and saw Jolie inside the reed basket, propped up on a blanket. Her toothless little mouth was smiling and her small arms and legs were waving as she made soft, cooing sounds.

The men were so busy making foolish baby

talk to her, they weren't even aware of Laura's presence. What amazed her the most, Fletch wore a wide, proud grin as though Jolie was his daughter and he was showing her off. If only he would always look at her with pride in his eyes, she thought, and passed on into Taylor's room.

"Aren't you going to go see Butterfly?" Taylor looked anxiously at her.

"I can't find your pistol in the cabin. I've looked everywhere for it."

Taylor slapped a hand to his forehead. "I'm sorry, honey, it's on that shelf over there next to the lantern. I brought it to the store to shoot rats."

Laura found the gun and slipped it into her jacket pocket. "I see Jolie is being entertained out front." She smiled down at Taylor.

"Yeah." Taylor grinned. "Shortly after you left, she started squirming and fussing, raising a racket. Fletch came and picked her up, and the little scamp was all smiles then. Just like a beautiful woman, she's been showing off for him and his friends."

"I think that little lady is becoming spoiled."

"She's older now and wants more attention."

"I'm surprised at the attention Fletch is giving her."

"I am too, considering how he treats her mother," Taylor griped.

Laura shrugged. "Babies are hard to resist. Don't let his behavior toward me bother you. The two of you are getting along now, and that's what's important. I don't mind how he acts."

Taylor knew she lied, but he said no more about it. "Are you headed for the Indian village now?" he asked as Laura rebuttoned her jacket.

Laura slanted him a teasing look. "Do you want me to give Butterfly any personal message?"

Taylor shook his head. "She knows I'll miss her."

"I've got a feeling she'll slip over here tonight after the post is closed. She'll want to see for herself if your leg has been properly set."

"You think so?" Taylor looked hopeful.

"I do," Laura said and opened the door.

The store was empty except for Fletch and Jolie when Laura entered the store. With her head held high and ignoring the glowering look that Fletch shot at her, she walked toward the outside door.

"Are you leaving the baby here again?" he demanded when she was midway to the door. "I don't have time to look after her."

"You won't have to. She'll be going back to sleep any minute."

"What are you doing up at the cabin that's so important you can't take her home with you?"

"Look." Laura swung around and glared at him. "I don't have to answer to you about anything, but I'm not going home. I have to go somewhere."

"Now where could that be, I wonder," Fletch

sneered. "You're not welcome in any of Big Pine's homes." His eyes narrowed to glittering slits. "Of course, you'd be welcome at Adam Beltran's place."

"That's right," Laura answered sweetly, then added, "As well as at all the other single men's cabins. Do you think that you and Adam are the only two men around here who would like to make love to me?"

With those cool remarks she walked outside, leaving a fuming Fletch behind her.

"Damn you, Laura," he muttered, going to the window to watch her walking swiftly away. "Why do I still let you get under my skin, still want you with an ache that never lets up? You're a worthless piece. You let a man sire a child on you, then manage to convince Pa to marry you, to give your bas . . . Jolie a name."

Fletch stopped short of calling the baby a bastard. Something inside him wouldn't let the word come out. She was a sweet little baby and didn't deserve such a handle put on her.

He watched Laura pass out of sight, his gut twisting as he thought of her and Beltran in the man's bed, doing what they had once done together. He wanted to go after her, demand that she turn around, pick up her baby, and go home where she belonged.

You can't do that, you fool, his inner voice warned. *You don't have the right. You lost that privilege when you went gadding off to Canada.*

That was the damnedest fool thing you ever did in your life.

Fletch turned back into the room.

As Laura walked fast in the frozen forest there was no sound except the crunch of her feet and the creaking of pines rubbing against each other.

She had never been inside the Indian village and she became a little wary as she neared the settlement. How would Butterfly's people greet her? Would they associate her with Pa and not hinder her from making her way to the woman's dome-shaped wigwam? This village was of a Chippewa tribe, and with the exception of a few renegades who had broken away from their chief, the rest were at peace with the whites at the present.

The village suddenly stood before Laura, spread out along the lake. The only signs of habitation were blue smoke spiraling from each hut, and the pack of thin-ribbed dogs that came barking toward her. She stopped short, her hand on the pistol in her jacket pocket. If she shot into the air, would that hold them until someone came to see why they were making such a racket?

The animals were only yards away when a strident order sent them skidding to a halt with only deep growls issuing from their throats.

She recognized Red Fox, Fletch's friend, coming toward her. Her heartbeat slowed and she said with a nervous laugh, "I can't tell you how relieved I am to see you, Red Fox. I thought my end had come."

A slow smile curved the handsome brave's lips. "They do look vicious, but they wouldn't have attacked you unless given the order to do so. What brings my friend's sister out in such weather, and alone? Has something happened to him?"

"No, Fletch is fine. It's Pa. This morning he slipped in the snow and broke his leg."

"Ah, that is too bad," Red Fox said, then grinned in understanding. "It is Butterfly you want to see, and why you have come alone." Laura nodded, and he said, "Come with me. I will take you to her wigwam."

Laura didn't explain that she knew where Butterfly's home was. She didn't want this son of Chief Muga to know that she had sneaked along behind Pa all those years back, prying into something that was none of her business. She followed him silently on the shoveled path and stood behind him as he knocked on the door of the wigwam that stood several yards away from the rest of the village.

"Who is there?" Butterfly's soft voice asked.

"You have a visitor," Red Fox announced as he pushed the door open.

Butterfly's pretty face grew ashen when she saw Laura. She rose slowly from her seat of furs before the fire in the middle of the room. Her hands clasped together, she half whispered, "What has happened to Taylor?"

"Nothing bad, Butterfly." Laura hurried toward her. "Early this morning Pa slipped in the snow and broke his leg."

The blood flowed back into Butterfly's face and she breathed a deep sigh of relief. Her man wasn't dead. "Come sit by the fire and tell me about it. How bad is the break and is he in pain?"

"It's a clean break and should heal nicely, according to Fletch's friend Daniel who set it," Laura said, unbuttoning her jacket, then sitting down on one of the furs that ringed the fire. "He does have some discomfort." She smiled at Taylor's lover. "He wishes that you could take care of him. He says that you would give him something for his pain."

Butterfly nodded solemnly. "That is my wish also. But I'm afraid it is impossible. I can, however, brew him a tea that will dull his pain. It would take a few hours, though, and you have a baby to get back to."

Laura slipped her hand into her jacket pocket.

"Tonight when the post is closed and the village sleeps, you could take it to him yourself." She opened her hand revealing a key lying in her palm.

Butterfly looked at her in disbelief. "Is that a key to the fur post?"

"Yes, it is. You can visit Pa every night if you want to."

Butterfly took the key, her lips tilted, her

white teeth flashing. "I shall go to him tonight when the post grows dark.

"Now, before your cold walk back to your village you must have a cup of my herb tea while you tell me how things are going in your life. Taylor told me his son has returned and that he is angry about your marriage to Taylor."

Laura gave a short, derisive laugh as she accepted a small steaming gourd cup from her host. "Angry is hardly the word to describe how Fletch feels about our marriage. Outraged is more like it. Especially toward me. He, like everyone else in Big Pine, is convinced that Adam Beltran fathered my child and that I used Pa to give Jolie a name."

Butterfly shook her head. "As if this Beltran wouldn't gladly marry you for any reason. Jealousy is keeping Taylor's son from thinking straight."

"Jealousy?" Laura looked at Butterfly as though the woman were dull-witted.

"Of course, jealousy. Why else would he carry on so? He wants you for himself."

Laura's lips twisted into a crooked smile. "Pa is always telling me what a wise woman you are. But this time you are very mistaken. Fletch had his chance to marry me and he wasn't interested."

Butterfly studied her downcast face a moment, then said, "We shall see who is right."

"This tea is delicious." Laura changed the subject as she drained the last of the herb mixture. "I've got to get home now. Jolie will be waking up soon, hungry as a bear. She has a strong set of lungs."

"Red Fox will walk home with you," Butterfly said as she rose with Laura. "The wolves will be out in full force now."

"Won't it be dangerous for you to walk through the woods tonight?" Laura asked as she buttoned up her jacket.

"I'll be safe enough. I'll take along two of our meanest dogs. There will be no danger for me."

Red Fox was waiting for her when she stepped out of the wigwam. Very little was said between them as they crunched through the snow.

As Laura left the Indian village, Milly Howard was knocking on the door of the deserted cabin that Fletch and Daniel had taken over. She was there to make peace with Maida and Daniel, to apologize for her rudeness the last time she was there. She had not only angered them, but she was sure that Fletch was out of sorts with her also. He hadn't intimated that he would like to take up where they had left off when he went to Canada.

Milly still looked down on the plain-faced girl with the dowdy, unbecoming clothes, but since Fletch called them friends she'd pretend a liking for the pair out of the wilds of Canada.

Milly was disconcerted when Daniel opened the door and said coldly, "Fletch ain't here."

He was about to close the door in her face

when she hurried to say, "I'm not here to see Fletch. I came to see you and Maida."

Daniel's lips curled in a cynical smile. This one wasn't fooling him for a minute. She wanted to mend her broken fences so she could continue to come here to be with Fletch.

Avoiding his eyes, Milly said, "Actually, it's Maida I want to see, to talk to."

"Oh? Did you think up some insult you didn't hurl at her the other day?"

Milly looked uncomfortable a moment, then said as Daniel watched her closely, "I didn't mean to sound insulting, the words just came out wrong."

"They sure as hell did," Daniel growled. "I don't know if Maida will accept your apology."

"Maybe Fletch would want me to." Maida had walked up quietly to stand beside Daniel. "You will be welcome in our home."

When Daniel started to object, Milly rushed in to speak over him. "Thank you, Maida. I'll be over to visit tonight." She was off the porch and halfway down the path as she finished her sentence.

"Why did you say that?" Daniel frowned at Maida as they closed the door.

"It's possible that Fletch does want her to come here in the evenings. I'm sure they were lovers once, and maybe he wants to pick up with her again."

"I doubt it, but it's his home too, so it will be up to him if he wants to sleep with her again."

* * *

Fletch had no desire to sleep with Milly, but he did want it known that she spent a lot of time at his and Daniel's place. He wanted that to get back to Laura.

I'm afraid it wouldn't bother her though, he thought gloomily. *Her interest lies in that fox-face Beltran.*

He walked over to the basket and looked down on the sleeping Jolie and studied her small features. Thank God she didn't resemble her father except for the color of her hair and eyes. But who did the small one look like? Not her mother, although Jolie did have curly hair like Laura's. Jolie didn't look like anyone he knew.

He had just walked to the other end of the counter when Laura came hurrying through the door. "I'll just have a word with Pa and then I'll take Jolie off your hands," she said, walking toward the storage room.

"He's sleeping." Fletch stopped her.

"Oh, then I'll see him later when I bring him his supper." As she carefully pulled Jolie's blanket around her, then picked her up, Fletch's gaze went over her face, looking for signs that she had just made love.

There were no swollen lips, no flushed cheeks, nor any love bites on her throat.

Beltran can't be much of a lover, he thought with some satisfaction. If he had just spent an hour with her she would bear the marks of it.

With the baby clasped to her chest, Laura left the store without further words. Fletch stared at the door she had closed behind her, feeling empty inside.

Chapter Eight

Laura raised her attention from the round of dough she was kneading and gazed out the window toward the post. She saw the backs of two young women disappearing into the long, low building.

She gave the piece of raw sourdough an unnecessarily hard whack. That was the sixth simpering young miss she'd seen go in there since nine o'clock this morning. Ordinarily they wouldn't make more than one visit to the store in a week. And that would be when their mothers forced them to do so. But since Fletch was in charge of the store now, they came every day to buy such piddling things as a spool of thread, some rock candy, and even to request something that they knew the store didn't carry.

And they always came in pairs, giggling and blushing as they stood around, casting fast glances at Fletch. He had shaved off his beard and was again devilishly handsome. As far as she could tell, though, he paid them scant attention.

There was one female, however, who always came alone. Milly Howard. That one didn't want any competition hanging around when she was there. She always came in the afternoon after she knew the younger ones had made their daily trip.

"She sees him every night," Laura muttered as she shaped the dough into three loaves and placed them in long, narrow pans to rise again. "Why does she have to hang around the store every day?"

Her friend Justine had told her that Fletch and Milly were courting again, that every evening after the store was closed Milly went to the cabin that Fletch shared with Daniel and Maida, and that no one knew when she left.

Justine was busy with wedding plans these days. Tommy had put the roof on the cabin the day before the blizzard. At the moment it held a stove, a bed, a table, and two chairs that didn't match. But the two young people were so much in love they'd be willing to sleep on the floor, and Justine wouldn't mind cooking over a fire in the fireplace.

Justine's mother had donated the bed, table, and chairs, but Tommy's mother hadn't given the couple so much as bed linens, she was that upset that Tommy was marrying and leaving her to live alone.

A long sigh feathered through Laura's lips. Justine was insisting that Laura stand up with her when she and Tommy took their vows. Laura had warned her young friend that she might be ruining her wedding by having Laura Thomas stand up with her. She pointed out that some people might stay away because of the shameless woman who had borne Adam Beltran's baby, pretending that it belonged to poor Taylor Thomas.

Justine had laughingly remarked, "They'll be there, every last one of them. They'll watch your every move, gathering every little bit they can gossip about later."

And she's probably right, Laura thought. Everybody except Pa and Mrs. Weatherford and the whores . . . and Jolie. Jolie would be with Pa. He could manage her until Butterfly slipped in to visit him. She would be able to come early that night because Fletch was closing the store around seven so that he could attend the reception in the tavern part of the building. It was the only place in the village big enough to hold everyone.

Taylor's leg was healing rapidly, thanks to Butterfly's doctoring, he claimed. Everything had worked out very well for him and his lover.

Instead of seeing her once a week, he now got to see her every night.

Laura glanced at the clock. Did she have time to work on the dress she was making for the wedding before she took Pa his lunch?

She decided she could work on it an hour or so, and walking over to her favorite rocker, she picked up the partially finished dress and ran a palm over the fabric. It was going to be one of the prettiest dresses she had ever owned.

The material was a pale blue brocade that Bertha Higgins, the madam, had ordered for her girls long before. It had taken the material a month to arrive, coming by boat down Lake Erie. Pa had been fighting mad when the red-headed Bertha had refused to take it, claiming it was too light a color for her girls. It had lain on a shelf in the store close to a year.

Laura held the half-finished garment up and ran her gaze over the bodice. That part of the dress was finished except for the wide ecru lace collar she would add later.

She had used the pattern from an old dress, and because her breasts were considerably larger since giving birth to Jolie, she would be showing more bosom than usual.

She had made the bodice to hug her ribcage, then come to a point a couple inches below her waist, which had returned to its trim size. A full gathered skirt would be added, and because of the material's weight it would fall in soft folds to her ankles.

Would Fletch look at her and think she was pretty? she wondered as the needle flashed, gathering the skirt to fit the waist. She shook her head at her foolish thought. In all likelihood he wouldn't even look at her. All his attention would be on Milly.

Laura tried to tell herself that she wouldn't care, but she knew better. She would care; she would care deeply. "More fool me," she muttered.

When the clock chimed the noon hour, all Laura had left to do to the dress was hem the skirt and attach the collar. She carefully folded it over a chair back, then went to check on her bread.

The dough had risen to twice its size, and she slid the three pans into the oven before bundling Jolie into a heavy blanket, then slipping into her jacket. She picked up Jolie and the cloth-wrapped ham sandwiches she had made and left the cabin.

When Laura entered the post, Fletch had only one customer. Daniel's Maida. The new wife greeted her with a friendly smile, then looked eagerly at the bundle in her arms.

"How's the little one taking to this cold weather?" she asked. "Daniel tells me she's the prettiest little thing he ever saw."

Knowing that Maida was hinting to see Jolie, Laura folded back the blanket and the little one gave them her ready smile.

"Oh, isn't she precious," Maida whispered in

some awe. "She does look like a live doll." She trailed a finger down Jolie's smooth cheek and said with yearning in her voice, "I can't wait to have a baby of my own."

"Would you like to hold her?"

"Yes, I would," Maida answered eagerly.

"Let's go into the back room where you can sit down," Laura said and led the way.

Fletch's dark eyes bored into Laura's back. Not once had the little witch looked at him. She acted as though he were a part of the merchandise stacked on the shelves behind him. When Milly entered the store a few minutes later, he scowled at her instead of returning her smile.

Taylor was sitting up in bed playing a lonely game of solitaire when Laura and Maida entered his room. Laura had fixed the storage room up the best she could. She felt that if Taylor had to spend at least two months there he didn't have to lie amid boxes and crates and rubble that had accumulated over the years. He had even saved a sled she had used as a youngster. Someday Jolie would use it.

After she had swept out the room, she had hung a pair of heavy drapes over the small window. No one could look in now when Butterfly came visiting at night. The next day she had had Elisha bring a rocker and a small table from her attic room while she carried a couple of colorful rugs. She nodded her head in satisfaction every time she entered the room.

Taylor's face lit up with a wide smile. "My,

my, two beautiful women coming to visit me at the same time," he said. "Or should I say three beautiful females. Let me see that little scutter, Jolie."

Laura gave Maida an apologetic look as she lifted her daughter out of the blanket and laid her in Taylor's lap. Jolie immediately began chortling, happy to see Taylor. As he gently chucked her under the chin, it was clear they shared a mutual love.

Laura had noticed that the little one was becoming attached to Fletch also, which always brought a sour smile to her lips. Poor baby, she didn't know what a rotter her father was.

When Jolie sneezed suddenly, Taylor looked alarmed. "I'm going to miss seeing this little one, but I don't think it is wise for you to be bringing her out in the cold every day. From now on Fletch can pick up my meals. We surely don't want this one coming down with pneumonia."

Laura didn't want that to happen either, but she didn't like the idea of Fletch coming to the cabin while she was alone.

But what could she say? Pa and Fletch were back on their close footing, and certainly she didn't want to cause trouble between them again. Pa would be curious and wouldn't stop questioning her until he, God forbid, got the whole truth out of her.

So she nodded agreement and, taking Jolie from Taylor, gave her over to Maida. Taylor bit into his sandwich, and it grew silent except for Maida's soft talk to Jolie and Milly's gay chatter in the store and Fletch's occasional gruff answer to some question or other.

Taylor grinned over a mouthful of ham. "That one is in here every day, and I think Fletch is getting tired of her always hanging around."

"I'm not surprised." Maida lifted her head from looking at Jolie. "She comes to our cabin every night. When she's ready to go home she hints to Fletch to walk with her, but he never does."

Laura could believe that. Fletch was an uncaring brute. It was just like him to use a woman and then put her out of his mind. Hadn't he done the same thing to her?

Laura and Maida were preparing to leave when they heard Bertha, the madam, bustle into the store. "Whew," she exclaimed, "it's cold enough out there to freeze the balls off a wooden Indian." Fletch's laugh was the first real one Laura'd had heard from him since her return.

Fletch liked the loudmouthed madam, and her girls as well. A man always knew where he stood with them. All they expected was a fast romp and then good-bye. There was no clinging on, no hinting at marriage.

"What can I do for you, Bertha?" he asked with a wide smile.

"Well, you could come visit my girls. They're complainin' that you haven't been to the pleasure house since you returned home."

"I'm sorry about that." Fletch grinned. "But I've been pretty busy with the store and all."

Milly laid a proprietary hand on Fletch's arm and said to Bertha with a warning in her voice, "I guess you know what the 'and all' means."

Bertha looked at the hand gripping Fletch's arm, then up to his frowning face. Her lips lifted in an amused smile. "If you say so, Miss Howard."

Fletch started to jerk his arm free, then saw Laura and Maida come from the back room. He not only let Milly's hand lie where it was, he covered it with his own hand, an action for Laura's benefit.

If Laura saw it, he wasn't aware of it. She was busy greeting Bertha with a friendly smile. "Bertha, meet Maida. She and her husband are newcomers to Big Pine." Bertha and Maida smiled at each other; then Laura asked, "How have you been? I haven't see you or your girls since the blizzard."

"I'm fine, honey, and so are those lazy girls of mine. I tried to get them to come over to the store but they won't budge from the stove."

"You mean they ain't still in bed, restin' up from a busy night?" Milly sneered.

Bertha raked contemptuous eyes over the speaker's plump body. "How come *you're* up so early, talking about busy nights?"

"Well, I never!" Milly huffed.

"The hell you ain't," Bertha came right back

at her. "You've been on your back more times than any of my girls."

Milly's face became an angry red when Maida giggled and Taylor's loud guffaw sounded from his room. When Milly felt Fletch's arm shaking in silent mirth, she jerked away from him and stamped across the floor. The outside door shuddered, she slammed it so hard behind her.

With some difficulty Laura and Maida brought a semblance of sobriety to their faces. They discussed Justine's wedding, and Maida shyly asked Laura if she would help her make a dress for the affair.

"Certainly. I'd be happy to. Do you have the material?"

"Not yet. Daniel said I should pick out what I want. I was hoping you'd help me choose."

"That will be fun." Laura smiled at the girl/woman. "I love looking at material. Pa got in some new a couple weeks ago. There's some lovely woolens."

They made plans to meet at the store the next day to choose a dress length and get started on the dress. When Laura left she ignored Fletch again.

"She's such a nice person," Maida said before telling Fletch that she would like five pounds of flour, a pail of lard, and a box of baking soda.

Fletch only grunted and went about filling her order.

* * *

Laura was growing more nervous by the minute. It was nearly five o'clock, and any minute Fletch would be coming to pick up Taylor's supper. She had it ready in a cloth-covered basket. There was a small pail of venison stew, half a loaf of freshly baked bread, and several butter cookies. The basket sat on the table, handy for her to pick up and pass to him through the door. She didn't want him coming inside the cabin. Something warned her that it would be dangerous to let him walk through the door.

As it happened, Fletch was inside the cabin before she was aware he was anywhere near it. She remembered that he could walk as quietly as an Indian if he wanted to, and that of course he wouldn't knock on his own father's door.

"Why do you look so shocked to see me?" Fletch scowled at her. "You did talk Pa into sending me for his supper . . . all his meals from now on."

"I did no such thing," Laura denied sharply. "It was all his idea. He's afraid Jolie will catch cold, being brought out in the freezing temperature."

"Yes, after you put the idea in his head."

"That's not true. He said it after Jolie sneezed."

After a moment's silence, Fletch asked gruffly, "Do you think Beltran would care that much for your baby? I think not. He didn't even care enough about it to marry you. To give the little one his name."

Dragging in a deep breath, Laura said, "Pa's supper is in that basket. Will you please take it and leave?"

"There's no rush," Fletch said, pulling a chair away from the table and sitting down. "Elisha is minding the store while I'm gone." He studied her frowning face a moment, then bit out harshly, "How often does Beltran sneak over here after everyone is asleep?"

I will not cry, Laura thought fiercely, although she felt her heart was breaking. There was no way in the world she could make this man believe her. She forced all emotion from her face and out of her voice as she said, "That's none of your business. I don't ask you how often Milly comes to visit you."

Fletch's eyes watched her closely as he said, "She visits me every night."

Laura's heart gave a lurch, but she managed to say in a cool voice, "My, aren't you the lucky fellow?"

Fletch gave her a mocking smile and drawled, "Of course, you meant to say, 'Isn't she a lucky woman?' "

"No, I didn't mean any such thing, you egotistical timber wolf."

"Come on, Laura." Fletch stood up and came toward her. "Stop pretending you didn't love the things I did to you in the barn that time. Remember?"

Yes, I remember, Laura screamed inside. She could almost feel his hands and lips on her body now—making her lose control, doing things that had made her blush in the daylight.

She drew a shuddering breath, and Fletch's eyes lingered on the pulse throbbing in her throat. "Ah, Laura," he said with gruff tenderness, "I can't get you out of my mind. All the time I was gone I thought of you."

His hands came out to grip her elbows and draw her to him. "Why did you get yourself mixed up with Beltran?" And while Laura gazed up at him in openmouthed surprise, he bent his head and crushed her lips beneath his with a desperate hunger.

Laura tried to pull away from him, reminding herself that Fletch Taylor did not love her, the person. He only wanted to use her.

And though his grip was firm, he wasn't hurting her, as instead of loosing his hold he drew her tighter against the hard length of his body. She felt his manhood rising, growing hard and throbbing against her stomach. She tried again to free herself. A hunger of her own was growing inside her and she was desperate not to give in to it. She had done that once and look where it had led. An unplanned baby and a farce of a marriage, not to mention her good name ruined.

"Please, Fletch," she whispered against his lips. "I don't want this."

"Yes, you do," he answered hoarsely as he swiftly undid the buttons of her bodice and pulled free a throbbing breast. "Look at that hard little beauty." He brushed his thumb back and forth across the nipple. "It's begging me to take it into my mouth. It remembers the delight I can give it."

"No!" Laura denied vehemently. "It remembers nothing."

"But you do," he whispered passionately as he leaned against the table and drew her between his spread legs.

Laura pressed her hands against his chest and arched away from him. The action only brought her breasts forward, and his lips swept down to draw one into his mouth.

She still fought to repress the desire that was building inside her, but as he licked and suckled and nibbled, her body took over her mind. She gave up the battle and let her body relax against his. She threaded her fingers through his hair, and Fletch groaned his relief.

"Hold me, Laura," he whispered. "Caress me the way only you can do."

Laura slid her hand down between their bodies and deftly unlaced his buckskins. His thick, hard length sprang free and her palm gently closed over it. Her fingers found the hard ridge that led down to where his desire waited and slowly stroked it. Fletch groaned and suckled her harder.

Her hand still caressing him, and Fletch's mouth still on her breast, he scooped her up and carried her into what was now her bedroom. There he stood her on her feet, and together they feverishly undressed each other.

"You are so beautiful," Fletch breathed and went down on his knees before her. Holding her hips, he rained kisses on her stomach, always moving downward to the dark curls that hid what he was dying to have.

Laura gasped and held on to his shoulders when he parted the curls and his tongue sought out the little nub that waited for him.

It had been so long since her body's needs had been taken care of, it took but a couple minutes before her fingers were biting into his shoulders and her head was thrown back in mind-shattering release.

When Laura's body stopped shuddering, Fletch kissed his way up her body until he came to her mouth. He kissed her lips deeply, then gently nudged her to her knees. She cupped his full sacs in one hand and closed the other one around his pulsating length. She ran her tongue all over it, gently nibbling on the ridge that led to the part she held in her hand. When she felt that she had teased him to the point where he would go mad, she opened her mouth and slid her lips over as much length as she could manage.

Fletch watched her through passion-filled eyes as he traced a finger around her drawing lips. How many nights he had lain in his cold bed in Canada and dreamed of watching her do this.

When his manhood began to jerk and throb,

Laura knew it was time to release him. She let her lips slide slowly off him and rose to her feet.

"Thank you, honey," he whispered huskily, then lifted her up and laid her on the bed.

Her arms and legs opened for him and he eagerly went into them. For a moment he just lay on top of her, relishing the feel of her soft skin, her nipples burning into his chest. He levered himself up on his elbows then, and without being told, Laura slipped her hand between them, and taking him in her hand, she guided him inside her.

"You're still so tight," he whispered in wonderment as he drove inside her, stretching her walls to take his large size.

Like the first time they made love, they reached a fast release together. Also like the first time, Fletch was still hard and wanting, and barely stopped the lift and fall of his hips. He slid his hands beneath Laura's hips, and holding steady, slowly pumped inside her, taking his time, savoring every thrust of his maleness.

Five minutes passed and both their bodies wore a thin film of sweat. Another five minutes passed as they made love to each other, Laura reaching to meet his every long thrust.

The time came when neither body would be denied the need raging inside them. Their cries of release rang through the room.

Fletch slumped his full weight on Laura for several seconds as he fought to return his breath to normal. He rolled off her then and lay on his back staring up at the ceiling. Laura wanted to curl up against him, have him wrap his arms around her. Something warned her not to. There was a strange tightness about him.

A few minutes later she was glad she hadn't. For when Jolie fussed from her cradle in the family room, Fletch rose, drew on his clothes, and silently left the room. When she had dressed and followed him a few minutes later, he was gone, along with the basket holding Taylor's supper.

Shamed tears ran down her cheeks. She had let him use her again.

Chapter Nine

It was snowing again, but lightly, as Laura and Maida stood in the kitchen of the Thomas cabin. "I really like this dark green you chose, Maida," Laura said as she unrolled the woolen dress length on the table. "It will look very pretty with your brown hair and eyes."

"Actually, Daniel picked it out," Maida said shyly. "He said the same thing about my eyes and hair."

"Your husband cares deeply for you," Laura said, picking up a pattern she had trimmed down considerably to fit her young friend's boyish figure. "Anyone can see that," she added as she carefully placed the paper on the material. "You are very fortunate to have such a loving husband." She picked up the scissors and, taking the first step in making Maida's new dress, cut into the green woolen.

"Yes, I am," Maida agreed, watching the scissors snip away, "and I love him the same way. I know that people look at us and wonder what I see in a man so much older than myself, and that some doubt that I love him. But they are mistaken. They don't know the hell Daniel saved me from."

When Laura gave her a questioning look, Maida began telling her story, pouring out words that had been bottled up inside her too long.

"I was fourteen years old when my pa, Claude Henderson, was killed in a knife fight. Ma didn't even have time to grieve for him before this trapper, Festus Carter, without my ma's permission, moved in with us. She was outraged and ordered him to leave immediately. He laughed in her face and said, 'You need a man, woman. A female can't make it alone in Canada.' He grabbed her by the arm then and dragged her into the bedroom.

"I heard Ma yell angrily, 'Take your hands off me.' Then I heard the sharp slap of that brute striking her. A minute later the bed's headboard was thumping against the wall and Ma was crying in pain. She stopped after a while, but the bed continued to creak for a long time.

"When it finally stopped I heard him order, 'Get your ass in there and make me something to eat.'

"Poor Ma. She looked so ashamed when she walked out of the room, Festus right behind her. I ran to comfort her, and his big hand slapped me up against the head, knocking me to the floor. 'I'll have none of that,' he said, sitting down in Pa's favorite rocker. When I sat up he growled, 'Crawl over here and pull off my boots.' That was to be my job from then on. That and to wait on him hand and foot.

"And my mother, it was her job to cook for him and go into the bedroom any time he told her to. Until it snowed and we were frozen in, every time Festus went hunting for fresh meat he took me with him. He knew that Ma would never go off without me.

"Festus began to bring an occasional man home with him. Money would pass between them; then Festus would force Ma to go into the bedroom with the man. I'd lie on my pallet in a corner and listen to the bed creak, hating him with every beat of my heart.

"That went on all winter, and Ma grew paler and paler and thinner and thinner. Festus no longer bothered to take me with him when he went hunting. He knew that she didn't have the strength to run away. Then when spring arrived and most of the snow had melted, Ma caught pneumonia, and in her weakened condition, died two days later."

"Ah, honey, I'm so sorry," Laura began, but Maida held up a hand, stopping her.

"I'm not finished, Laura. Let me tell it all once

and for all. Hopefully, then I can put it out of my mind forever."

Laura nodded, and Maida continued. "That night after Ma had been buried back in the woods, I sat before the fire numb with grief, knowing that I must escape Festus but having no idea where to go after I ran away from him. Festus asked suddenly, 'How old are you, girl?' Without thinking, I answered that I was fourteen. 'Hell,' he swore, 'you're plenty old. Your small size has fooled me. You should have been bringing in money a long time ago.'

"He stood up and jerked me to my feet. 'Come on to bed,' he ordered. 'I'll break you in tonight, get you ready to start entertaining my friends.'

"When he started dragging me toward the bedroom, I thought of my mother dying in there and no way in hell was he going to get me on that bed. I started struggling with him. I finally broke free. I wrenched open the door and his hands missed me by inches as I dove into the darkness. I heard the door slam and the latch click. He had locked me out.

" 'When you change your mind I'll let you back in,' he yelled from inside. I didn't bother to yell back that I'd let the wolves eat me before I would ever go back to him.

"It was raining, one of those steady, soaking rains, and in minutes I was wet to the skin. Shivering, my teeth chattering, I crawled beneath a big pine tree and huddled up close to its trunk.

"And that is where Daniel found me. I don't think I'll ever forget how the water-laden branches of my hiding place were suddenly parted and I saw this bear of a man peering down at me. He was bearded and shaggy-haired, but by the light of the lantern he carried I could see his eyes and they were warm and kind. I trusted him right off.

" 'What are you doing out here in the rain, young'un?' " he asked.

"I didn't want to tell him everything, so all I said was, 'My stepfather locked me out of the cabin.' I saw those kind-looking eyes turn real mean-looking then. He helped me from under the tree, saying that he wanted to see what kind of bastard would do that to a young'un. When we got to the cabin he practically kicked the door open.

"I guess Festus thought one of his friends had come calling when the door banged open. He stood up with a wide smile on his face. It was wiped off real fast, though, when he saw Daniel's angry face and heard him demand, 'Is this your young'un?'

" 'Kind of,' Festus answered uneasily. 'Her and her ma have been living with me. We buried her ma today.'

" 'What's she doin' out there in the rain, without a coat or boots? She's near froze.' Daniel took a threatening step toward Festus.

" 'She could come in anytime she wanted to.' Festus took a step back. 'All she had to do was say she would mind me.'

" 'What was it she wouldn't obey you about tonight?' Daniel growled at him. Before Festus could tell him some lie, I hurried up and told him everything. How he had treated my mother and his intention to rape me tonight.

"Daniel stared real hard at Festus for a long time. Then he turned to me and asked, 'Are you warmed up yet, gal?' I nodded, and he said, 'Bundle yourself up. I'm takin' you out of here.'

"Festus started yelling and swearing and went for his hunting knife. Quick as lightning Daniel jerked a knife out of his belt and met Festus head-on. The long blade pierced Festus's heart, and he fell to the floor, blood trickling out of his mouth and nose.

"We left the cabin as soon as I got my coat and boots on. Daniel lingered long enough to set fire to the building, explaining that if anyone came along they would think that me and Festus had lost our lives in the fire.

"He took me to this deserted cabin he'd been living in about ten miles away. We spent the summer there, just lazin' around, hunting and fishing, getting to know each other. Then when fall approached we packed up and trekked along Lake Superior for about fifteen miles where we stopped and Daniel built a cabin. When the first freeze came, Daniel set out his trapline in the new territory."

Maida paused and looked at Laura, who had long since laid down the scissors, giving her entire attention to Maida. Maida continued then with some shyness. "Daniel knew I had been scarred by what Festus had done to my ma, the men and all, and he waited until I was sixteen before he asked me to go to bed with him."

Humor gleamed in Maida's eyes. "Our first time together was an experience, I tell you. I was as wary as a young doe, scared but still wanting Daniel to make love to me. You see, I had been in love with him for a long time.

"He was ever so gentle with me, taking his time, stroking and kissing me all over. He got me so roused up I hardly felt the pain when he broke through my maidenhead."

It grew quiet in the room. Maida had finally wound down, and Laura was too amazed to speak. What a life this young girl has lived, she thought. She had already experienced more than most women would in a lifetime. And how lucky she was to have Daniel, big and rough and yet so gentle when it came to his gal.

Maida broke the silence, saying very seriously, "I have never told my story to anyone else, Laura. I trust you will not repeat it."

"You have my word of honor I will never speak of it to anyone," Laura answered just as seriously.

The subject was dropped as though it had never come up, and Laura picked up the scissors and began cutting out the dress that Maida would wear to Justine's wedding.

"I suppose Fletch will be taking Milly to the

party," Laura said after a while, trying to sound as though she didn't care whom he brought.

"I imagine she'll manage that," Maida said dryly. "But Daniel says he doesn't want her hanging around us. He really doesn't like her. We both know that she only pretends to be our friend so that she can come to the cabin every night to see Fletch." She gave a short amused laugh. "About all she says to me all evening is hello and good-bye. The rest of the time she's fawning all over Fletch."

There was a slight catch in Laura's voice when she said, "Milly always did want to marry him."

"Daniel says that she will never get him to the altar; that he would never marry a piece of used goods like her."

Laura grasped Daniel's prediction and hung on to it as though it were gospel. She suddenly felt more lighthearted than she had in a long time.

A short time later she laid the scissors down and smiled. "Well, Maida, your dress is cut out. Are you handy with a needle?"

"Not very," Maida apologized. "My ma always did most of the sewing. I do sew a straight stitch, though."

"That's fine. You can help baste the pieces together so that we can see how it's going to fit before the permanent stitches are put in."

It was nearly four o'clock, time for both women to start their evening meals, when they left off working on the first stage of the dress. Even though it only hung together by long, loose stitches, it was taking shape. Maida's eyes danced with excitement. It would be her first new dress in a long time.

"How long do you think it will take to finish it?" she asked as she pulled on her heavy, short coat.

"I should think a couple days will do it. I'll work on it this evening, finish the basting. What will take the most time is working the buttonholes."

"Then I'll see you tomorrow?"

"Yes. I'll look forward to seeing you, Maida. I've enjoyed our afternoon together."

"Me too." Maida's eyes looked suspiciously wet. "I've never had a woman friend to talk to before."

They stood talking a minute longer, Maida suggesting that she and Daniel walk to the church with Laura, then stay together at the party. It had not escaped the kind girl's notice how Laura was shunned by the women of the settlement.

When Maida had gone, her eyes bright and her step bouncy, Laura checked the pot of ham and beans that had been simmering all afternoon. They were done, and she lifted the pot to the back of the stove to keep warm.

She nursed Jolie, then began getting Taylor's supper together. Since that time Fletch had walked into the cabin, she kept watch at the kitchen window, watching for him to come toward the cabin to pick up the basket that held Taylor's evening meal. When she'd see him open the store door she would set the basket outside on the porch, then bar the door against him.

It kept him out, but she could hear his mocking laughter as he walked back to the post. He knew that she didn't trust herself to be alone with him.

Chapter Ten

Laura awakened to bright sunlight shining through her bedroom window. She smiled and stretched her arms toward the ceiling. It was going to be a beautiful day for Justine and Tommy's wedding.

The ceremony was to take place at four o'clock, and the party would begin at seven. She ticked off in her mind the things she had to do before the big event.

She had promised Maida to help her with her hair. She had to wrap up a set of sheets and pillowcases, her wedding gift. She had suggested to Maida that she might give the newlyweds a nice warm blanket and she wondered if the teenager had remembered to purchase it.

Maida was almost as excited as Justine about the wedding.

Laura smiled ruefully. Pa had suggested the most important thing on her list: someone to watch Jolie while she was in church.

She had thought he was joking when he said, "Why don't you ask Bertha to come over and sit with Jolie? She'd jump at the chance."

"Oh, sure," she'd laughed. "I can just see a whore taking care of my daughter."

When Taylor didn't laugh back, she knew he was serious. "I don't think that would be a good idea, Pa." She frowned.

"Why not? Bertha is one of the finest women I know. I grant you she's loud and don't act like a lady, but she's got one of the softest hearts you could find in any woman."

"But, Pa, she . . ."

"Not anymore, she don't. She hasn't taken a man to bed in ten years."

"But what about the girls who work for her?"

"You want to know something about those girls?" Taylor said, his voice a little sharp. "Every last one of them would be dead by now if Bertha hadn't taken them off the streets in Detroit and brought them here. They were sleeping in doorways, alleys, anyplace they could find, until Bertha came along. It's too late for them to find a husband and raise a family, but you can be sure that before they found themselves doing anything to keep alive, they dreamed of a different life. A man to love them, children to tend to, respectability."

Laura had never thought of the whores in that vein before. She had always imagined that they had deliberately chosen such a life.

"I guess I'd better go talk to Bertha," she thought out loud. "But Pa could be mistaken. The redheaded madam might not want to be bothered with a baby."

Laura sat up, swung her feet to the floor, and shoved her feet into her moccasins. She grabbed up her robe and shrugged into it as she left the chilly bedroom. She hurried to the fireplace and stirred up the fire. After adding several lengths of wood to the red coals, she checked on Jolie all wrapped up in her cradle. When she touched the smooth little cheeks and found them warm she went into the kitchen and after building a fire in the stove, put a pot of coffee to brewing.

By the time she got dressed, nursed Jolie, and had breakfast, Jebbie Morse was knocking on the door, ready to milk the cow.

As she handed him the pail she asked, "When you've finished milking, would you sit with Jolie for a short while? I have an errand to do."

Jebbie readily agreed. He was used to babies always being around. It seemed his mother, Agnes, had one about every year. He could handle them as deftly as any mother.

It was a cold and still day, and Laura buried her chin in the collar of her heavy jacket as she stepped off the porch and headed toward the cabin tucked in the pines back of the post. She wondered how many curious eyes were watching her from behind curtains and asking themselves what in the world was that shameless Laura Thomas doing, going to the madam's house. A sour smile darkened her eyes. The women would get together later in the day and tell each other that she was working for Bertha now.

As she knocked on Bertha's heavy door, Laura glanced at the lantern with its red chimney, hanging on the wall. Its light had been blown out, not to be lit again until nightfall. She remembered the many nights as a young girl she had lain in her attic room staring at the red glow, watching the men come and go, and wondering what went on in the pleasure house.

She had a pretty good idea now of what went on, thanks to Fletcher Thomas.

Bertha looked startled when she opened the door and saw Laura standing there. Laura looked just as startled. The madam's face was clean of the heavy powder and paint it showed to the public, and the fading red hair was done up in paper curlers. Her uncorseted figure was quite lumpy beneath the loose woolen robe she wore.

She looks like some child's grandmother, Laura thought when she got over her shock.

"I thought you were one of the girls coming back from the privy," Bertha said, disgruntled about her appearance.

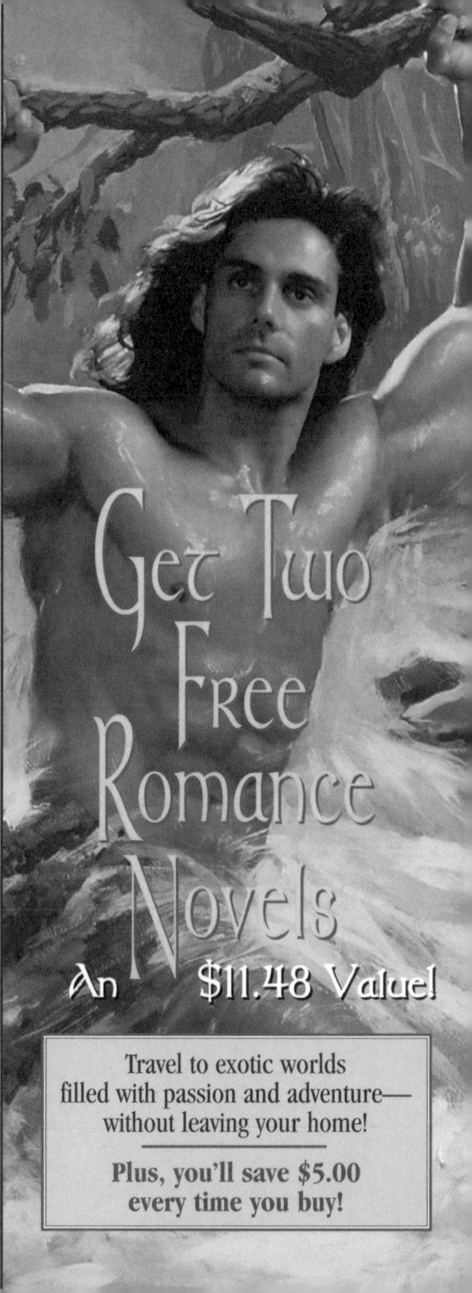

GET YOUR 2 FREE BOOKS NOW—AN $11.48 VALUE!

Mail the Free Book Certificate Today!

Free Books Certificate

YES! I want to subscribe to the Love Spell Romance Book Club. Please send me my 2 FREE BOOKS. Then every other month I'll receive the four newest Love Spell selections to Preview FREE for 10 days. If I decide to keep them, I will pay the Special Member's Only discounted price of just $4.49 each, a total of $17.96. This is a SAVINGS of at least $5.00 off the bookstore price. There are no shipping, handling, or other charges. There is no minimum number of books I must buy and I may cancel the program at any time. In any case, the 2 FREE BOOKS are mine to keep—A BIG $11.48 Value!

Offer valid only in the U.S.A.

Name ______________________

Address ______________________

City ______________________

State ______________ *Zip* __________

Telephone ______________________

Signature ______________________

If under 18, Parent or Guardian must sign. Terms, prices and conditions subject to change. Subscription subject to acceptance. Leisure Books reserves the right to reject any order or cancel any subscription.

Laura remembered that the madam and her girls kept different hours than the rest of the village. "I'm sorry, Bertha, I shouldn't have come so early. I'll come back later."

"Nonsense." Bertha motioned her inside. "I'm sure you won't spread the word that Bertha Higgins looks like an old hag before she gets her war paint on."

"Of course I won't," Laura said, shrugging out of her hip-length coat, "and you don't look like an old hag. You look like the rest of the women in the village. I like you without your war paint."

"I do get tired of wearing it, but it's expected of me." She pulled a chair away from the table. "I just brewed a pot of coffee. Sit down and tell me why you've come calling while we have a cup."

While Bertha placed sugar and cream on the table, then poured the coffee, Laura glanced around the large room. There wasn't a housewife in the village who kept a cleaner kitchen. It was immaculate, from the polished black range to the well-scrubbed floor.

When the aging madam took a seat across from her, Laura pulled the sugar bowl toward her, saying, "If you say no to what I'm going to ask of you, Bertha, I'll understand. Would you sit with Jolie while I'm at church this afternoon? Justine Fraser and Tommy Weatherford are getting married and I'm standing up with Justine."

For several seconds Bertha stared at Laura in

total surprise. Then, her face beaming with a wide smile, she said, "I'd be honored to, Laura. I haven't held a baby since I used to help out with my younger brothers and sisters at home."

"Then you've never been married or had a family of your own?"

Bertha looked down at her coffee, shaking her head. "I almost got married when I was sixteen." She looked up at Laura. "My birthday present that year was to lose my entire family, plus my intended, to influenza. Half our village was wiped out."

"What a heartbreaking thing to happen to you," Laura exclaimed softly, laying her hand on Bertha's.

Bertha nodded. "It near killed me. Our family was very close to each other, and I loved Ben dearly."

After a short silence Laura said, "I know you couldn't replace your family, but couldn't you have found another young man to love after a while?"

Bertha gave a short, mirthless laugh. "I didn't have the time or the inclination to look for love again. I had to worry about keeping body and soul together. There were no jobs to be had in our little village, and everyone there was too poor to take in another mouth to feed. So . . ." Bertha took a deep breath. "I packed my duds in an old leather satchel and headed for Detroit, about fifteen miles away. I was sure I'd find employment there.

"I didn't know that times were bad then, and that jobs were just as scarce in that big city as they were at home. Finally, when I was near to starving, down to the last sandwich I had brought along with me, I found a job, working in a tavern, serving drinks to the drunks that stumbled in. The pay was miserly, hardly enough to rent a room my ma wouldn't have kept her chickens in, and furnish me with one scant meal a day. What with the hard work and poor meals, I began to lose weight and felt sickly all the time."

Bertha looked up at Laura and said, "That's when I started selling my body." There was a defensive tone in her voice.

"I am so sorry, Bertha," Laura said over the tears that had welled up in her throat as she listened to the story of the big woman's hard life. One never knew what paths might lie ahead of them.

Bertha shrugged. "It wasn't too bad. I hated it at first and I felt so ashamed. But after a while it became just a job that furnished me better living quarters and all the food I wanted. But always I wanted to get out of the business, get out of the back streets of Detroit. I longed for the clean wooded hills of the country."

A rueful smile curved Bertha's lips. "It was a long time coming, but I finally convinced those four women sleeping in there to strike out with me. We landed here in Big Pine."

"Are you ever sorry you settled here?"

"Never. This is truly God's country, and though me and the girls are mostly shunned by the women in the village, we love it here."

"I know what it feels like to be shunned," Laura said with a wry smile. "It hurts."

"Don't let it, Laura. You have a friend in that Justine girl, and that little Maida thinks the world of you. She doesn't think the sun comes up until you're out of bed. Two such good friends are worth a hundred acquaintances who will turn on you without mercy."

"You're right, of course, and I'll get used to the noses that are turned up at me. Well," Laura said as she pushed her empty cup away, "I'd better get home. Jebbie Morse is with Jolie, and I imagine he's getting impatient for me to get back. Besides, I have a lot of things to do before four o'clock. For one thing, I have to wash this mop of hair." She fingered her black curls.

"So," she said, standing up, "shall I look for you around three o'clock?"

"I'll be there." Bertha nodded as she opened the door for her.

The day went swiftly for Laura as she straightened up the cabin, and put a beef roast in the oven for Taylor's supper. After she nursed Jolie and changed her into clean, dry clothes, she packed Taylor's lunch of ham sandwiches in the basket, ready to set outside the minute she saw Fletch leave the post.

It was almost two o'clock by the time she got

around to washing her hair and brushing the curls dry before the fire. She had just donned her new blue brocade when the clock struck three and Bertha knocked on the door.

"My, my, you're gonna knock everybody's eyes out, you look so beautiful," Bertha said as she stepped inside. She looked the dress over and said pensively, "I should have kept that dress material. It sure made up pretty."

"Jolie is sleeping now." Laura helped Bertha out of her fur coat. "She may sleep all the time I'm gone."

"I hope not," Bertha said, going over to the cradle and looking down at the baby. "I'll be disappointed if I don't get to hold her."

"If she doesn't wake up, you'll have to come visiting some morning when she's awake." Laura smiled at the madam, whose face wasn't as painted as it usually was. Nor was her dress as flamboyant as usual. Bertha looked almost respectable, Laura thought with a smile.

"I'd like that just fine." Bertha sat down in a rocker and opened a book she had brought with her.

Maida, who had been waiting on tenterhooks, excited to get her new dress on, jerked the door open before Laura could knock. "I've kept my robe on because I knew you were going to wash my hair and fix it," she explained, ushering Laura inside.

"Yes, I am." Laura smiled and held up a bar

of the rose-scented soap Taylor always ordered for her from Detroit. She reached into her pocket and brought out two strips of green ribbon. "This is for your hair."

"Oh, Laura, I've never had ribbons for my hair before." Maida lovingly fingered the velvet strips.

"Well, if I know your Daniel, you're going to have all the ribbons you want from now on. Now, let's get started with washing your hair."

"That sure smells good," Maida said a few minutes later, bent over a basin of water as Laura gave her hair a good sudsing. "I've only ever used lye soap on my hair before."

"This soap will make your hair silky soft and shiny. I'll leave it with you."

"Thank you, Laura. I've never had anyone be so nice to me."

After a good toweling, Maida's fine-textured hair dried fast before the fire. As Laura had promised, it was silky with red highlights and fell softly around the girl's narrow shoulders.

After Maida had slipped the green dress over her head, Laura tied the matching ribbon into a bow over each ear. When she told Maida to go look at herself in the mirror, her narrow little face flushed with excitement. She saw that she looked quite pretty.

"Oh, Laura, I can't believe it's me," she said softly, stroking the lace collar that lay beneath her chin. "I wish Daniel could see me."

"He will see you, silly," Laura teased. "When

we go to the wedding party tonight." She looked at the clock. "I guess we'd better get started for the church. It's almost four o'clock."

Laura could hear the whispering going on behind her stiffly held back. She knew what the women were saying to each other: What was Justine thinking of, having that hussy stand up for her? She slid a look at the best man, Tommy's cousin. What was he thinking? Did he feel like everyone else?

The wink she received from him told her that he was only amused at the scandalized women.

It was over finally. Reverend Stiles had been overly long in binding the young couple together. Even after the vows had been spoken, he had gone on to say that they must always cling to each other, work together, have a large family. Everyone had become a little impatient, wanting to get out of the cold church and home to their warm cabins.

After congratulating the happy pair, Laura headed for the door, walking so fast Maida almost had to run to keep up with her.

"Don't let them gossipers make you feel bad, Laura," she said when they got outside.

"They don't make me feel bad, Maida. They make me mad as hell."

"That's good. Daniel says that a person can get over anger faster than he can get over hurt."

Laura made no response, and when they came to the cutoff that led to her cabin, Maida said anxiously, "Me and Daniel will come for you around seven o'clock, all right?"

The cold air and brisk walk had calmed Laura down somewhat and she answered calmly, "I'll be ready."

Laura had to smile when she walked into the cabin. Bertha was rocking a cooing Jolie as she softly sang her a bawdy tavern song. "Bertha," she laughingly said, "that is hardly a nursery song."

Bertha grinned. "I know it, but it's one of my favorites. The little one doesn't understand the words, and she likes the way I sing it."

Jolie heard her mother's voice and turned her blond head, looking for her. "I'll bet you're hungry, aren't you?" Laura tickled her under the chin. "Let me get my coat off."

"Well, how did everything go?" Bertha asked when Laura had settled Jolie to her breast.

"The ceremony was beautiful even if it did run on too long. As for the rest of it, it was as I expected it would be. Whispers and cold looks."

"Laura, you mustn't let them narrow-minded women get to you. They're not worth a minute's fretting over. You just hold your head high and go on with your life."

"That's exactly what I'm going to do. I made up my mind walking back from church that I intend to get out of life all it can give me. I'll ignore the looks and slurs, as well as Fletch's insults."

"His insults bother you more than all the rest, don't they?"

"They used to, but from now on he's going to find that he's dealing with a different woman. He and his slut, Milly Howard."

"Now, that's the way I like to hear you talk," Bertha said, rising from the rocker. "I'm gonna go home now and get those lazy girls out of bed. They're gonna be plenty busy tonight. After the party is over, the single fellers are gonna come looking for some lovin'."

"Thank you for watching Jolie for me, and don't forget to come visiting," Laura said as Bertha opened the door.

"It was my pleasure, and I'll drop in on you once in a while. Don't forget, though, you can come calling on me. I get awfully tired just talking to the girls. They haven't got a good brain between the four of them. Poor souls, the only thing they know to talk about are men and the next new dress they're going to buy."

As the madam hurried away, Laura thought that the women of Big Pine didn't know what they were missing by not accepting Bertha into their midst.

She turned back into the kitchen thinking that would never happen.

Chapter Eleven

Laura was late getting Taylor's supper packed. Jolie had fussed, wanting to be held some more after Bertha left. It had taken her quite a while to rock the baby back to sleep.

She had just spread a cloth over the basket when Fletch opened the door and stepped into the kitchen. His eyes widened a fraction when he saw Laura in her new dress. Anger came into them then, and he lowered his lids to slits as he studied her.

"Aren't you afraid you're gonna fall out of that thing?" he taunted sarcastically. "But then, maybe that's your intent. Start fights between the men who will be ogling you."

When Laura made no response, he sneered, "What's Beltran going to say about you showing yourself like that . . . looking like one of Bertha's girls?"

"Why should he say anything?" Laura was finally goaded into responding to Fletch's insults. "He's nothing to me. It's none of his business if I walk into the party buck naked."

"Since when?"

Laura's eyes shone wickedly. "Since I have my eye on a new man," she lied.

"Who?" Fletch demanded, going toward her, looking as though he might strike her.

"Go to hell, Fletcher Thomas." Laura's condemnation brought him up short. "I don't have to answer to you about anything. Just stay out of my life from now on."

Fletch glared at her for several seconds, then warned savagely, "I'll be watching you tonight. If you do one thing to shame Pa, I'll haul you out of there."

"I think not. The man I have in mind wouldn't like that."

Fletch continued to glare at her another few seconds, then mumbling some incoherent word, he snatched up the basket and slammed out of the cabin. Laura watched him stride toward the post, a wide smile of satisfaction on her face. She had given back as well as she had received.

"Your face looks like a storm cloud, son," Taylor said when Fletch stomped into his room and began transferring the food from the basket onto a tray. "Did you and Laura have words?"

"Yes, we had words. That one is getting way too smart with her tongue."

Taylor picked up a knife and fork and cut into a slice of beef. "You've got to remember Laura's not just your little sister anymore. She's a grown woman, married and with a baby. I imagine she can talk any way she pleases."

"She could at least speak respectful to a person."

"It depends if a person is speaking respectful to her. Do you speak respectful to her?"

When Fletch made no answer to his father's question, Taylor asked, "What did you get into it about?"

"The dress she's going to wear to the wedding party."

"What's wrong with it? It was one of the prettiest dress lengths I've ever had in the store."

"I'm not saying that the material isn't nice, and so is the color. It's the way she made the dress. It shows too much of her . . . top."

"You mean her breasts?"

"Yes! It's not decent."

"I can't imagine Laura ever doing anything that wasn't decent."

"Hah!" Fletch snorted and walked back into the store.

For a moment Taylor stared unseeing at his supper. It had just struck him that his son was in love with Laura. "Ah hell, what a mess we're in," he whispered, pushing away the plate, his appetite gone. He stared up at the ceiling, wondering how it was all going to end. He finally decided he would speak to Butterfly about it tonight, but he doubted there was much she could do this time to straighten out matters.

It was shortly before seven when most of the people living in Big Pine began arriving at the tavern. Everyone was in high spirits, talking and laughing, children running about, squealing and carrying on in general.

"Bar the door, Fletch," Taylor called. "I don't want any of them tramping in here."

"I already have, Pa," Fletch answered, his attention on the three people walking toward the store. Actually, there were four. Daniel was carrying Jolie.

I hope she's bundled up good and warm, Fletch thought, then grew impatient with himself for caring.

His face wore a dark scowl when the three walked into the store, bright smiles on their faces, looking forward to an enjoyable evening.

Daniel gave him a big grin and said, "Maida's got your clean clothes laid out, Fletch. You can go on up to the cabin and change now."

Fletch looked at Laura's animated face, her sparkling eyes and smiling red lips, and decided that he wasn't going to attend the affair. He'd be sure to get into a fight over her before the night was over, and feed more fodder to the gossips.

He was about to announce his decision when

he was reminded that if he was alone in the cabin Milly would hotfoot it over to join him. There would be no Daniel and Maida to keep her from saying, "Let's go to bed."

And what could he answer her? "I'm sorry, Milly, but I don't want you anymore. There's only one woman I want in my bed, and she's married to my father." When that word got out, tongues would really wag.

With a sigh of helplessness he pulled on his jacket, dreading the evening ahead.

By the time Laura settled Jolie in beside Taylor, and Daniel and Maida visited with him a few minutes, they entered the tavern almost at the same time as Fletch did. Daniel was just helping Laura and Maida out of their coats when he arrived.

Like a magnet Laura's eyes went straight to Fletch. How handsome he is, she thought, watching him hang his jacket on one of the pegs pounded into the wall for that purpose. He wore a new set of buckskins, the supple leather molding the muscles of his broad chest and long legs. He had laced the neck opening only halfway up, revealing a couple of inches of chest curls. His black hair waved loosely to his shoulders, and the moody look in his dark eyes made him all the more attractive.

He's the handsomest man here, she thought, then caught sight of Hunter O'Hara, the bartender. Hunter was handsome also. He was built much like Fletch, had the same curling black hair, worn long. But his eyes were the green of dark moss and somehow haunted-looking. A long scar on his right cheek gave a wicked look to his handsome face. Women were drawn to him as much as they were to Fletch.

As though the bartender sensed her studying him, he looked up from the tittering young women gathered around him and gave her a broad wink. She blushed but couldn't help smiling at him.

Fletch turned from hanging up his jacket and caught the interaction between them. He shot a dark scowl at Hunter, who ignored it. He glared at Laura then, and she glared back. When Milly came hurrying up to him, he gave her a smile that wasn't reflected in his eyes. But Milly, blind to anything she didn't want to see, grabbed hold of his arm and hung on.

Laura and Maida placed their wedding gifts on a table where other packages already lay. They talked to Justine and Tommy standing near the table a few minutes, then went and sat down on one of the benches that had been lined up against two walls. From under her lowered lids Laura saw that almost all eyes were upon her. The women who were already scornful of her became more so when they honed in on the neckline of the pale blue dress. That most of the other young women wore a dress cut equally as low, maybe even a little lower, didn't count. They didn't look as lush and lovely as Laura Thomas did.

Laura also saw that most of the men in the tavern were ogling her, single *and* married ones. She looked across the room where Fletch and Milly had taken seats, and seeing them smiling at each other like lovers, she began to give the single men a little smile when she caught their eye. After all, every last one of them had courted her before her marriage, and it was only being polite to nod and smile at them, she told herself.

Maida whispered, amusement in her voice, "Are you flirting with those young men, you wicked girl?"

"Maybe just a little," Laura whispered back. "But actually I'm just being neighborly." At which Maida gave a snorting laugh.

But Fletch didn't see it as being neighborly. To his way of thinking, Laura was flirting with the men, plain and simple, and he wouldn't have it. He started to stand up, to go give her fair warning to keep her eyes and smiles to herself, then eased back down. There had come the scrape of a fiddle, the picking of a banjo, and the pounding on the beat-up piano in a corner. The same piano and the same player who had pounded it every night for the young men and trappers of the village to dance with the tavern whores.

When couples swarmed onto the floor and started dancing to the rollicking tune of "Camptown Races," Milly urged Fletch to dance with her. He shook his head and sat watching the men who were trying to get up the nerve to approach Laura, who now sat alone. Daniel had grabbed Maida and they were hopping around on the floor like everyone else.

At one point Adam Beltran stuck his head in the door, but Fletch gave him such a dark look he quickly pulled back and closed the door.

Since Fletch's return the young man had grown sorry that he hadn't spoken up a long time ago and denied that Laura's child was his. At first he'd given no thought to the possibility that sooner or later the big man would return, and perhaps beat him to a pulp. Now he had waited so long, he didn't know how to go about telling the truth.

The men continued to look at Laura, and Fletch continued to warn them off with dark, threatening stares. Then Hunter O'Hara, idle for a moment, walked from behind the bar and, making his way through the dancers, bent over Laura.

"Would you honor me with a dance?" He smiled down at her.

She darted a glance at Fletch and received a glowering look that dared her to dance with the handsome bartender. She gave Hunter a dazzling smile and said, "I'd love to."

As Hunter swung her smoothly onto the floor, gliding among the other dancers, he looked at Laura with a crooked grin. "I notice that the young bucks would like to ask you to dance but Fletch glares at them every time they make a move toward you."

"And you're not afraid of him?" Laura arched a questioning brow at him.

"No. Fletch and I have already tested our strength against each other. We're pretty evenly matched. He knows that he'd be in for one hell of a fight if we tangled. He also knows that Taylor wouldn't like it one bit, his fighting over his wife."

"In that case, then, let's enjoy ourselves." Laura gave Hunter a smile that set Fletch's teeth on edge.

He sat and fumed as the couple danced to every tune played in the next hour. Milly fumed also. All that good music going to waste while Fletch sat like a frog sunning itself on a log.

To Fletch's relief, the music makers finally took a break, wiping their sweaty faces as they headed for the bar. Hunter escorted Laura back to her seat beside Maida. "I have to go pour some drinks now, but we'll dance again, all right?"

"Yes, I'll look forward to it." Laura smiled up at him.

"Laura," Maida warned, "he looks pretty taken with you. Are you leading him on? There's going to be trouble. Fletch looks like a bear that's been shot in the rump."

"There's not going to be any trouble, Maida, and I couldn't care less how angry Fletch is. Let him take care of his business and I'll take care of mine."

"But the women are talking about you something fierce."

Laura shrugged indifferently. "As if they don't always do that."

Daniel returned with a cup of sweet cider for each of them and the subject was dropped.

The music makers returned to their instruments and began tuning up for another round of dancing. Fletch left an irate Milly and walked across the floor to join Laura and Maida and Daniel. He sat down next to Laura and practically growled, "The next dance is with me."

"I'm sorry, but it's already promised," Laura delighted in saying.

"Look, everyone will think it strange if I don't dance with you at least once."

That was just an excuse, Laura knew. He only wanted to get her on the dance floor where she couldn't get away from his threats and taunts. But he was right in one respect. It would be wondered why Taylor's wife and son ignored each other and didn't once dance together. The onlookers would come up with their own reasons, which would be many and varied.

When the music struck up again, and Fletch took hold of her arm and said, "Let's go," Laura stood up and they moved among the other dancers.

How good it feels to be in his arms, Laura thought. His own special clean male scent engulfed her, and she repressed the desire to lay her head on his chest, to lift her arm and curl it around his neck. Instead, she forced herself to hold her body stiff and well away from his.

They circled the floor once in silence. Then Fletch sneered, "If you're wondering why your friend Beltran isn't here, I saw to it that he didn't show up."

"Really? I hadn't noticed his absence."

Her tone told Fletch that she really hadn't missed Beltran. His fingers bit cruelly into her waist as he rasped angrily, "You remind me of a woman-chasing man. You tire of one lover, then move on to another. Now that you know all about lovemaking, you're choosing the older, more experienced ones."

"You mean like yourself?" Laura smiled up at him, wanting instead to slap his hateful face. "Is that what you think?"

"That's what I damn well know, you little bitch, and be warned that you can't play games with Hunter O'Hara. You won't be able to drop him so easily."

"What if I decide not to drop him? He's awfully nice . . . and handsome," she added.

"Then he'll drop you when he tires of you."

"What if he doesn't? What will you do about it? Will you challenge him to a fight?"

Fletch gave her a suspicious look. "I see you've heard that we've tangled before. We came out pretty even that time. It was just a case of pitting our strength against each other. But if we ever go at it again, I'll beat the living hell out of him. I'll have good cause to. I'll not let any man shame my father."

"Oh, really?" Laura's voice shook with the anger that had been building up inside her. "What about the way you have shamed him?"

"How have I ever shamed him?" Fletcher glared at her.

"By seducing his wife."

Stunned by the truth of Laura's words, Fletcher could only look at Laura for several seconds. It had only struck him now that he had put horns on his father. He finally defended himself by saying, "I, unlike the other men, have known for some time that you and Pa don't have a normal marriage, so I don't feel that I shamed Pa in any way."

"Of course you don't," Laura snapped. "You wouldn't feel shame about anything."

The dance number came to an end, and before Fletcher could respond to her charge she stepped out of his arms and went back to Maida and Daniel who were still sipping their drinks. Fighting to keep his features from showing the rage inside him, Fletcher walked across the floor and sat down beside Milly. If he heard any of her complaints he paid no attention to them. When the music started up again and Hunter approached Laura and held out his hand for another dance, Fletch wordlessly stood up, pulling Milly up with him.

It was a slow dance this time, "Swanee River," and Hunter was very quiet. Laura knew by the way he talked, slow and soft, that he was from the South. She suspected that the song held sad memories for him. She looked up at him and asked softly, "Do you miss the Southland? Your home? Your family?"

She felt the ragged sigh that came up from his chest. "Yes, I miss it. I miss it terribly. But the life I once knew there is gone forever. As for family, they're all gone, and so is my home. While I was away fighting in the war the home place was burned and my father was killed trying to protect it. My mother died two weeks later from a broken heart."

"I'm so sorry, Hunter." Laura squeezed his hand. She lightly drew a finger down his scarred cheek. "Did you receive this in the war?"

"Yes, and a few other wounds also," Hunter said, bleakness in his eyes. "I spent two months in a Yankee hospital, more dead than alive."

When Laura's eyes grew misty in sympathy, he said huskily, "That was a long time ago, Laura. I'd almost forgotten it until the song brought it all back. Now smile and let's enjoy ourselves, make old Fletch squirm some."

They gave themselves over to the music, laughing and talking like everyone else. Laura was thinking that she had never enjoyed herself more when Hunter bent his head so she could hear him over the music and stomping feet as he said, "Another thing I have missed since coming north is being with a true lady. I enjoy your company very much, Laura Thomas."

"Thank you, Hunter. I enjoy the company of

a gentleman for a change."

"Are you referring to Fletch?" Hunter grinned.

Laura's laughter pealed out. "I sure am."

Fletch and Milly, dancing nearby, heard Laura's gay, amused laughter, and Fletch's arm tightened so hard around his partner's waist that she cried out. A few minutes later when Laura missed the couple on the dance floor, she looked across to where they had sat for most of the evening.

Milly sat there alone, a very cross look on her face.

A fast glance around the room showed Laura no sign of Fletch being in it. A pleased grin lifted the corners of her lips. He had gone off and left his lady love.

Where had he gone? Laura wondered. If he had returned to the cabin he shared with Daniel and Maida, Milly would have gone with him. Unless, of course, he had ordered her not to. He was rude enough to tell her not to follow him.

But whatever the case, a few minutes later Milly was dancing with one of the trappers, her body pressed tight against his, leaving nobody to guess who she would be spending the night with, or at least a good part of it.

It was growing late, the clock over the bar showing a quarter to midnight. "This will be the last dance, ladies and gentlemen," the fiddler said and drew the bow across the strings, sending out the opening notes of "Beautiful Dreamer."

"I'd like to see you again, Laura," Hunter said soberly.

"I'd enjoy that, Hunter," Laura said wistfully. He was such entertaining company. "You couldn't come to my cabin, of course, but we could run into each other sometimes." Her eyes twinkled. "Like when I go visiting Bertha. She would always give us a cup of coffee to visit over."

Hunter laughed and gave her a quick hug. "I do believe you do have some Irish in you, girl. You've got a devious little mind. What if I drop in on Bertha next Thursday around noon?"

"Make it around one o'clock. I have to make Pa's . . . Taylor's lunch. And I'll probably have my baby with me."

Although Hunter wondered at her slip-up, almost calling her husband Pa, he only said, "I'd like to see your little daughter. Everyone I talk to tells me how pretty she is."

"I guess you've also heard it said that Adam Beltran is her father."

"Yes, I've heard that rumor, but I could never believe that one so beautiful as you would ever have anything to do with that sneaky man. And now that I've gotten to know you, I'm convinced it isn't true."

"Thank you, Hunter," Laura said gravely, wrapping a blue shawl around her shoulders. "There are very few people in Big Pine who think that Jolie is a Thomas."

"Well, I do," Hunter said, opening the door

for her. "I'll see you Thursday," he added as she left to step next door to pick up her daughter.

Ever since Fletch's threatening look had scared him off, Adam Beltran had been standing back in the pines waiting for the party to break up. He had worked up the nerve to approach Fletch, to tell him, hoping to make him believe, that he was not the father of Laura's baby. He knew it would be difficult because he had let it go too long, and had let the village believe it.

He started when he saw Fletch leave the party long before it was over. He almost lost his nerve to speak to the big man when he saw the black scowl on his face. He could crush me with his hands, he thought as he stepped fearfully out of the shadows.

Beltran cleared his throat and called nervously, "Fletch, I'd like to talk to you a minute."

Fletch stopped in midstride and glared at the man he'd like to kill. His eyes cold and dangerous-looking, he demanded, "What could you possibly tell me that I would want to listen to?"

"I could tell you, and truthfully, that I am not the father of Laura's baby. I could tell you that I've never so much as kissed her, let alone do anything else with her."

For some reason Fletch thought Beltran was telling the truth. "Why are you telling me this now? I've been home for some time."

Adam looked away, shame and embarrassment on his face. "I liked having the men think that me and Laura had been lovers. They had all tried to get next to her, and she wouldn't have anything to do with them except to flirt a little."

"Who do you think is the father of Laura's daughter?"

Adam shook his head. "I haven't the slightest idea. She never walked out with any of the men who were always hangin' round her." He waited a moment, then ventured, "Maybe the baby is Taylor's."

When Fletch made no response, Adam said, "Now, don't go gettin' mad, but it's possible that the child's father is a married man. There's a couple blond-headed Swedes in the village."

Fletch gave a grating laugh. "Yeah, one's sixty if he's a day, and the other one is fat and way past fifty."

"Well, there are some young men with light brown hair who might have been blond when they were babies. I've been lookin' around, and there are lots of fellows with blue eyes."

Fletch found it hard to continue discussing who Laura's lover might be and said sharply, "Look, Beltran, I'm satisfied that you're not the father, so let's leave it at that."

"Oh, sure," Beltran hurried to agree. "I just thought I'd mention my ideas."

Fletcher turned and walked away without further words to Adam. He didn't know whom to hate now. Thanks to the little rat, now he'd suspect any man who had blue eyes and light brown hair. It comforted him to know, though, that he could at least eliminate Hunter O'Hara. That one was as dark as Fletch himself.

Damn the man, Hunter had his eye on Laura, and she, blast her beautiful hide, was looking back at him.

When he entered the cabin a few minutes later, Fletch also damned the blizzard that had locked him into Big Pine until spring.

Chapter Twelve

Hunter was on Laura's mind as she made up the bed and then began tidying up the family room. The truth of it was she thought about him a lot, but not in a romantic way. She looked on him as a very good friend, a friend she could relax with, speak her thoughts to whether they be serious or sometimes even foolish.

What puzzled her, made her think of him so often, was that he, unlike all the other single men in the village, acted as though all he was looking for from her was friendship.

She and Hunter had met at Bertha's pleasure house three Thursdays in a row. They had enjoyed themselves thoroughly, sitting over coffee, listening to the wild tales Bertha told about her past and present. She never mentioned names, but some of her stories about the men who came visiting her girls had Laura and Hunter holding their sides with laughter.

Laura always took Jolie and left Bertha's place first, as Hunter stayed behind another half hour. She had asked Bertha once if he used that time to visit one of her girls.

"No," Bertha answered, somewhat puzzled, "he never goes beyond my kitchen. Not that the girls wouldn't love to get that handsome devil into their beds. But he doesn't seem the least bit interested in what they offer.

"He's awfully nice to them, though. He sees to it that they don't get manhandled in the tavern by the drunks. The girls and I have come to the conclusion that a woman in his past hurt him so deeply that he's soured on the rest of us women."

Or maybe he still loves the woman, Laura thought, straightening up from raking the dead ashes from beneath the large grate in the fireplace.

Hunter O'Hara slipped from Laura's mind when she opened the door to set the pail of wood residue on the porch. Maida stood there, her hand raised to knock on the door. They laughed together; then Maida carefully wiped her feet before stepping into the kitchen.

"You know, Laura," Maida said, taking off her jacket and sitting down at the table, "I think that your Upper Peninsula is just as cold as my Canada is."

"Maybe it's because of the wind that blows off the lake," Laura suggested as she poured them both cups of coffee.

Laura pushed a plate of cookies toward Maida and asked, "How's the gift you're knitting for Daniel coming along? Christmas is only a week away."

Maida grinned ruefully. "I shouldn't have attempted a sweater for him. He's so gosh-awful big. But I think I'll have it finished in time. I have only one sleeve left to do. Have you finished Taylor's afghan?"

"Yes, last week. I'm working on a sweater for Jolie now."

After a moment's silence Maida remarked, "I don't suppose you're going to give Fletch a gift for Christmas."

"You suppose right. Unless it's to bake him a hemlock pie."

"I do wish you two got along together," Maida said wistfully. "The four of us could get together in the evenings, play cards and cribbage. Then I wouldn't have to put up with that awful Howard person every night. Not that she bothers to talk to me and Daniel. Most of the time she acts like we're not even there as she practically crawls all over Fletch."

"He must not mind or he'd put a stop to it."

"Sometimes he does. She embarrasses him a lot with her carrying on."

Laura didn't want to talk about Milly and Fletch anymore. It was too painful. She changed the subject. "I heard that two of the trappers are down with influenza. Bertha has been taking care of them, I believe."

"That's what I heard. I hope it doesn't spread. It's very contagious, you know."

Laura nodded. She knew of entire families being wiped out by the virus.

The clock struck eleven and Maida drank the last of her coffee. "I've got to get home," she said. "I left a bowl of sourdough rising. It's probably ready to be shaped into loaves by now."

As Laura helped her friend into her jacket she glanced out the window and noted that there were several people going into the store. Fletch would be busy waiting on them. She decided she would take Taylor's lunch to him. She hadn't visited him but twice this week. He was probably feeling neglected.

Fletch looked startled to see her when Laura stepped inside the store, but he didn't remark on it. The three women he was waiting on gave her a cool, disdainful look as she walked past them, heading for Taylor's room.

"It's about time you came to see me," Taylor said. "Let me see that Jolie baby. I don't see her often enough."

Jolie began to squirm as soon as she heard Taylor's voice, and she was all smiles when Laura laid her on the cot and folded back the blanket she was wrapped in.

After Taylor had played with the baby awhile, he looked up at Laura and said with concern in his voice, "I think something is wrong with Butterfly. She hasn't been here for the past two nights."

An uneasiness gripped Laura as she remembered the two trappers sick with influenza. Was the Indian village in the grip of the virus? It wasn't like Butterfly to miss even one night's visit to Pa, let alone two nights running.

Laura stood up and put her jacket back on. "I'm going over to the village and find out what's keeping her away."

"Would you, Laura?" Taylor said, relief in his voice. "I know something is wrong."

"Maybe not," Laura tried to soothe him. "I won't be gone long. Jolie nursed not long ago and shouldn't fuss until I get back."

The store was empty of customers when Laura sailed through it and Fletch called after her, "Where are you going, leaving Jolie here for me to mind?"

Laura didn't bother to answer him, only slammed the door behind her.

Like the other time Laura was there, as soon as she set foot in the Indian village the pack of vicious dogs came bounding toward her, their hackles raised and barking shrilly. She waited for someone to call them off. When no one appeared, she remembered Red Fox saying that they wouldn't attack unless ordered to. Still, her pulse raced a little when she started walking toward Butterfly's wigwam, the barking dogs at her heels.

The village seemed strangely quiet, Laura thought as she called in at Butterfly's wigwam. Usually at this hour someone was stirring about outside. She had to call twice before she was huskily told to enter.

The first thing she noticed when she entered the dim interior was Butterfly lying on her pallet of furs, the covers pulled up to her chin. The next thing to catch her eye was the fire in its rock pit. It was almost out. The wigwam was decidedly cold.

"Stay back, Laura," Butterfly rasped when she started forward. "I have the white man's influenza. You must not catch it and take it back to Jolie and Taylor."

"Don't worry about that, Butterfly." Laura knelt down beside the bed of furs and laid her hand on the sick woman's forehead. "Whites are used to catching it in the winter and have cures for it. You have a fever. Do your bones ache?"

Butterfly nodded. "Every one in my body."

"Are any of your people down with it?"

"Yes, and they are dying like flies. Even Chief Muga is sick. The medicine man is spending all his time with him."

"When did you eat last, Butterfly?" Laura asked.

"I'm not sure," Butterfly answered weakly. "Two days ago, I think."

Laura shook her head. The woman should have been drinking a lot of meat broth. "Butterfly, after I build up your fire I'm going back to my village to bring back some food and remedies that will help you get better." She knew she must get help to Butterfly and the village as soon as possible.

"Well, that was fast," Fletch said, surprised when Laura returned so soon. "Didn't your new boyfriend want to be bothered with you today?"

Again he received no answer from Laura. She had no time to exchange insults with him today.

Taylor's face turned as white as the pillow his head lay on when Laura said, "Pa, Butterfly has influenza. As you know, Indians have have no inborn resistance to it. I won't lie to you, Pa. She is very ill. Many of her people have died from it. I guess Chief Muga is at death's door."

When Taylor pushed himself up to a sitting position, cursing his inability to go to the woman he loved, Laura said, "I'm going back as soon as I can gather up a piece of beef and the remedies I need to fight the virus." She paused, then said, "I don't know what to do about Jolie. I may be gone for some time."

"While you get everything together, I'll take Jolie to Maida," Fletch said from the doorway where he had heard everything that had been said. "She's old enough now to be put on cow's milk. Send Elisha over to Agnes Morse to borrow a bottle and nipple."

Laura nodded her thanks and was halfway out of the store when Fletch said, "I've got a young doe hanging in a tree outside. We'll bring that too. Venison broth is stronger than beef."

We? Laura paused for a moment. Was Fletch going with her to the Indian village? She remembered then the friendship between him and Red Fox and wasn't surprised that he would be concerned about the Indian and his people.

Hurrying up the snow-trampled path to the cabin, Laura burst into the kitchen. It took her but a few minutes to whip up a poultice of kerosene, turpentine, and lard to place on Butterfly's chest to break up the congestion there. She placed it in a basket, along with a square of woolen cloth to put under the mixture so that it wouldn't burn her skin. To help the concoction along, she put a handful of rock candy in a pint of whiskey. She would give Butterfly several spoonfuls every couple hours.

To help cure the influenza, Laura added to the basket a small bottle of quinine. A teaspoon of it added to a glass of water should also help bring down the fever. The last thing she put in the basket was a pot of clear beef broth she had planned to make soup with.

Laura didn't know how the word had spread so fast, but when she stepped outside, Fletch was waiting for her, a dozen of Big Pines' population with him. She knew from the women's pale faces they were frightened of an epidemic that could take half, or all, of their families.

"Don't go bringin' their sickness back with you," Milly said sullenly, angry that Fletch was going off with Laura.

"What are you talking about?" Fletch glared at her. "Two of our trappers are already down with it; have been for a couple weeks. They probably took it to the Indians."

The mothers' pinched faces looked more frightened at this piece of news, and they huddled together when Fletch and Laura struck off toward the Indian village.

Laura deliberately led the way along the narrow path in the high snow. Had Fletch been in front with his long strides she'd have had to practically run to keep up with him.

They hadn't gone far when the threatening skies that had hung overhead all day opened up and great white flakes of snow began to fall. There was a stillness in the air as it fell silently and straight down. Neither broke the silence with talk.

When they arrived at the village, the dogs were waiting. Laura had the feeling they were in the same spot where she had left them earlier.

Again, no one appeared at their wild barking. Was Red Fox ill, she wondered, or was he with his father, Chief Muga?

Butterfly was in much the same position in which Laura had left her. Laura hurried to feel her forehead, then the pulse in her wrist. The pulse was fast and her brow burning hot. Taking off her jacket, she looked at Fletch. "Will you please add some more wood to the fire, then bring in some more? You'll find where Pa stacked it behind the wigwam."

After Fletch had stirred up the fire and left to bring in more wood, Laura placed the tin pail of broth on some red coals to heat, then returned to Butterfly.

She drew the covers down to the sick woman's waist and laid back the blanket-robe she wore. When she had placed the woolen square and poultice on Butterfly's chest, then covered her up again, she found that the broth had warmed. She filled a small gourd cup from the pail, then added a teaspoon of quinine.

Laura had lifted Butterfly's head and was holding the cup to her lips when Fletch entered, his arms full of wood. "How is she?" he asked quietly.

"She's very ill and burning up with fever. Will you please bring me a pail of snow? I'll rub it on her face and hands, try to keep the fever down. There's quinine in this broth. It should start working in about half an hour."

Fletch picked up a wooden bucket, recognizing it as coming from their store. He stepped outside and within seconds had it packed full of snow. "I'm going over to Red Fox's wigwam now," he said, placing the bucket next to Laura. "I want to see if everything is all right with him and his family."

Laura nodded and began to smooth the snow over Butterfly's face. It melted almost immediately on touching her burning-hot skin. She next formed a small, firm snowball and laid it on Butterfly's dry, cracked lips. Butterfly lifted a hand and eagerly held it there, sipping at the water that thawed and dripped from it.

Laura lost count of time. The snow had melted in the pail and she was now able to dip a piece of cloth into its icy coolness and properly bathe the hot flesh.

She had given Butterfly a second dose of quinine when Fletch and Red Fox entered the wigwam. The Indian looked tired, but not unwell. So far he hadn't been hit by the virus.

"How is your father?" Laura gave him a tired smile.

"His fever has finally broken and the congestion in his chest is loose now. The medicine man says he will not die."

"I'm sure that you, and your people, are happy about that," Laura said, wringing out the cloth and bathing Butterfly's arm. "Are your wife and children well?"

"Yes. All is well with them so far." Red Fox knelt down beside her. "How is my sister responding to your care?"

Surprise flickered in Laura's eyes. She hadn't known that Pa's lover was related to Chief Muga. "She's no worse." She dropped the cloth back into the water. "I think she may be a little better. Her skin doesn't seem to be as hot as it was before."

Fletch picked up the bottle of whiskey with the rock candy in it. "I see you've given her several doses of this."

"Yes. It seems to calm her."

Fletch and Red Fox exchanged amused grins, thinking to themselves that unknowingly Laura was keeping her patient half drunk.

"How are the other sick ones?" Laura asked.

"Not so good," Red Fox answered. "Fletch has been doing what he can for them. I'll be giving him a hand now, and so will the medicine man now that my father is recovering."

Laura looked at Fletch. "We need more help. There are too many sick ones."

"It's not so much that we need more help as we need some of what you've been giving Butterfly," Fletch said.

"Look!" Red Fox broke in on them. "My sister's fever has broken."

Laura jerked her gaze to the sick woman and gave a glad little cry. Beads of sweat had broken out on Butterfly's forehead. "I can start giving her the broth now, build up her strength."

Mopping at the smooth brow, Laura started issuing orders. "Fletch, go back to the house and get my bottle of quinine. It's in the cupboard next to the drysink. Then pick up a quart of whiskey and a pound of rock candy from the store.

"And Red Fox, you can dress out that doe Fletch brought and set the women to making broth out of it."

Neither man stopped to think that they were taking orders from a woman as they hurried to obey her.

Within an hour pots were boiling throughout

the village, sending out the delicious smell of cooking meat. Fletch had made record time in returning with the items Laura had requested, taking only the time to tell Taylor that it looked like Laura was going to pull Butterfly through.

The Indian women who hadn't succumbed to the virus were spooning Laura's remedies down dry throats, and pails of snow were being used on fevered bodies.

It was around two in the morning when Fletch stepped into Butterfly's wigwam and found Laura, her head bowed, sound asleep. He gently eased her down on her side and covered her with a bright Indian blanket he found folded on top of a pile of furs. He knelt beside her a long time, stroking her hair and wishing he hadn't gone off to Canada last spring. Had he stayed, things would be different now.

Before he left, Fletch felt Butterfly's forehead and found it cool. He noted that she was also breathing easily now. Pa's love was going to live, thanks to Laura who had worked so hard to make it so.

Laura and Fletch stayed on at the village three more days, helping to attend the sick. They congratulated each other that no more patients had died.

In the late afternoon of the third day Fletch came to Butterfly's wigwam. His eyes were red-rimmed from not enough sleep, and his jaw was dark with unshaven stubble. "I think we can go home now, Laura," he said. "Everyone is recovering and no one else has come down with the virus."

"Yes, you must go, Laura," Butterfly urged. Although weak, the Indian woman was now able to take care of herself.

"I would like to see Jolie," Laura said and looked up at Fletch. "If you think it's all right, then let's get going. I notice that it has started snowing again. We don't want to get caught out in a blizzard."

She took Butterfly's hands and they looked deeply into each other's eyes. A firm friendship which nothing could break had formed between them. Only Butterfly's eyes thanked her for all that she had done. It was not the Indian custom to speak aloud their gratitude. The favor received would be returned someday.

Red Fox was waiting for them outside the wigwam. Two vicious-looking dogs sat at his feet, a rope tied around their necks. He handed them over to Fletch, saying, "They're mean devils and won't let any wolves attack you." He and Fletch gripped hands; then Red Fox laid a hand on Laura's head as though in blessing.

"I'll drop by tomorrow," Fletch said, then led off down the path.

They had walked but a short distance when the snow thickened and a wind came up. It became so violent that a nearby tree, stiff with frost, came crashing down. The snow seemed to blow in all directions, stinging their faces and blinding their eyes. Fletch knew that he must find shelter for them, and soon. They could not battle this storm.

He peered through the slashing white curtain until he spotted a huge, low-spreading pine only feet away from the path. "Come on." He grabbed Laura's hand. "Let's get under that tree."

Laura's eyes were so tear-filled from the wind and snow, she couldn't see the tree, but she blindly followed Fletch, once stumbling into one of the dogs whose rope Fletch still held on to.

They finally crawled beneath the interlacing boughs, and Fletch immediately began scraping the snow away and piling it into three walls. Then, while Laura waited in the small enclosure, no larger than three feet by three feet, her teeth chattering uncontrollably, Fetch took one of the dogs and went searching for broken boughs and limbs beneath other trees.

It seemed like hours to Laura, but only about 15 minutes had passed when Fletch returned, dragging a good-sized lightning-blasted tree and carrying an armful of spruce boughs he had cut from a tree.

He quickly built a fire, and Laura and the dogs huddled around it while he spread the fir branches on the ground.

When he had them placed to his satisfaction, he lay down on them and said, "Come on, let's try to get some sleep."

Laura hesitated only a moment before scooting away from the fire and crawling onto the makeshift pallet. They lay spoon fashion, her back curled up into the nest of Fletch's chest and drawn up knees. He put his free arm across her waist and pulled her close to him.

Night had fallen, and as Fletch's body heat and the warmth of the fire seeped into Laura's body, she fell asleep.

The dogs, curled as close to the flames as it was safe, growled and snarled a couple times, but only Fletch knew that wolves were smelling around. And he was barely aware of it, he was so firmly fixed on having Laura in his arms.

Chapter Thirteen

Laura roused to a silent world. The wind had ceased to blow and the snow had stopped falling. She lay in a fuzzy state for a moment, gazing at a pile of red glowing coals which the two dogs curled close to. It was several seconds before she became aware that her jacket was unbuttoned and that a hand was thrust into her bodice. Her eyes widened. Lean fingers were stroking her breasts.

She jerked fully awake and flipped over on her back, slapping Fletch's hand away.

"What do you think you're doing?" she demanded sharply.

Fletch came up on an elbow and leaned over her, desire in his dark eyes. "You know what I was doing," he said huskily, "and don't bother to deny you liked it." He rubbed his thumb across her lips.

"I did not! I was asleep!"

He looked significantly at her hardened nipples pressing against her bodice. "See, you even desire me in your sleep."

"I wasn't desiring you." Laura sat up and rebuttoned her jacket. "I was dreaming about somebody else."

"Who? Hunter O'Hara?" Fletch grabbed her wrist when she started to stand up and demanded, his eyes blazing, "Was he making love to you in your dream?"

"Look, I'm cold and hungry and I want to get home to my daughter. I'm not going to sit here in the snow and answer questions that are none of your business."

Jerking her wrist free and standing up, she looked down at the hard ridge riding the front of his buckskins and said coolly, "I suggest you get hold of Milly as soon as possible. You look in a bad way."

As Fletch looked at her, half amused and half angry, she wheeled and walked around the fire that had warmed them through the night, and then struck off through the deep snow that half covered the path.

"Wait for me, you little fool." Fletch came hurrying behind her, the dogs trotting at his heels. "The wolves are still out hunting."

Laura stilled her steps until he caught up with

her, but the trip back to Big Pine was a silent one.

Elisha had just arrived at the store a short time ago after pushing his way through the new foot of snow. He looked up from adding wood to the fire that had burned all night and stared when Laura and Fletch stepped inside.

They were a sorry-looking pair. Their hair was in snarls, full of pine needles. Their clothes were wrinkled and their faces pinched and strained.

"Did you two get caught in the blizzard?" Elisha asked after running his gaze over them.

"We did," Fletch answered shortly, following Laura to the stove and holding his hands over the heat emanating from its top. "Along with a couple of Red Fox's dogs. They're tied up outside. Would you give them something to eat and then turn them loose?"

Elisha's lips curled in his toothless grin. "Widder Louden brought over a pot of stew last night. It was so tasteless me and Taylor ended up eatin' cheese and crackers for supper. Maybe the dogs will eat it."

"Do you think Red Fox would mind if I kept that one that looks half wolf?" Laura asked Fletch as she pulled off her jacket. "He and I became friendly during the time I spent in the village."

"I doubt if he'd even miss him, they've got so many dogs, always raising a racket," Fletch answered as he removed his jacket also.

"Hey, is that you, Laura and Fletcher?" Taylor called from his bed. "Come on in and tell me how everyone is at the village."

Laura smiled to herself as she hurried into what used to be the storeroom, Fletch following her. Pa had said everyone, but he meant how was Butterfly. She sat down on the edge of the cot and Fletch took the chair.

"The influenza is finally licked, Pa." Laura smiled down at his concerned face.

"Nineteen people died, though, before it was over," Fletch added.

"Butterfly was awfully sick for a while but she pulled through," Laura told Taylor. "She sends her regards and says she will come visiting as soon as she gets her strength back."

Taylor's chest heaved in a sigh of relief. "I was awfully worried about her. I was worried about you two also," he quickly added. "The women-folk wouldn't let anyone go to the village to find out how you were doing for fear they'd bring back the sickness. Hunter said he was going anyhow, but the mothers put up such a howl I told him he'd better not go."

Taylor looked at Fletch. "You were lucky no one saw you when you came back for Laura's remedies. Them scared mothers might have driven you away."

"How are the two trappers who were down with the influenza?" Laura asked.

"They're fine. Big Bertha wouldn't let anyone near them, so the sickness didn't spread."

Laura leaned over and kissed Taylor's cheek. "I'm going to fight my way to the cabin now to take a bath and get into some clean clothes. Then I'm going to get my daughter. I can't tell you how much I've missed her. Is she all right? Does cow's milk agree with her?"

"According to Daniel, she took to the bottle without any trouble." He grinned. "Daniel also said that Maida has spoiled the little one rotten. Claims his wife holds her all the time."

"I've kept a fire going in your cabin all the time you was gone, Laura." Elisha walked into the room. "We didn't know when you'd get back and we didn't want you returnin' to a freezin' cold cabin."

Fletch shook his head as he thought to himself that it didn't matter to these two men that Laura had brought shame to the Thomas name. They still doted on her, treated her like a princess.

It didn't occur to him that he was doing much the same thing when he said, "There's no need for you to go fetch Jolie. I'll send Maida over with her."

Laura didn't look at it as if Fletch were doing her a favor, however. To her it only meant that he wanted his cabin free of Maida so that he could be alone with Milly when she came hotfooting it to see him. She merely nodded at Fletch and left the store.

Outside, she found the wolf-looking dog still tied up. Evidently the other one had gone home after helping to eat the widow's stew. She untied the rope from a supporting post, saying, "Come on, boy," then struck out for the cabin.

"I'd better keep you tied up a couple days," she said as she reached the porch. She rubbed the dog's rough head and was repaid with a friendly tail thumping on the floorboards. "When you learn that you're going to get two hearty meals every day, I won't be able to drive you away." She went inside the cabin, returning shortly with an old rug and a moth-eaten blanket. As soon as she spread it in a corner where the wind didn't hit so hard, the dog curled up on the bed she had made for him.

"Tomorrow I'll ask Hunter to build you a doghouse." She gave her new pet a final pat on the head and went back into the cabin.

The cabin wasn't overly warm, but the chill was broken in it. As she added wood to the cook stove, then did the same to the fireplace, she thought how different her life was compared to that of the Indian women. They had few comforts. But, she supposed, one didn't miss what one had never had. Nevertheless, she wished that Butterfly could have things easier.

Would Pa ever marry the Indian woman? she wondered. He loved Butterfly dearly. Laura would be happy for him if he did, but the women of Big Pine would gossip their heads off. Of course, if Pa got it in his head to make Butterfly his wife, it wouldn't bother him in the least what people said.

But how could he marry the woman he loved when he was married to Laura Morris? Her mood was gloomy as she brought clean underclothing and a dress into the kitchen and sponge-bathed before changing into the fresh garments.

Laura had just finished brushing the snarls and pine needles out of her hair when she saw Maida walking toward the cabin. She smiled when she saw Hunter with her, carrying Jolie. She flung open the door, eager to get her hands on her daughter.

"It's good to see you back, Laura." Maida wore a wide smile as she stepped inside. Hunter's face reflected the same gladness as he handed over Jolie.

"I'm very happy to be back," Laura said, lifting the blanket off Jolie's face and kissing her fat little cheeks. "I've missed this little one so," she said softly.

Maida set a basket on the table. "Here's her clothes, all nice and clean. And a bottle that Agnes Morse gave us. Jolie is used to cow's milk now. You can wean her if you want to."

Laura was happy to hear that. Her milk had probably dried up by now.

"Sit down and I'll make us some coffee after I hold this one a bit." Laura kissed Jolie again.

"Thanks, Laura, but I'd better get over to the tavern," Hunter said. "I've got to stock the bar and clean the floor. None of the men ever bother to wipe off their boots before tramping in."

Standing behind the seated Maida, Laura mouthed, "I'll see you tomorrow." Hunter's smiling eyes said that he understood her and he turned to leave.

"I wanted to ask you something, Hunter." Laura stayed him. "I've taken over one of the Indian dogs. I guess you noticed when you stepped up on the porch and heard his growling." When Hunter nodded, she asked, "Do you think you could build him a house?"

Amusement shone in Hunter's eyes. "I expect I could knock one together. But, Laura, you must realize that animal has never had the comfort of his own quarters."

"I don't care," Laura said stubbornly. "That doesn't mean he won't appreciate having a place to crawl into when it snows and the wind blows."

"All right. I'll work on it today when business is slow."

"Thank you, Hunter. Make it big enough for him to be comfortable in."

"Should I put a door on it so he can have his privacy too?" Hunter teased.

"If you want to," Laura said laughingly. "He's smart enough to open and close it."

When Hunter had left, laughing and shaking his head, Maida jumped up, saying, "I'll put the coffee on while you take care of Jolie. I'm just dying to tell you something."

As Laura took Jolie into the family room, talking to her all the while, she wondered what new gossip had sprung up in her absence. No doubt something about her and Fletch.

When the baby's lids grew heavy and she yawned, Laura laid her in her cradle and walked back into the kitchen. "Well," she said, sitting down at the table and smiling at the eager-looking Maida, "what is it you're dying to tell me?"

"Daniel and I are expecting, Laura! I am finally going to get my fondest wish."

"Oh, Maida, I'm so happy for you, for both of you." Laura hugged the young girl. "When?"

"I think sometime next August. We started trying on our wedding night."

"What do you want, a boy or girl?" Laura asked when they had sat down to cups of steaming coffee.

"I don't really care, but Daniel wants it to be a boy. A son who will take care of his mother when his father is gone. He worries a lot about him dying, leaving me with no one to take care of me."

Laura wondered if it had ever occurred to Daniel that if he lived another 20 years Maida would still be a young woman and would in all likelihood marry again. But all Laura said was, "Daniel cares deeply for you." A tinge of sadness in her voice said that she wished someone cared for her like that.

As Laura and Maida sipped their coffee they excitedly talked about baby clothes. Laura would help the young girl make them and she would start knitting baby blankets tonight. Maida bragged that Daniel had already started making a cradle.

An hour later when Maida left, Laura stood at the window watching her wade through the snow and thought that the women of Big Pine wouldn't look down their noses at her little friend when her baby arrived.

"Of course, I'm glad of that," she said, turning from the window. She looked at the clock and decided that she had time for a short nap before it was time to make Pa's lunch.

Fletch had looked forward to a nap also. His sleep had been broken last night what with not being overly warm, desiring Laura, and waking up every time the dogs growled.

He had just made himself comfortable and was falling asleep when there came a rapping on the door and Milly called his name. "Damn," he growled, wondering if she was brazen enough to just walk in without being invited.

He soon discovered that she was, as he heard the outside door creak open. Swearing under his breath, he pulled the covers up over his head. Maybe she would leave him alone if she thought he was sleeping.

Fletch knew that was a foolish thought seconds before Milly was shaking his shoulder.

"Fletch, honey, we've got the cabin to ourselves. Push over and I'll get in beside you."

There was a roaring in Fletch's head, he became so enraged. He flung the cover off his head and, glowering at her, ground out, "I don't want you in bed with me. All I want to do is sleep. I haven't had much lately, you know."

"Well," Milly snapped, offended at his rough manner, "you shouldn't have spent so much time in that little bitch's bed. I hope you know that she only let you bed her because Hunter O'Hara wasn't there to satisfy her."

Fletch jerked up in bed, his rage making Milly catch her breath. "If you don't get off this bed right now, I swear I'll knock you off."

Milly jumped to her feet and moved out of his reach as she continued, "Just because you don't want to hear the truth doesn't mean it isn't so. She meets O'Hara at Big Bertha's place every Thursday. If you don't believe me, just watch around one o'clock tomorrow and you'll see her leave her cabin and walk toward the pleasure house. Then, if you keep watchin', you'll see O'Hara leave his place and go to Big Bertha's too. They always stay there at least a couple hours."

"You're lying, woman." Fletch glared at Milly. "You forget that he bartends in the tavern. I'd know if he left it."

"And you forget that he doesn't work on Thursdays," Millie shot back. "Old Elisha fills in for him."

Was Milly telling the truth? Fletch thought rapidly. Now that he remembered, O'Hara didn't work on Thursdays. Did he and Laura meet at the pleasure house then? Jealousy was added to the rage inside him as he remembered Laura repulsing him this morning. Was it because she was involved with the Southerner?

A thought struck him that made his eyes glitter. Had it been Hunter O'Hara all the time? Was he Jolie's father? There could be blonds among his relatives. His mother or his father.

His voice was dangerously quiet when he looked at Milly and ordered, "Get out."

Milly wished that she could recall every word she had said as she spun around and practically ran from the room. The very devil had shone out of Fletch's eyes. She feared that she had ruined any chances of ever getting Fletch for her husband. Before she got home, however, she had convinced herself that after Fletch cooled down she could eventually get back to her old footing with him.

Sleep deserted Fletch. He was too torn up inside even to close his eyes. Milly had sounded too truthful when she said that Laura met O'Hara at Bertha's every week. He couldn't say he was surprised. O'Hara was handsome, had courtly ways, and always acted the gentleman, even with the whores.

But why hadn't Laura married him when she found that she was carrying his baby? Why foster it off on Pa?

Because Hunter O'Hara has nothing, the little voice inside him whispered. *He couldn't provide for her and a child. He couldn't even buy the land to build her a shack on. Miss Laura wouldn't want to lose her comfortable home and easy living. She'd also want her child to have the same good life.*

"And carry on with the Southerner as usual," Fletch growled to himself.

Suddenly he felt that he had to get out of the cabin, to walk around outside, try to decide what in the world he was going to do. He couldn't endure the way things were much longer.

Fletch avoided the shoveled paths, striking out through the woods in back of the cabin. He didn't want to run into anyone and have to talk while his mind was in such turmoil.

It wasn't hard walking. The trees grew so close together there was scarcely eight inches of snow on the ground. Fletch had walked for about half an hour, thinking and rethinking his suspicions about Laura and Hunter O'Hara, when he heard female voices from back of the Morse place. He wondered if lazy George had sent his women out to hunt or gather wood for their fireplace. He had done it before, according to gossip.

I'll give them a hand, he thought, and walked in the direction of the voices. He stopped short when he rounded a large pine. A few yards away Agnes and her oldest daughter, Mary, each gripping an ankle of George, were dragging him through the snow. The way the fat man's head wobbled, Fletch knew he was dead.

Which of the family had killed him? he asked himself. That had to be the case, otherwise why were they taking George out into the woods for the wolves to find him?

The teenager Jebbie wasn't involved, Fletch decided. Otherwise he instead of his sister would be helping his mother. Had it been the girl who had done George in? He thought not. George had been a worthless father in not providing for his children, but to Fletch's knowledge he had never mistreated them.

That left Agnes. God knew she had ample reason to kill the man. She was worn out from his using her, breeding her as if she were one of his cows and bragging about it, shaming her.

I guess I should just turn around and walk away, Fletch decided, and at that moment Agnes looked up and saw him. Her face, which had been red from exertion, turned deathly white.

They stood gazing at each other for several seconds; then Fletch walked up to Agnes and said gently, "Let me give you a hand, Agnes."

Agnes's mouth gaped open a moment; then she stepped aside, letting Fletch take her place. He smiled at Mary and they moved forward.

"It was an accident, Fletch," Agnes said, walking alongside him. "This morning while I was milking the cow he came into the barn and ordered me to lie down. I've had a misery in my side all winter and I knew I couldn't bear his weight on me. I rose as if to mind him, but instead I grabbed up the pitchfork lying nearby and held it in front of me. It was the first time I ever tried to defend myself, and he let out a roar and charged at me. He rammed against the fork. I guess one of the tines pierced his heart, because he fell down dead."

She looked up at Fletch, tears running down her thin cheeks. "I guess you'll tell the village folks."

"I guess you're wrong, Agnes," Fletcher answered quietly. "I'm not telling you anything except how to handle this."

While Agnes and Mary waited, their eyes glued hopefully on him, Fletcher told them what he had hurriedly thought out. "First, I'm going to roll George's body into that ravine about a dozen yards from here. Then tonight when it's full dark, Agnes, you go to the post and tell whoever is there that George went hunting and hasn't returned home yet. Say that you're afraid he might have been set upon by wolves.

"Now, there will only be a sickle moon tonight, plus it's cloudy. The men won't be in no hurry to go out into them wolf-infested woods to look for a man they don't like in the first place. But if by chance one or two should stir themselves, you point them in the opposite direction from here."

"God bless you, Fletch," young Mary said when her mother was too choked with tears to voice her thanks.

When they came to the shallow ravine, Fletch

said, "Agnes, you and Mary look about frozen. Go on back to your cabin and I'll take care of the rest."

Agnes squeezed his arm with thin, gloveless fingers; then she and her daughter turned around and trudged back toward the shack they called home.

When they were out of sight, Fletch dragged the heavy body to the edge of the depression in the earth, and with one shove sent it rolling down into it. "Too bad you were such a bastard, George Morse," he said. "May God have mercy on your soul."

The next morning Fletch learned that Agnes had done as he had advised her. When full darkness settled in, she had gone to the tavern, a lantern in her hand and Jebbie at her side. Her announcement that George hadn't come home from hunting hadn't made much of an impression on the men gathered there. One man expressed the opinion that it was too dark for him to go looking, and the others agreed, saying that they'd search the woods tomorrow morning.

"He went into the north woods," Agnes said as she opened the door and left, Jebbie behind her.

When she and the teenager were out of hearing distance, one of the trappers voiced everybody's thought. "It'll be a useless, cold trip. We won't find anything but ole George's clothes and a pile of bones."

Chapter Fourteen

Two weeks had passed and George Morse's disappearance had made only a slight stir in the village. Four men had made a halfhearted attempt to search the forest back of the post. They had returned within an hour saying that they had found no trace of the man.

As far as anyone knew, only his sister, Martha Louden, had shed any tears when it was decided that the wolves had gotten the fat man. Martha, however, showed no sympathy toward her sister-in-law, nieces, and nephews. When asked if she would be helping them out over the winter months, she had answered coolly, "No, I will not. Agnes would only waste the money."

"You mean like buying food with it?" old

Elisha had asked sarcastically, which the widow ignored.

But others had pitched in to help out Agnes and her brood. Fletch looked at the big glass pickle jar he had placed on the counter for donations. It was almost full of greenbacks and loose change. Reverend Stiles had passed the basket for the Morses at last Sunday's meeting and was pleased with his parishioners' generosity. All last week Big Bertha had charged the men a little extra for the use of her girls and had turned that money over to the store to be used for provisions for the Morse family.

Maida and Justine had gone to the families with children, asking for any clothing they could spare. And the day after George's disappearance, Taylor had sent over a side of beef, a hundred-pound bag of potatoes, and other staples the family might be out of.

Fletch felt a real sense of pride for the people of Big Pine. They looked out for each other. He looked up at the clock. It was time to pick up Pa's lunch. As he shrugged into his jacket he knew that Laura would be watching for him through the window. As soon as she saw him coming she would set the basket out on the porch, then lock the door behind her.

She is wise to do that, he thought wryly. He ached for her so badly, he would surely try to seduce her.

As Fletch made his way up the tunnel-like path to the cabin he remembered that it was

Thursday. Laura would be meeting O'Hara at Big Bertha's place today.

Milly hadn't lied when she told him that if he watched he would see the two of them go to the pleasure house about ten minutes apart. When he had seen it happen, it had taken all his willpower not to go after them. He had wanted so badly to beat O'Hara to a pulp and haul Laura home. But she'd had Jolie with her, and he didn't want to fight in front of the little one.

But how it had hurt, thinking how the baby's father would play with her and hold her for a while before taking her mother into one of Bertha's back bedrooms. His stomach had tied in knots as he visualized them in bed together, making love. Did Laura respond to the Irishman the same way she did with him?

As he had expected, the basket sat waiting on the porch for him. The wolf dog that Laura had named Brave stuck his head out of the doghouse that someone had made for him. The growl in his throat died away when he recognized Fletch.

"You're getting to be quite handsome with all that good food you get now, aren't you, fellow?" Fletch said, wishing he dared pat the large head. So far, the dog allowed only Laura to touch him. He acted like a foolish puppy with her, jumping around, wanting her to play with him.

Fletch picked up the pail, muttering sourly, "You're like all the other males in Big Pine. They all want to play with her too.

"But none as badly as me," he added as he struck off for the post.

Taylor was sitting on the edge of the cot when Fletch brought the lunch basket to him. Daniel had made him a pair of crutches, and each day as his leg mended, he used them a little longer. He spent a lot of his daylight hours in the store and tavern, happy to have the company of friends and neighbors again.

As Fletch transferred Taylor's lunch onto a tray and placed it on the bed beside him he noted the bright afghan around his shoulders. "Where'd you get that? I've never seen it before." He arched a teasing eyebrow at his father. "Did Widow Louden knit it for you?"

"I wouldn't be wearing it if she did." Taylor dipped a spoon into the potato soup Laura had sent him. "Laura gave it to me last week. It's my Christmas gift from her and Jolie."

Fletch realized with a start that Christmas had come and gone while he and Laura were at the Indian village. "Did the usual celebrating go on?" Fletch asked.

"No, it was kinda gloomy. No one had the holiday spirit, worrying if influenza was going to spread to the village. But thanks to you and Laura, there's no more threat of that."

Butterfly had visited Taylor last night, the first time in two weeks. Fletch wondered if they had managed to make love, what with Pa's leg in splints. He remembered the old saying,

Where there's a will there's a way. Pa looked so relaxed today, Fletch was pretty sure they had found a way.

It seemed to him that everybody except himself had found ways of making love. Milly had wheedled her way back into their cabin, and last night in a desperate effort to banish Laura from his mind he had given in to Milly's urging and had taken her to bed. He had been embarrassed and Milly had been enraged when, despite everything she tried, he remained flaccid.

She had finally jumped out of bed, yelling, "Did you freeze that damn thing when you were in Canada, or is it that whorin' little bitch Laura that has you actin' like a gelded stallion?" She had flounced out of the cabin, and hadn't been back. In one sense he was relieved, in another a little disappointed. If she wasn't hanging around him, how could he pretend to Laura that they were lovers?

"How are Laura and the little one?" Taylor asked after taking a swallow of coffee. "Did you tell her I wanted to see them?"

"I forgot to," Fletch lied. He didn't want Taylor to know that things were worse than ever between him and Laura.

"That was real nice of Hunter to make Laura's dog a house, wasn't it?"

"Oh, yes, O'Hara's a very obliging fellow," Fletch said.

Taylor heard the sarcasm in Fletch's tone and, frowning at him, said, "I thought you and

Hunter had made it up since your fight. You sound like you're ready to fight him again. Have you had words?"

You don't know how badly I want to fight him again, Pa, Fletch thought, a nerve jerking in his jaw. *I'd like to tear him apart.* But what he said was, "No, we haven't had words. Sometimes he just rubs me the wrong way."

Taylor's eyes twinkled. "I imagine sometimes you do the same thing to him. You two remind me of two bull moose, each afraid the other is going to move in on his territory."

Fletch gave his father a narrowed look, wondering what he meant by that. He didn't ask him, though, as he picked up the tray and went back into the store. He idled about a bit, swearing that he would not watch out of the window to see if Laura went to Bertha's this Thursday.

But no matter how hard he tried not to, his eyes kept straying toward the window. His hands clenched into fists when in about 15 minutes the cabin door opened and Laura stepped out onto the porch. A bundled-up Jolie was clasped to her breast. He waited a few minutes, then, knowing that he was chancing a blow to his heart but unable to help himself, he went into the tavern and stood at the window that gave him a view of the pleasure house.

He hadn't long to wait before Hunter approached the building. When Bertha opened the door to the Southerner, Fletch wheeled around, his face stony, not answering Elisha when the old man said, "I'm gonna need more whiskey, Fletch."

Bertha had coffee and cookies waiting for Laura and Hunter. The big woman was mystified about the relationship between the pair. They were very fond of each other, there was no doubt about that. But they never asked to be alone together. They seemed content to sit at her table and visit with her.

And that was the poser. Every single man, and many married ones, would almost sell his soul to the devil to make love to Laura Thomas, and the single girls were crazy about Hunter O'Hara. Yet neither seemed eager to get into bed together.

Bertha decided that today she was going to invent some excuse to leave the pair alone together. She would give them the opportunity to use one of her rooms without having to ask, if that was their problem.

Laura and Hunter had been in her kitchen about 20 minutes, she holding Jolie, when Bertha asked, "Is it all right if I take the little one into the parlor so the girls can play with her awhile? I'll stay and keep an eye on her."

"Of course." Laura smiled. "The little scamp loves being made a fuss over."

When the madam left the kitchen, a chortling Jolie grabbing at her frizzed hair, Laura looked at Hunter with an amused grin. "She thinks we want to be alone."

Hunter nodded, his eyes twinkling. Then looking soberly at Laura he said, "Laura, you must have wondered why I haven't tried to make our friendship into something more serious."

"Not really, Hunter. But since you've brought it up, why haven't you?"

Hunter hesitated a minute, fingering the scar on his cheek. Then he said, "Do you recall me telling you I got this in the war and that I have other scars?" Laura nodded, and he went on. "The other scar that I carry robbed me of my manhood. There will never be a wife and children for me."

Shocked, Laura could only stare at Hunter, the misery in his eyes. Then making a sound of sympathy, she stood up and rounded the table to press his head against her breasts. "I am so sorry, my dear friend," she whispered.

Hunter put his arms around her waist and they stayed that way for several seconds, tears in both their eyes.

"Don't feel bad for me, Laura," Hunter said, dropping his arms from around her. "I've gotten used to it. It was hell at first. I only felt like half a man. Then an old wise Indian pointed out to me that the thing that hung between a man's legs didn't necessarily make him a man. It was what he carried inside him."

"He was so right, Hunter." Laura returned to her chair. "I have never known any man who was more manly than you."

The subject was dropped, and they talked of Taylor's birthday coming up next week and the party Laura planned for him. When Bertha returned an hour later, she found them where she had left them, having a second cup of coffee and debating whether Taylor's party should be a surprise or not.

Laura and Hunter winked at each other, seeing the disappointment on the painted face.

Pushing back her frustration, Bertha handed the baby to Laura and poured herself a cup of coffee. The three sat around discussing the Morse family, wondering how they were getting on. "Much better, I'd think, with that lazy-ass George out of their lives," Bertha said.

Hunter agreed. "They do look happier these days. That pinched, hungry look is gone from their faces."

"And what a change in Agnes," Laura said. "you can tell that she was once a very attractive woman."

Bertha agreed and added, "And she will be again once she gains some weight."

"I don't suppose she'll ever marry again. There's not many men who would want to take on her brood and raise them," Laura said.

Bertha gazed thoughtfully into her coffee. "I doubt that Agnes would want to ever marry again. She told me emphatically that she would never again share a bed with a man. Being married to George cured her of ever wanting another man in a biblical sense, not even if he was an angel sent down from heaven."

Later, when Laura had said good-bye and was walking home, she still had Agnes on her mind.

What if Agnes and Hunter got together? They were around the same age. Agnes had no use for men, in her bed at least, and poor Hunter wouldn't want or need that part of a relationship. He loved children and would have a ready-made family. Also, having a wife, he would appear like every other man in the village.

She would throw the two together every chance she got, Laura continued to daydream. Agnes must come to Pa's birthday party. Maida would be happy to lend her one of her new dresses, and Agnes had beautiful thick hair if taken out of the tight knot she kept it in.

Her face glowed with the thought of playing Cupid.

Chapter Fifteen

As Laura visited with the Morse family, she urged for the third time, "Please come to Taylor's birthday party, Agnes. You and your children will be the only family who won't be there."

"But, Laura, you know I've never attended any of the affairs in the village," Agnes reminded her.

"I know that, and it's high time that you did. You would be more than welcome at any get-together."

Agnes looked down at her worn but neat dress. "Anyhow, I haven't got anything nice to wear." She looked up at Laura. "I'll send Mary and Jebbie. They've never been to a party before and will look forward to it. Thanks to the neighbors, they can can get dressed up pretty good."

"And so can you. Maida would be pleased to loan you one of her dresses. She's never been to a party before and she's real excited about finally attending one."

"I don't know, Laura," Agnes said, weakening. "It's been so long since I've been with a group of people. I don't know if I can remember how to act."

"You'll act just fine, don't worry about it, just be your own sweet self."

"Do you really think the women will talk to me?"

"Of course they will," Laura answered, then gave a little derisive laugh. "I'm the one they won't talk to. They look on me as a fallen woman, you know."

"I've heard that mean gossip and I think it's a shame, all because your little one has blond hair. Three of my children were born with blond hair, and God knows I never lay with any man other than George. I wouldn't have had the strength nor the opportunity to do so. It could be that either you or Taylor had white-haired relatives some generations back. It just came out in Jolie."

"Me and Ma will talk to you, Laura," young Mary said from her seat beside the fireplace. "Won't we, Ma?"

"We certainly will." Agnes's eyes snapped angrily. "I don't know how some folks can be so mean. I know they've been good to me and my children, but I can't help holding it against them, talking about you the way they do."

Laura shrugged a slim shoulder. "I don't let it bother me anymore. It used to hurt at first. I've known those women all my life. But I have Justine and Maida, and now you, for friends." Her lips tilted in a grin. "And I mustn't forget Big Bertha."

"All those gossipers are going to be sorry the way they've treated you someday. You just wait and see," Agnes said with conviction. "As your little one grows older she's going to start looking like a Thomas. Either her hair will darken or her features will take on the look of Taylor. It never fails. The truth most always comes out. I've seen it happen with my own children."

"Do you really think so, Agnes?" Laura asked eagerly.

"I know so."

A few minutes later Laura left the small two-room cabin that was now snug and warm. Some of the village men had spent a day recaulking between the logs and cutting wood. Agnes now had enough wood to last her through the winter, plus enough money to provide food for the family. Any time she needed something from the store, Fletch took the cost from the big pickle jar. Come spring, rested and strong again, Agnes and her children would put in crops and be able to support themselves.

Laura was so deep in thought she almost forgot to stop at the store and collect Jolie. "You've been gone long enough." Fletch glowered at her when she stepped inside. "I can't believe you've spent all this time with Agnes Morse. Are you stringing a new man along now?"

"Yes, I am." An impish devil glittered in Laura's eyes. "He's a trapper friend of yours. I really like him. I may hold on to him for a while."

Rage darkened Fletch's face so much that Laura took a step back, sure that this time he would strike her. But he made no move toward her. His eyes icy bleak, he said, "You've turned into quite a slut, haven't you?" When Laura merely shrugged, he grated out, "Take your bastard and get out of my sight."

Laura gasped from the pain Fletch's words caused her. In all his name-calling he had never attacked Jolie before. Tears sprang into her eyes as she picked the baby up out of her basket.

She was halfway to the door when Fletch came after her, saying thickly, "I'm sorry, Laura, I didn't mean that about Jolie. I care deeply for her, you know that."

Laura stared up at him, mockery glittering in her tear-wet eyes. "But underneath that deep caring you look upon her as a bastard. Your anger let it slip out."

"That's not true. I admit that anger made me say it, but I have never, ever thought of the little one that way."

"Hah!" Laura snorted sharply and slammed

out the door, leaving Fletch standing there, utter defeat on his face.

Laura would hate him until the day she died, he thought.

Laura wiped her eyes as she approached the cabin and saw a young Indian waiting for her on the porch. He was hunkered down beside Brave, rubbing his head and talking to him. When she stepped up on the porch, the boy jumped to his feet. She vaguely remembered seeing him in the Indian village.

She smiled at him and he said, "I am Chief Muga's grandson. He has sent me to give you this." He handed her a small, flat package.

Laura thanked him and took the package. "Please come inside while I lay my daughter down. I don't want her to catch cold."

The teenager hesitated a moment, then, having always wondered what the white man's cabins looked like inside, nodded and followed her.

"Have a seat." Laura motioned toward the rocking chair. "I'll just be a minute."

The boy's black, curious eyes scanned the room, taking in the furnishings, the pictures on the walls, the clock whose ticking fascinated him, the bright woven rugs on the floor. He relaxed after a moment and sat back in the chair. His movement set the chair to rocking, and, startled, he began to jump to his feet. Then he discovered that it wasn't going to spill him to the floor, and he moved it to make it rock again.

When Laura returned a minute later he had the chair rocking madly, a wide smile on his face. He's going to tip it over, Laura thought with concern and hurried to say, "Come sit at the table and have some cookies and milk."

When Laura poured the milk and placed a plate of the sugar delicacies before the lad, he eyed the sweets curiously. "Taste one, you'll like it," Laura urged.

The young Indian picked up one of the round, flat sweets and cautiously bit into it. He chewed and swallowed; then a grin spread across his face. "Good," he said and reached for another one.

"You're Red Fox's son, aren't you?" Laura asked, recognizing the smile as similar to that of Fletch's Indian friend.

"Yes. I am called Little Fox," Laura was answered proudly. "I am my parents' firstborn. It was my father's face that I saw when I opened my eyes."

Laura picked up the package from Little Fox's grandfather and opened the square of tanned animal skin. Her eyes widened at the beautiful necklace that lay there. A large piece of turquoise was framed in beaten silver and hung from a leather thong. In its center was carved an Indian symbol. As she rubbed a finger over it, Little Fox explained, "It is a sign that if any of our tribe see this around your neck, they will never harm you. There might come a time when they will help you if you need it."

"Please tell your grandfather that I will treasure his gift. I will wear it every time I leave the vicinity of the village."

"He will be pleased to hear that," Little Fox said, reaching for yet another cookie.

The teenager proved to be quite a talker. He spoke of his family, and until the cookie plate was empty, he boasted of hunting trips he had gone on. When he finally rose to leave, Laura invited, "Come visit me anytime. I bake cookies almost every day."

When Little Fox closed the door behind him, Laura took Chief Muga's gift into her bedroom and laid it in a small cedar chest that Fletch had made for her on her fourteenth birthday. It joined a string of beads, a pair of earbobs, and a brooch. Items precious to her. They had belonged to mother Marie.

Closing the lid on the fragrant cedar, she went back to the kitchen and started preparing supper. Fletch would arrive within the next hour to pick up Taylor's evening meal, and she wanted to be sure the basket was outside waiting for him. She wished that she need never again see or talk with him. Insulting her baby had been the last straw.

As she peeled potatoes and carrots to add to the beef stew, Laura knew it was impossible not to see Fletch again, but she wouldn't have to talk to him. She had to visit Pa at least every other day or he would want to know why she was staying away. If she told him why, Lord knew what he might say to Fletch in anger. That she wanted to avoid at all costs.

Stars shone coldly in the sky as Laura hurried toward the Morse cabin. She was late. Big Bertha had come to take care of Jolie while Laura attended Taylor's birthday party, and she had lingered too long visiting with the madam.

As she stepped up on the sagging porch, a glance through the window showed the Morses waiting for her. "I could never bring myself to face all the neighbors alone," Agnes had said a couple days ago. It had been agreed then that the family would walk into the tavern with Laura.

When Laura stepped into the room crowded with children and they all greeted her excitedly, she thought what a difference a short time had made in them. They had lost their shaggy appearance, and the hungry look was gone from their eyes. Their faces had been scrubbed shiny clean, and the boys all wore trimmed hair. The donated clothes they wore had been neatly ironed.

The biggest change was in Agnes. The attractiveness that had once been hers was slowly returning. Her new hairstyle softened the thinness of her features and brought to attention her soft, magnificent brown eyes. The beaten look in them was almost gone.

Taylor's birthday party had already begun

when Laura and the Morses arrived. A dance set had just finished when they stepped inside, and the cold air that rushed in behind them brought everyone's eyes swinging their way. The women, smiles on their faces, came forward to welcome Agnes, elbowing Laura out of the way.

Two men saw that happen and neither one liked it. It pained Fletch to see her ostracized by her onetime friends. He started to step forward, to buffer their harsh treatment of Laura, then stopped. Hunter O'Hara was making his way to her, his lips curved in a wide smile. Fletch turned away when Laura smiled back at Hunter.

The three musicians struck up another tune, but when Hunter would have swung her out onto the floor, Laura hung back. "I must speak to P . . . Taylor first. Wish him a happy birthday."

She had decided not to surprise Taylor with the celebration, but to give him warning so that he could spruce himself up a bit. Which he had done, she had noticed earlier as he talked to the friends and neighbors who had gathered around him. He had managed to get his splinted leg into a new pair of trousers and pull on his favorite blue flannel shirt.

He doesn't look sixty, she thought, or act like it. He still had the muscle tone of a man much younger and had all his hair, although it was mostly gray now. And she mustn't forget Butterfly. He still had a love life.

It's too bad, Laura thought as she and Hunter approached Taylor, that Butterfly isn't by his side tonight.

"Happy birthday, Taylor." Laura placed a kiss on his cheek.

"Thank you, daughter," Taylor said, drawing many curious looks. Unaware that he had erred, he shook hands with Hunter when the bartender offered his best wishes. They chatted awhile; then Hunter noted that three men were waiting for drinks at the bar.

He took Laura's arm and escorted her across the room where Maida made room for her on the bench. "Remember, the next dance is mine," he said to Laura, then returned to the bar and began dispensing drinks to the thirsty men. They had complained at first about being served only hard cider, then had grumblingly agreed it was only proper that nothing stronger was being served with a lot of children running around.

Justine and Tommy came over to sit with Maida and Laura, and after a while Agnes managed to get away from those who had snubbed her friend and joined the small group of Laura's supporters. In a short time Daniel appeared with a tray of sweet cider which had been provided for the women. Soon they had their own private little party going. Their laughter at some joke would ring out, making the young single women look at them with envy as they were kept at their mothers' sides.

Sometimes Agnes's laughter pealed out louder than the others'. Her flushed cheeks and sparkling eyes made the older bachelors watch her with interest. But when the music started up again and the men approached her, asking her to dance, she refused.

"Why don't you dance with them, Agnes?" Laura asked. "They're all nice, decent men."

Agnes shivered. "I don't think I'll ever be able to get that close to a man again, Laura."

"If Hunter O'Hara asks you to dance, please oblige him. You will have no aversion to him. He's the kindest, gentlest man you could ever meet."

Agnes hesitated for several seconds before answering, "If he asks me, I'll try, just to please you, Laura."

A minute later Hunter was pulling Laura to her feet, swinging her among the other dancers who had taken to the floor. As they circled around, dodging stamping feet and whirling bodies, they smiled and talked and laughed. The watching women raised their eyebrows and made remarks behind their hands.

Nearing the end of a waltz, Laura looked up at Hunter and asked, "Will you ask Agnes to dance the next set?"

"But she turned down the other men."

"I don't think she'll refuse you." Her eyes twinkled mischievously. "I told her what a grand fellow you are and that you wouldn't step on her feet."

Hunter threw back his head and laughed. "I'm convinced that you've got Irish in you." He gave her a tight, affectionate hug that didn't go unnoticed by Fletch, who had seldom taken his eyes off Laura since she arrived.

"I'd better get the hell out of here before I beat him to a pulp," Fletch muttered to himself and yanked his jacket off the wall. He opened the store and got a bottle of whiskey, and left.

When Hunter asked Agnes to dance, she accepted, though it was obvious she was a little nervous about it. Holding her loosely, keeping several inches between them, Hunter was surprised how well she danced, how light she was on her feet as he swung her around the room. He thought how very pretty she would be with a few pounds of weight added to her small frame. He talked quietly to her as one would a frightened deer. He spoke of their long, hard winter and complimented her on how nicely her children behaved. Once he even coaxed a shy, timid smile from her.

When the set was over, Hunter led Agnes back to where Laura was waiting and thanked her graciously for the dance. When he and Laura were back on the dance floor, he said, "Did you know that Agnes is from Georgia?"

"No, I didn't. I was of the opinion she was from the South, though, from her soft speech, the way she talks."

"She's so frail looking it makes a man want to take care of her."

"Maybe some men would feel that way, but certainly her dead husband didn't. He treated her shamefully."

"That beast should have been shot minutes after he was born," Hunter gritted through his teeth.

Agnes danced with Hunter twice more but refused the other men who tried again to get her to dance with them.

When the party broke up at midnight and Agnes began gathering her brood, Hunter walked over to her. "I'll walk you and the children home." When she demurred, he said forcefully, "It's not safe for you and the young ones to be walking alone in the woods."

Laura, along with others, lifted an eyebrow when Hunter escorted Agnes and her family through the door. Most of the women asked each other what did that handsome Southerner see in skinny Agnes Morse? They didn't know, as Laura knew, that Hunter had recognized a kindred spirit in Agnes's beautiful, haunted eyes. They both had wounds that went deep into their souls.

Everyone trooped out of the tavern, and Laura said good night to Maida and Justine and walked the short distance home. She found Jolie asleep in her cradle and Bertha asleep in the rocker. She gently shook the madam awake.

"How was the party?" Bertha asked at the end of a wide yawn. "Did you have a good time?"

"It was a fine get-together. Taylor enjoyed

himself, visiting with his friends again."

"What about you? Did you have a good time?"

"Oh yes. Hunter and I danced a lot."

Bertha said no more. Laura's tone had told her what she wanted to know. The young woman would have preferred to stay home.

Later, lying in bed, Laura wondered why Fletch had left the party so early, and why he hadn't danced with anyone. Milly was there, dancing with any man who asked her. Had that made him angry? Jealous?

Before Laura fell asleep she hoped that Milly gave him the same pain he had given her when he called their daughter a bastard.

Chapter Sixteen

Laura turned the calendar to February. The new year was a month old. She sighed. She couldn't see that her life would be any different in the new year than it had been before. She would still be married to Pa, each day slipping into another, nothing changing.

The years ahead looked very bleak. She would always stand on the sideline, watching the changes that would come into her friends' lives as they raised their children, wives and husbands working together, loving each other, making love at night.

None of that was in her future, Laura thought gloomily, carrying her cup of coffee to the window and looking out on the white world. Laura Thomas would raise her child alone, her little daughter most likely being shunned as her mother was. She had no doubt that most of the people in Big Pine looked on Jolie as Fletch did. A bastard.

Laura saw Daniel leave the store and was reminded that she was supposed to visit Maida that afternoon. Maida certainly had a lot to look forward to. Her girlish figure had a small protrusion in the stomach now. And though she claimed she had never felt better, Daniel watched over her like a mother wolf with one pup.

Laura's mood lightened somewhat when she saw Little Fox trotting up the path to the cabin. He showed up two or three times a week to visit and to eat cookies. Yesterday she had baked his favorites, oatmeal and raisin.

Little Fox paused on the porch to stroke Brave's head and talk to him in Indian language. Laura had learned only recently that the wolf dog had belonged to him before she had taken him. She had felt badly and offered to return the animal to him.

Little Fox had shaken his head and said, "He is better off with you. Here he has a dry place to sleep and plenty to eat. I will come visit him if you don't mind."

Laura had managed to keep a straight face, knowing that his visit would be mainly an excuse to eat some cookies. She wore a welcoming smile when she opened the door at his knock. Her smile was returned; then the teenager went to the table and sat down in the chair he always used. She placed milk and cookies before him, and, his eyes shining like polished black beads, Little Fox helped himself.

The young Indian was a bright lad and Laura always enjoyed his company. After politely asking about his family, she brought up a subject they often discussed—the Isle Royale in Lake Superior.

In one of the long talks they'd had while Butterfly was recovering from the flu, the Indian woman had described the island. "It has a serene beauty about it," she said; "calm and peaceful, with the water lapping at its shores. There's an old log cabin almost hidden by the tall pines that grow around it. A trapper built it many years ago. No one knows what happened to him, but it is believed that he was killed by wolves one winter.

"When the boys of the village reach a certain age, they are sent alone to the island to test their courage, to become men."

Laura had often thought of that place after that, especially on days when she was sunk in a gloom of despair, longing to get away from the disdainful looks and the whispers that went on behind her back. But most of all she thought of escaping the contempt in Fletcher's eyes every time she came near him, the scorch of hot desire from his dark eyes as they skimmed over her body.

Laura gave herself a mental shake and came

back to the present as Little Fox was saying, "Come spring I will be going alone to the island. I will spend a month there, living off the land. I will kill rabbits and quail to eat, and when I grow tired of meat I will fish for perch and bass. In between I will lie in the sun and listen to the songs of robins and meadowlarks and bluebirds as I meditate."

"What about wolves? Don't they frighten you?"

"A little. Of course I will always have to be on the alert for them."

As Little Fox talked on about the small piece of land in the same glowing terms Butterfly had used, there grew in Laura the determination that when the lad went there next spring, she would go with him. She would have to follow him secretly, though, for no doubt he wouldn't want her with him. The rule was that he had to live alone on the island.

As Little Fox continued to talk and eat cookies, half-formed plans grew in Laura's mind. She would ride the mare, of course. Jolie was getting too big to carry any distance. And for their protection she would take a pistol and a rifle and the dog. Once they arrived at the island they would have shelter in the old cabin.

When the cookie plate was empty, Little Fox said it was time he left. "I am going hunting with my father," he said proudly. When Laura closed the door behind him, she wrapped Jolie in a heavy blanket and hurried along to Maida's cabin, her feet crunching crisply in the snow, her nose puffing little clouds of white vapor.

Maida swung open the door as soon as Laura stepped up on the porch. "You're late," she said. "I thought you weren't coming." When Laura stepped inside, Maida took Jolie so that her mother could take off her jacket.

"Little Fox stopped by," Laura said, hurrying over to the fire as Maida unwrapped Jolie and sat her in the high chair that had been purchased for her own baby that was on its way. "We got to talking about Isle Royale, and time got away from me."

Giving Jolie a string of colorful wooden beads to play with, she asked, "Where is Isle Royale?"

"A place where the Indians go from time to time. Little Fox has gone there many times to hunt and fish with his father." As Laura sat down at the well-scrubbed table, something told her not to mention that the boy would be going there in the spring. When she left Big Pine she didn't want anyone to suspect where she had gone.

"You'll never guess who came to visit me yesterday," Maida said after she had poured coffee and sliced a piece of apple pie for both of them.

"Big Bertha," Laura guessed.

Maida shook her head. "Agnes Morse."

"I can't believe it," Laura said. "I think it's wonderful that she is coming out of her shell and getting to finally know her neighbors. What did you talk about?"

"Oh, I don't know. Just things like you and I talk about. Cooking, sewing, and of course the weather." She laughed shortly. "Nobody ever talks long without mentioning that. She sure is sour on men. Every time a man was mentioned, her face got all stony looking."

"Yes," Laura agreed. "I'm afraid Agnes will never get over the way George treated her. She'll probably go to her grave never letting a man touch her intimately again."

"It's a shame, too. She could use the help of a man, trying to raise all those children by herself."

"You know what seemed odd," Laura said thoughtfully. "Agnes turned down several men who invited her to dance, then danced three times with Hunter."

"What struck everyone as odd was that she let him walk her and her brood home. What do you make of that?"

"I think it was because Hunter didn't scare her. He has a gentleness about him that makes women trust him."

"I've noticed that about him." Maida nodded. "That would appeal to Agnes, never having had any kindness from that awful George. The poor woman must be starved for affection."

Laura was about to agree when Jolie began to fuss and rubbed her eyes. She stood up and reached for her jacket. "She's ready for her nap, and I might as well take her home and put her to bed. If I don't, she'll raise a racket that all the neighbors can hear."

"I'll walk with you," Maida said as Laura wrapped her irritable daughter back into the blanket. "I need to pick up a few things at the store."

They had walked but a short distance when a feminine voice called out Maida's name. "What does that gossip want?" Maida muttered as they both turned their heads to watch Martha Louden hurrying toward them.

Ignoring Laura as though she were one of the snow-covered stumps scattered about the area, Martha smiled at Maida and said, "I just wanted to remind you that tomorrow we're to meet at the church hall to work on the quilt we ladies are makin' for poor Agnes."

A frown etching her forehead, Maida said shortly, "I remember," then hurried after Laura, who had walked on ahead. Martha stared after her, indignation in her stance as she stood with her hands on her hips. She turned around so fast to head back to her cabin, she slipped on the icy snow and sat down hard. As she struggled to her feet, gales of laughter trilled from the throats of Big Bertha's girls who had just stepped outside to take a short, brisk walk.

Her chin in the air, Martha moved on down the path, walking as quickly as she dared on the frozen snow, the sound of the whores' amusement following her.

"I can't stand that old bitch." Maida's eyes

snapped angrily when she caught up with Laura. "She's mean and spiteful. Justine told me that Martha's got it in for you because she wanted to land Taylor herself. And I think it's just awful that she isn't helping out with her nephews and nieces. The only reason she's helping with the quilt is so she can hear the latest gossip."

"Of which I'm the prime subject, I'm sure," Laura said bitterly.

"Your name is not mentioned when Justine and I are there," Maida declared. "The first time ole Louden started to bad-mouth you, Justine and I jumped all over her. Justine pointed out to her that if Taylor ever got wind of anyone talking bad about you, he'd probably refuse to let them in his store. I'll bet there's very little talk going on about you these days."

Amusement sparkled in the young wife's eyes. "It's a thirty-mile trip to the next village and fur post. There'd be some mighty angry husbands if they had to make that trip very often. Especially when they learned why Taylor wouldn't sell them anything."

"Maybe I'm not their favorite topic anymore, but I'm sure there's a few of them that get together and rip me up the back. Their attitude toward me hasn't changed." Laura smiled warmly at her young friend. "Thank you, Maida, for standing up for me."

Maida smiled back. "It gave me a lot of pleasure to tear into that old biddy," she said as they came to the path that branched off toward the Thomas cabin. They said good-bye, Laura hurrying home and Maida going on to the store, walking carefully so as not to slip on patches of ice.

Chapter Seventeen

February and March passed in much the same way as the months before them, cold and snowy and gloomy. It was now a week into April, and except for scattered patches that still hung on in shaded spots, the snow had melted. The paths that meandered around stumps that dotted the area were now ankle-deep quagmires. Women were constantly nagging husbands and children to wipe their feet before entering the cabin. Big Bertha made her customers take off their boots before entering her establishment.

Stands of birch were sprouting new leaves the size of a squirrel's ear, and the willows along the lake were putting on a soft misty green. The trappers had brought in their traps and hung them up until the first frost of the next season.

All of Big Pine had taken a new lease on life. Changes had taken place in the Thomas cabin also. Jolie, nearly ten months old, had grown out of her infant clothes, and it seemed to Laura that she spent half her time sewing new ones for her. She was crawling now and getting into everything she could reach. Laura expected her to start walking any day. For the past two weeks the little blond-haired beauty had been pulling herself up to chairs and walking around them as her chubby fingers hung on to the seat. Butterfly had made her a beautiful pair of moccasins, butter soft and bead-trimmed. It was difficult for her mother to keep them on her little feet, she was so fascinated with the colorful beadwork and wanted to play with them.

Jolie had trained easily to her own little chamber pot and now took her meals with her mother. She sat in the same high chair that Laura had used before her, banging on the tray with her small fists if food wasn't promptly put into her rosebud of a mouth. She had a small vocabulary: mama, eat, wawa, and dada. Ironically, she used the last word for both Taylor and Fletch.

It gave Laura great satisfaction to hear her daughter refer to Fletch as dada. She never corrected her. Although he became very flustered when called that endearing name, when Jolie reached her arms to him to be held, Fletch never hesitated to take her.

Laura smiled wryly as she stood in the open

doorway looking out on the bright spring morning. She and Fletch had exchanged bitter words a couple weeks ago. Not that that was unusual for them, but this had been their worst to date.

One morning, shortly after breakfast, her stomach had felt unsettled and she had visited the privy. She was on her way back to the cabin when without warning bile rose in her throat and she bent over, losing her morning meal. She had finished and was leaning weakly against a tree when Fletch spoke from a few feet behind her.

"You're in a family way again, aren't you?" he asked, his voice tight with accusation.

It was on Laura's tongue to deny his words, knowing that she had just finished her menses. Then she had thought, why bother? After all, she didn't care what he thought of her. Time would prove him wrong.

She looked him full in the face and said defiantly, "Yes, I am."

Fletch sucked in his breath, his face going a shade paler. "By the same bastard, I suppose," he finally spoke.

Laura knew he was referring to Hunter, and turning her face away from him so that he wouldn't see the amusement in her eyes, she answered, "Yes, by the same bastard."

There was a moment of tense silence; then Fletch rasped, "This is going to break Pa's heart, you know." When Laura made no response, he swallowed a couple times, then asked dully,

"Why don't you set aside your marriage to Pa and marry the man who has fathered two children on you? You can't go on hurting people this way."

"I suppose when you say *people* you're referring to Pa. I can't imagine that I'd hurt anyone else. At any rate, I have no desire to marry Jolie's father. Something happened between us that showed me he isn't the type of man I'd care to share my life with."

"Look," Fletch began, but before he could continue, Daniel walked out of the woods and joined them. Laura smiled at the big man and grabbed the opportunity to get away from Fletch and into the house.

Laura sighed as she picked up the broom to sweep the kitchen floor. This coming Sunday she would begin the trip that would take her away from the hurt and pain she had suffered ever since her marriage to Pa. Yesterday when Little Fox visited her he had said with shining eyes that he would start his big adventure on that day. She had casually questioned him about the hour he would leave his village and how he planned to cross the lake to get to the island.

"I'll be leaving at first light," he had answered. "And it will be a simple matter to get to the island. My people keep several canoes hidden in the reeds along the narrowest and shallowest stretch of the lake."

Several times Laura had weakened in her determination to leave the security of the home she had grown up in. She had no idea what awaited her on that lonely strip of land. She asked herself if a woman, alone with a baby, could make it. Could she live the simple life the Indians did?

"I'll have to," she told herself each time doubts assailed her. She could no longer endure being gossiped about, snubbed by most of Big Pine's female population.

But how she dreaded the good-byes to those who had stood by her through it all. They wouldn't know, of course, that she was wishing them farewell, and they would be very upset at her disappearance.

And Pa. Although it was a coward's way, she was leaving him a note. He deserved an explanation. It's time I get his lunch ready, she thought when the clock struck the half hour.

Slipping an apron over her head, she wrapped the ties around her waist twice. She had lost a lot of weight the past couple weeks. She'd had so much on her mind that she had lost her appetite and her sleep was restless. Some mornings she awakened as tired as she had been on retiring.

"Please, God," she prayed as she started a thick slice of ham frying in the cast-iron skillet, "make Fletch Thomas pay for what he has done to my life. Make him feel some of the mental pain I have suffered all these many months."

Half an hour later, Taylor's lunch packed in

the usual basket, she went to set it out on the porch for Fletch to pick up. Her heart sank when she saw Fletch standing on the bottom step. He had arrived early.

He stared at her, stony-faced, for a moment, then took the basket from her. He gave a significant look at her stomach and asked, "When are you going to tell Pa?"

Laura looked up at him, her eyes expressionless. After a moment she answered tiredly, "Sunday. He'll know all there is to know on Sunday."

She knew by the way Fletch shifted his feet that he wanted to linger, that he was itching to draw her into an argument. She stopped him neatly by turning around and walking back into the kitchen. He had to content himself with growling, "Make sure you do," before stepping off the porch and stalking toward the post.

Fletch hadn't noticed, but he too had lost weight. His face had thinned out considerably, and like Laura, he wore a haunted look in his eyes.

But Taylor had noticed the change in his son, and when he had finished his lunch and they were having a cup of coffee he spoke about it. "Something is bothering you, son," he came straight to the point. "Do you want to talk about it?"

Fletch gave him a startled look, then answered, "There's nothing bothering me, Pa."

When Taylor gave him a look that said he knew he was lying, Fletch added, "I admit I'm getting a little tired of being cooped up in the store all the time. I guess I need to carouse with my friends for a change."

"I thought maybe you'd had an argument with that Milly Howard and were feeling bad about it."

Fletch gave Taylor a disapproving look. "I thought you'd give me more credit than that, Pa. I care more for Big Bertha's girls than I do for that one. The whores aren't mean and vicious."

"I'm sure glad to hear that. A few months back she was spreading it around that you were going to marry her."

"I sure hope nobody swallowed that as gospel," Fletch said at the end of a snorting laugh. He didn't add that at the time he'd wanted Laura to believe it.

Taylor set his empty cup down. "Give me another week and I can take the store over. We can both get back to our normal way of living. It's been damned hard staying in that back room all this time."

"I can imagine," Fletch said, thinking that life would never be normal for him again. The woman he loved with every breath he drew had allowed a man who *didn't* love her to father a second child on her. How could he ever live with that?

Why did he keep staying on in Big Pine?

Fletch asked himself later, standing in the doorway of the store, listening to mothers call their children into supper. *Because you won't let Laura go,* his inner voice answered. *You unconsciously keep thinking and hoping that someday she will be yours."*

I don't think that! Fletch denied vehemently.

Yes, you do, and you're a damn fool for thinking it. She will never forgive you for calling her child a bastard. You let that jealous temper of yours get away from you once too often.

Fletch made no response to that charge. He could not deny it. And the first statement the pesky voice had made was true also. The wish that Laura was his was always on his mind. He would gladly marry her if he could, and he would raise her children as if they were his own. He already loved Jolie dearly and he felt that he would love the one yet to be born just as much. After all, they were a part of Laura. How could he not love them?

Fletch left off thinking of Laura when he saw a couple trapper friends coming toward the post. "How you doin', Fletch?" Red Southern, a tall, slender man with red hair to his shoulders, asked as he entered the store. His companion, Jake Crawford, short, dark, and squat, stepped in behind him.

"Let's put it this way." Fletch grinned. "When Pa takes over the store next week, I'll feel like I'm being let out of prison."

"Yeah, it sure is too fine weather to be cooped

up inside," Red said, crossing the room and sitting down at a table in a corner. "We thought maybe we could help you spend some time playin' a few hands of pinochle if Taylor feels like joinin' us. Me and him can be partners against you and Jake."

"Sounds good to me," Taylor said as he limped into the room. A deck of cards lay on the table where the last players had left it.

When everyone had taken their seats, Jake dealt out the cards. There was silence in the room as the men arranged their hands; then Taylor spoke.

"What's new in the village, men? I've not heard much of anything the past few months stuck back there in that storage room."

"You haven't missed much," Red answered. "The farmers are plowin' and seedin', the womenfolk are all doin' spring cleanin'. The only thing of any interest is the talk of the big cabin Hunter O'Hara is buildin'. Four rooms plus a loft room."

Fletch lifted his head, a startled look on his face. "Why would he build a place so large for just himself?"

"Rumor has it he's gettin' married," Red said, starting the game with a jack.

"To who?" Fletch held his breath.

"It's hard to believe, but to Agnes Morse."

"Agnes Morse!" Fletch and Taylor said in unison. "He's taking on that brood of hers?" Taylor added.

Red nodded. "That's why he's buildin' such a large cabin."

"That sure beats all." Taylor shook his head. "Hunter never struck me as the marrying kind. I sure can't see him settling down with little ole skinny Agnes."

"I guess you haven't seen Agnes lately," Jake said, covering Red's jack with a queen. "She's put on weight and she's not bad lookin' at all."

The men settled into the game, and the subject of Hunter and Agnes was dropped. Not by Fletch, though. The pair was very much on his mind. Over and over he asked himself how could O'Hara marry another woman after knowing Laura?

Chapter Eighteen

Laura stepped out of the cabin, Jolie on her hip. It was Thursday, the day she and Hunter always visited with Big Bertha. It was the last time she would take the path to the madam's cabin back of the post, and she was going to miss the rough, tenderhearted woman. She felt guilty about not telling her she was leaving, or where she was going. But if her friend didn't know where she had gone, she could truthfully say so if she were asked.

And there was Maida whom she would pay a last visit to tomorrow. That tender soul would worry about her, she felt things so intensely. The birth of her baby, however, would occupy most of her mind. Would Daniel get the son he wished for? she wondered. A son who would take care of his mother after his father was gone?

Laura was a yard or so away from the pleasure cabin when Hunter called out to her. She turned around and waited for him to catch up.

"You're early." She smiled. "Aren't you afraid of being talked about; the neighbors seeing us going to visit Bertha together?" she teased. "You're going to ruin your good name, associating openly with Big Pine's fallen woman." Her eyes twinkled.

Hunter grinned. "I'll chance it," he said. "I don't think I'll be driven out of the village." His face took on a serious look. "I wanted to talk to you alone before we go inside."

"Oh?" Laura looked at him questioningly. "What about?"

"I guess you've heard I've been building a cabin."

"Yes, I heard that. Everyone is wondering why you're building such a large one."

"I'm getting married."

Laura could only gape at Hunter for a long moment before finally gasping, "You are? To who?"

"To the sweetest, kindest woman a man could ever meet."

Laura slowly nodded her understanding. "Agnes Morse," she said softly. She laid her hand on Hunter's arm and, looking deeply in his eyes, asked, "Do you really care for her, Hunter, or are you marrying her out of pity? Wedding someone because you feel sorry for them is not a good basis for a happy union."

"I know that, Laura," Hunter said quietly. "I do love Agnes. I love her the same way I love you; like a dear sister."

"But what if Agnes expects—"

"Agnes knows my secret," Hunter interrupted her. "She knows that's the only way I can ever love a woman, and it suits her fine. She had enough of that side of a marriage to last her a lifetime. That George was like a rutting moose.

"You know, Laura, the thing that bothered me the most about losing my manhood was the knowledge that I would never have a wife and a family, someone to spend my old age with. I've seen old bachelors sitting around, waiting to die, welcoming the grim reaper to come for them, take them away from their lonely existence."

"My dear friend." Laura smiled at Hunter through tear-glimmering eyes. "I am so happy for you. And Agnes too. I'm sure she's counting her blessings to get such a fine husband."

"Thank you, honey." Hunter thumbed away a tear that escaped her eyes. "I wish you could find the same happiness someday."

Laura's only answer was a wan smile.

Fletcher Thomas's fingers curled into fists as he stood in the post doorway and watched the tender gesture of Hunter's hand on Laura's cheek. He could not see the glistening tear, and to him it was a lover's caress. *Damn you, Laura,* he raged silently, *you said you were finished with Jolie's father. Are the two of you going to carry on as usual even after he's married?*

Pain and rage warring inside him, Fletch turned back into the store, and in so doing missed seeing Agnes join Laura and Hunter.

When Agnes walked up to Laura and Hunter, her husband-to-be put an arm around her shoulder, smiled down at her, and said, "I've just been telling Laura our good news."

"I'm so happy for you both." Laura stepped forward and kissed Agnes's cheek. "I know that you both will be very happy."

"Thank you, Laura," Agnes said shyly. "All the credit goes to you for getting us together. If you hadn't made me get out and mingle with my neighbors, I'd have never met this wonderful man."

As Hunter smiled fondly at her, Bertha called from her doorway, "Are you three gonna stand there and gab for the rest of the day? Should I pour out the coffee and put away the cake I baked?"

"Don't you dare," Hunter joked back. "I've been looking forward to your applesauce cake all week."

As soon as they stepped inside Bertha's comfortable kitchen, the big madam took Jolie from her mother. Talking baby nonsense to the little one, she placed her in a high chair that Hunter had crafted some months back. "My, she's getting big," she said, handing Jolie a sugar cookie. "Changing in looks too."

Bertha gave one of her rowdy laughs and added, "If I'm not mistaken, she's beginning to look like that hellion uncle of hers."

Everyone except Laura laughed. Her face paled and she grew very still. Only Hunter noticed her startled unease and thought with shock, That bastard is Jolie's father. He wondered at first if Fletch knew it, then decided that he didn't. The man was crazy about Jolie's mother.

Hunter thought back to when Laura and Taylor had married and remembered that Fletch had gone off to Canada a month before. In a panic to save her good name, the elder Thomas had married the young woman he had raised as a daughter. Did Taylor know that he was the baby's grandfather? Hunter asked himself. He thought not. Had the highly principled man known, he'd have gone after his son and brought him back to do the honorable thing by Laura.

Who had she named as the father? The question slipped into Hunter's mind. After thinking on the matter a moment, he decided that Laura hadn't named anyone. She had let Taylor, like everyone else, guess the man's identity.

To divert Bertha and Agnes from noticing Laura's strange silence, Hunter began talking about the cabin he was building. He ended by saying that all that was left to do was put on the roof. Laura regained enough composure to be aware of his adding, "And then Agnes and I are getting married."

By the time Bertha had congratulated the couple, Laura was able to join in the conversation and ask, "Do your children know yet, Agnes?"

Agnes's teeth flashed in a smile. "Yes, I told them last night. My two oldest, Jebbie and Mary, were uneasy at first, especially Mary. Poor girl, she likens all men to her father." Her soft brown eyes moved to Hunter. "I finally convinced them that my new husband would never hurt me. All of them are excited now about living in larger quarters."

"I expect you're happy about that, too," Bertha said. "Having that many young'uns underfoot all the time must be a bother."

"It is indeed." Agnes laughed. "Especially when I'm trying to get a meal together."

"You won't have to bother about that anymore," Hunter assured her. "The kitchen is a separate room, and when you cook you can keep everybody out if you want to."

Laura was finally able to relax, and she sat quietly, listening to and watching the three friends she would miss so badly. When it came time to break up the little gathering, she surprised Bertha by putting her arms around her and kissing her painted cheek. Although the action flustered the madam, the softness that came into her eyes said that she was touched, and pleased. The big woman didn't know that Laura was telling her good-bye.

Nor did Hunter, when outside Laura thanked him for being there for her when she was at her lowest. Smiling, he teased, "You're being awfully mushy today. I'll still be here for you anytime you need me."

Laura blinked against tears as she walked away from the friend she would never see again.

Later in the afternoon, near suppertime Laura took a pan of pasties out of the oven and set them on the table. Taylor was very fond of the mixture of meat, potatoes, and onions wrapped in dough and baked to a crusty, golden color. She wanted him to enjoy this last meal she would be cooking for him, she thought sadly as she sat down at the table.

She stopped the tears that were gathering in her eyes by mentally counting off the items she had packed in a heavy cloth bag yesterday. She hoped it was enough for the two-week trek Little Fox had said it would be to reach the island. There was a slab of salt pork, a bag of coffee, a jar of matches, two loaves of her bread wrapped in a cloth, several strips of pemmican, and her and Jolie's clothes. In the small barn back of the cabin she had a canvas tarpaulin and three heavy blankets ready to be strapped on the back of the saddle. She felt confident that she and Jolie would be warm enough in that bedding.

She glanced over at the haversack lying in a corner of the kitchen. Inside it was a battered coffeepot and a smoke-stained skillet, a knife and a spoon. The same gear she and Pa used when they went on overnight fishing trips.

That was another thing she would miss, Laura thought sadly. There were so many things, so many people she was going to miss. Although Maida hadn't known it, Laura had said good-bye to her yesterday. Though she hadn't known the young wife long, she was as fond of her as she was of her lifelong friend, Justine. She felt regret that she'd never see Maida's baby, never know if Daniel had got the son he wished for.

An hour later, heaving a ragged sigh, Laura began packing up Taylor's evening meal. She wasn't going to wait for Fletch to come for it today. She would deliver it herself and spend an hour or so visiting with the man who had raised her. She would stow in her mind this last time together, bringing the memory out to relive when missing him seemed unbearable.

To her surprised pleasure, Laura found Taylor minding the store when she arrived, Jolie on her hip and the food basket hanging from her arm. "Well, now, this is sure a nice surprise." Taylor's face beamed with a wide smile. He held his hands out to take Jolie from her mother. "Let me hold this little scrap. I don't see nearly enough of her."

His eyes skimmed over Laura's thin face.

"And I don't see enough of you either, young woman," he said, frowning. "Aren't you feeling well, honey? It seems like the few times I do see you that you have lost more weight. Is anything bothering you?"

"No, Pa, I'm fine," Laura hastened to say. "I guess being cooped up so much this past winter honed me down some. When you don't get much exercise you don't eat much."

"That will change." Taylor grinned as he followed her into the back room. "It's garden-making time, and you'll get plenty of exercise."

"How come you're minding the store alone? Do you really think you're up to it?" Laura asked as she set out the pasties and a tin cup of buttermilk. "Where is Fletch?"

"To answer your first question, my leg is almost as good as it ever was. Butterfly says it's time I start walking around on it, otherwise it will stiffen up on me. I plan on coming home tomorrow, sleep in my old room again. I'll be glad to see the last of this dungeon.

"As for Fletch, he went off with his friend Red Fox hunting for a few days. I told him I didn't need him in the store anymore." Taylor's lips twitched in a sheepish grin. "Truth to tell, I could have taken over the store a couple weeks ago. I just hated giving up my nights with Butterfly."

"I don't know why you don't marry the woman." Laura took Jolie from Taylor so that he could eat. "You love each other. It's a shame you have to hide it."

"I've thought about it," Taylor said after popping a forkful of pasty in his mouth. "There's a couple reasons keeping me from asking Butterfly to be my wife."

"And those are?"

"One, how will she be treated by the womenfolk around here? You, better than anyone, know how they can snub a person, curl their lips scornfully."

Laura nodded with a rueful smile. "I agree, they know how to hurt a person. What is your second reason?"

"Well, honey, that should be obvious." Taylor grinned at her. "I'm already married."

"Oh, for goodness sake, I forgot about that." Laura laughed merrily. She turned serious then. "You'd have no problem having our marriage dissolved. I think that by now all of Big Pine thinks our marriage is a sham."

"That could be, but what about Jolie? Would she still carry the Thomas name?"

"Sure she would. The preacher wrote it on her birth certificate. Jolie Thomas. She'll have that name until she gets married."

"I'll have to think on it," Taylor said, then resumed eating his supper.

Laura waited until the last crumb of pasty had disappeared and she and Taylor were having a cup of coffee before she started reminiscing of bygone days. She started by recalling out loud how she and Taylor and Fletch had been crushed by the death of mother Marie shortly after Laura's tenth birthday.

"It was a sad time," Taylor agreed. "She was the backbone of our small family. I never realized it until she was gone. She was the only mother you and Fletch had ever known. Especially Fletch. Marie came into his life when he was only a month old."

"You've never talked about your first wife, Pa," Laura said.

"No, I haven't," Taylor said after a short pause. "It's such a long time ago that I lost her. Thirty years now." His eyes took on a look of remembering.

"Mavis was my first love, the love of my youth. She was the prettiest little thing, curly blond hair, so delicate; much too delicate to give birth to Fletch. She lived only long enough to gaze a few minutes at her son and to make me promise that I would marry a nice woman who would raise her baby, be good to him. She closed her lovely blue eyes then and was gone.

"I didn't love Marie when I married her a month later, nor did she love me. I was still eaten up with grief over losing Mavis, but I needed someone to take care of my son. An Indian maiden had been tending Fletch, but suddenly her people were moving their wigwams several miles away and she wanted to go with them. She didn't want to be parted from her intended.

"A week before she left, Marie came to live with an aunt and uncle over on Camp Lake. She was a comely looking young woman with a gentle nature. I knew the first time I met her that she would be good to my boy.

"When I asked her to marry me the next day, she was reluctant. She knew nothing about me except that I was grieving over a dead wife and that I had a baby who needed tending. I'm sure she was pressured by her relatives to accept my proposal. At any rate, we were married the day before the young Indian woman took off with her people.

"I never dreamed that I could love again, but over the years I grew to love Marie dearly. Who could not love such a gentle woman?

"Then, after she passed away, several months later to my surprise I found that I could love a third time. One day while fishing for brook trout I met Butterfly digging roots in the forest. I was struck by her beauty right off and felt like a teenager falling in love for the first time. I was so taken with her, I didn't even notice when a big trout swam by and took my bait along with my pole.

"Butterfly laughed so hard she had to sit down. As we talked, I learned that she too had lost a mate a couple years back but hadn't found a man in her village she would want to marry. Before we parted, we made plans to meet the next afternoon at the same place. We met like that once a week until cold weather set in.

That's when Butterfly invited me to come to her wigwam."

Taylor heaved a long sigh. "After seeing her every night all winter, it's going to be hard only visiting her on a Thursday."

"That's another good reason the two of you should get married," Laura said.

"Hey, who's minding the store?" Laura and Taylor recognized Daniel's deep voice in the other room.

"I'll be right with you," Laura called, standing up and handing Jolie back to Taylor. "I won't be gone long," she said. "Daniel's not one to stand around and gab."

"Take your time. Me and this little girl are going to play horsey."

It was while Taylor bounced Jolie on his good leg and her laughing eyes gleamed her pleasure that he gave a sudden start. He was remembering his description of Fletch's mother. He had said that she was a pretty little thing with her curly blond hair, then mentioned her lovely blue eyes.

It hit him like a rock to his stomach when he realized who Jolie had always reminded him of. Thirty years had dimmed his memory of his young first wife until he talked of her to Laura. Was it possible that Fletch was this little one's father?

Taylor commanded his racing pulse to calm down. It could be just a coincidence that both Jolie and Mavis had pale hair and blue eyes. A glint appeared in his eyes. He would tell Fletcher how the baby resembled his dead mother, then ask him straight out if he had ever made love to Laura. He didn't believe, or at least hoped, that his son wouldn't lie to him.

Taylor was still unconsciously bouncing Jolie on his knee when Laura walked back in the room. "I was right." She smiled. "Daniel asked for a spool of thread, paid for it, and after asking about my and Jolie's health he left."

Taylor forced an answering smile. "Yeah, Daniel is a man of few words. There's never any idle talk from him."

Laura began to get nervous. It was getting dark outside, time to say a silent good-bye to this man she loved so dearly.

"I guess I'd better get going, Pa," she said huskily. "Jolie is getting sleepy and I still have to bathe her." When she took the baby from him, she kissed Taylor's cheek, saying softly, "I love you, Pa."

"I love you, too, daughter." Surprise flickered in Taylor's eyes. Laura hadn't kissed him in a long time.

Chapter Nineteen

The first pink of dawn was coloring the eastern sky as Laura sat down at the kitchen table to write her good-bye letter to Taylor. She chewed on the stub of pencil a moment, then began to write.

Dear Pa,

Writing this letter is one of the hardest things I've ever had to do. I am taking Jolie and leaving Big Pine. I have come to the realization that my daughter has no future here. She will always be looked down upon and shunned as I have been. I do not want her to experience that pain.

I know that what I write next are empty words, but please try not to worry about us too much. I have a place to go to. It's not like I'm just striking off through the wilderness.

Pa, there are not enough words to explain how sorry I am for the pain I have caused you even though I loved you with all my heart while I was inflicting that pain on you. I will think of you every day and love you until the day I die. Please take care of yourself and say good-bye to Butterfly for me. Give some thought to what we discussed about her.

Your loving daughter,
Laura.

Propping the letter against the lamp where Taylor wouldn't miss it when he came for breakfast, she shrugged into her lightweight jacket and walked over to gaze down on her sleeping daughter. Working carefully so as not to awaken her, she wrapped a heavy blanket around Jolie and placed her in a hooded papoose carrying case that Little Fox had made for her. When Jolie was safely strapped inside the woven leather cradle, she lifted it to her back and settled the handles over her shoulders. Taking one last look around the kitchen, choking back tears, she took up the saddlebag and the rifle leaning beside the door and stepped outside.

Laura paused on the porch to untie Brave, who jumped around her, whining a greeting.

Then she set out for the barn.

In the dim interior of the small log building she bridled and saddled the mare mainly by touch. She led Beauty outside and it began to rain as she tightened the belly cinch. It was not a downpour but a steady, straight-down fall of water. And though it would wash away Beauty's tracks, for which Laura was grateful, it felt icy cold as she grasped the pommel and pulled herself onto the mare's back.

As Beauty pulled out, Laura had no fear of Jolie getting wet. The hood attached to the cradle extended well over Jolie's head and face, and the tanned bearskin that covered it all was liberally rubbed with bear grease. The rain would roll right off it.

The gray of dawn had arrived under the cloudy sky when Laura guided the mare into a stand of pine several yards from the Indian village where she would not miss seeing Little Fox take his leave of it. When she had been waiting about fifteen minutes and the boy hadn't appeared, she began to wonder. Had she arrived too late? Had Little Fox already left?

She saw him then, hurrying through the rain, the fringe on his leggings swaying back and forth with each step his moccasined feet took. A quiver of arrows was slung over his shoulder, and in his hand was a sturdy-looking bow. Laura shook her head. That was all the lad had for protection in his search for manhood.

Little Fox took off to his right, following a

path along the lake. Laura nudged Beauty into motion, keeping within the forest, out of the boy's sight. It was sometimes difficult to keep up with him, for he ran at a trot and the trees grew so closely together she sometimes lost sight of him as she guided Beauty through the trunks.

Taylor awakened to gray skies and falling rain. He lay staring up at the low ceiling, his mood as dismal as the weather. He didn't look forward to the day ahead.

Last night as he tried to go to sleep he decided that he was too upset to wait for Fletch to come home so that he could confront him with his suspicions. So this morning he planned to make Laura tell him what in the hell was going on between them.

But as he pulled on his trousers and boots he wondered if he should talk to Laura alone. Maybe the best thing to do was wait for Fletcher to come home, then face them together about Jolie. But it was going to be hard to keep his mouth shut as he had breakfast with Laura.

Limping toward the cabin a few minutes later, Taylor was surprised to see no smoke coming from the chimney. It was unusual for Laura to oversleep. And where was that damn wild dog that had tried to take his arm off yesterday? he wondered, stepping up on the porch.

A chill ran through Taylor when he pushed

open the door and stepped inside the kitchen. He knew instantly that the cabin was empty. He felt the stove and found it cold. There had not been a fire in it since yesterday.

Even though he knew the search would be fruitless, he walked through the family room and looked into the two bedrooms. Laura's bed was neatly made up and Jolie's little cradle sat at the foot of it.

Taylor walked back into the kitchen, his brow furrowed with worry. What had happened to Laura and the baby? Had renegade Indians come in the night and carried them away? Why hadn't that vicious dog raised hell, alerting him to her danger?

His eyes fell on the sheet of paper propped against the lamp, and with a sickening feeling in the pit of his stomach he hurried to snatch it up. When he had quickly scanned the short letter, his eyes glazed over and he sat down, shocked to his soul.

That foolish girl, he thought, his hands clenched to fists on his knees. Where had she gone? Who would she go to? Did anyone go with her? Maybe Hunter? They were on very friendly terms. But he was supposed to marry Agnes Morse any day.

As Taylor sat in the grayness of the kitchen, questions running through his mind, he slowly came to the conclusion that Laura hadn't gone off with anyone. She had taken her little girl and gone off on her own.

But where to? Would she try to make it to the nearest big city? Detroit perhaps? He jumped to his feet. She couldn't have too long a head start. He would get some men together and track her down.

Taylor walked back to the post as fast as his leg would permit and began pulling on the rope attached to the bell on top of the building. It was rung only in an emergency.

Men, women, and children started piling out of their cabins, unmindful of the rain falling on their heads. "What is it, Taylor?" someone called. "Is the post on fire? I don't smell any smoke."

"I wish to God that's all it was." Taylor's eyes ranged over the wild-eyed group, touching on every woman who had ever gossiped about Laura, shaming her, bringing tears to her lovely eyes. His voice was like ice when he said, "Due to you mean gossipmongers, and you all know who you are, you have forced Laura to take her little girl and run away. If anything has happened to her and that little one, be ready to pack up and get the hell out of here."

He looked at the shamefaced husbands and said with some sarcasm, "I would like for you men to join me in a search for Laura." Taylor paused, added, "If your wives will let you, that is."

"Have no fear about that," one husband spoke up, giving his wife a look that made her cringe.

Other wives were getting the same dire looks

from their mates as Hunter said quietly, "This rain will have washed away her tracks, Taylor. Do you know if she's walking or riding?"

"I don't know, Hunter," Taylor answered distractedly. "I was so upset after reading her letter, I didn't think to go to the barn and see if the mare was gone. She took the dog, though."

"Let's go take a look." Hunter nudged Taylor ahead of him.

To soothe the man he liked and respected so highly, the bartender said, "Laura will be fine if she took that dog of hers along. That's the meanest damn animal that ever lived. I heard that when he lived with the Indians one time he took on three wolves at once and killed every one of them."

"He couldn't stand up against a bullet, though," Taylor answered glumly. "What if she runs into some of those rough loggers or renegades?"

"Put that thought out of your head, Taylor," Hunter said as he swung open the door to the sturdy building that housed the Thomases' three horses and cow.

When they found Beauty's stall empty, both men were relieved somewhat. Taylor began saddling his horse, and Hunter hurried off to ready his roan.

When Taylor returned to the post, some 20 mounted men were waiting for him. Their wives, who had made Laura's life so miserable, had slunk off, avoiding each other's eyes.

"The rain has washed away all traces of Laura's mare," Taylor said when the slicker-clad riders had nudged their mounts up around him. "I guess the best thing to do is split up, half going to the right and the others left. Be sure to spread out so that every inch of the forest is covered. If one of you should find her, bring her back here and ring the bell. Otherwise we'll meet back here at sundown."

When the men had ridden out of sight, Big Bertha said to the other three women who had stayed, "Maida, you and Justine and Agnes come home with me and have some coffee. Laura's leaving has floored me, and I'd like to talk to her friends about it. I had no idea she meant to go away. Where in the world could she have gone?"

"Thank goodness," Laura muttered when after about four hours Little Fox stopped and sat down to rest. Jolie had awakened and was making hungry noises. If she didn't get something to eat pretty soon, the forest would ring with her angry cries. Laura leaned over and took from the saddlebag a short strip of pemmican, a small knife, and a long strip of rawhide. With the sharp point of the blade she bored a hole in one end of the meat mixture, threaded the strip of leather through it, and tied it off.

Jolie readily took it, and her two teeth on top and two on the bottom chewed at it greedily. After about five minutes Little Fox was on his feet and off again.

The rain continued to fall but not as heavily. It bothered Laura little, for now she rode beneath a canopy of trees that was like a huge umbrella. Still, she was damp to the skin and wished that she could sit in front of a roaring fire and warm her cold flesh.

Little Fox didn't stop for a noon meal. She saw him reach into a small pouch at his waist and pull out his own strip of pemmican. Jolie had fallen asleep again, and Laura tied the other end of the rawhide to one of the shoulder handles. It easily reached Jolie's mouth and would not fall to the ground and be lost. Indian mothers used this method to pacify their babies all the time. It was equivalent to a white mother's sugar teat.

The wet forest was so still, Laura was intensely conscious of the wilderness crowding in on her as she rode. The mare seemed attuned to her uneasiness as she nervously picked her way through the trees.

"It's all right, Beauty," she said, patting the mare on the shoulder. "We'll be just fine."

Because of the gloomy wet skies and early dusk setting in, up ahead Laura saw Little Fox stop for the night. Her eyes searched for a spot that would shield her and Jolie from the weather.

She spotted it, a tall pine with thick branches that swept the ground. It would probably be quite dry close to its huge trunk. There would also be small broken limbs, and resin-filled needles to kindle a fire with. Little Fox wouldn't be able to see a small fire through the heavy foliage. And the slight wind against her face would carry the scent of smoke away from him.

She reined Beauty in and slid off her back. She was about to crawl beneath the tree when she heard a rustling behind her and the dog growled low in his throat. She spun around, and her heart seemed to jump to her throat. A wolf stood only feet away, his gray body taut, his eyes red as he stood ready to spring at her. Every instinct in her urged her to run, but she was afraid to take the chance. The wolf could outdistance her, and Jolie was strapped on her back. He would get the baby first.

Suddenly the dog was in front of her, lunging at the wolf's throat. She saw his snapping teeth close around his mark. She felt as though the two animals rolled around on the wet ground for hours, but actually only about five minutes had passed when the wolf lay dead at the dog's feet.

Her heart racing, Laura gulped in deep breaths as her eyes scanned the forest for more wolves. When the dog lay down at her feet, breathing heavily, his tongue lolling out of his mouth, she knew there would be no more danger from wolves tonight. She quieted the mare down with soothing words, and was surprised that Jolie had slept through it all.

Laura crawled beneath the tree, and it was as she had expected. The rain had barely penetrated the heavy branches. She scraped twigs and needles together, took a match from her pocket, and struck it beneath the pile. When the dry material caught and flamed, she went back to Beauty and slid the saddle and bags off her back. Setting them aside, she led the mare up close to the pine tree and tied her to a branch.

With the dog close on her heels, she crawled back under the tree and slid the cradle board holding Jolie off her back. She placed it close enough to the fire so that Jolie could feel its heat, but well away from the flames. The little one was still sleeping. Ordering the dog to stay beside her, Laura went searching for more wood.

Within five minutes she returned, dragging a good-sized tree length of dead, seasoned maple. It would burn all night.

Squatting before the fire, she had barely warmed her chilled hands when Jolie awakened and began to fuss. Laura hurried to slip the pemmican between the child's small lips, hoping that would keep her content until she could fry up some salt pork.

She had become adept at cooking over an open fire in her camping trips with Taylor, and it was but a short time before the meat was sizzling in a battered frying pan and coffee was brewing in an equally beat-up coffeepot. As she turned the slices of meat over with her knife, she planned to set a snare before she went to bed. She felt sure she would catch a rabbit overnight.

While the meager supper continued cooking, Laura used her knife to cut branches off the tree and spread them on the ground. When she had a layer about six inches thick she covered the branches with the tarpaulin, then smoothed the blankets over them.

By then the meat was cooked to a crispy state and the coffee was ready. She took Jolie out of the carrier and, holding her in her lap, broke off small pieces of meat and fed them to her. When the child refused to eat any more, Laura changed her diaper and laid her down on the bed of pine. She and the dog then shared the meat and bread.

As Laura sat before the fire, fashioning her hair in a long braid, the dog lay down beside her and rested his head in her lap. The rain had slowed to a drizzle, and she could hear the steady drip of water falling off the lofty pine to the ground. She thought that by now Pa would have found her letter. Her eyes grew wet. He would be so upset.

The glimmer of a pale moon shone through the branches, and Laura gave a tired yawn. The strain of the day had caught up with her. She rose and, walking just a few steps from under the tree, she answered a call of nature, then set her trap. Back at the fire she removed only her shoes and crawled between the blankets of her pine-scented bed and pulled Jolie up close beside her. As she fell asleep she was full of bitterness toward Fletcher. Because of him, her life had been turned upside down.

The wind moaned in the trees, but the rain had finally stopped as Fletcher and Red Fox sat before their campfire finishing a meal of roasted rabbit.

It was the second day of their hunt, and yesterday they had been quite successful. Each one had shot a doe which now hung high in a tree, safe from marauding wolves.

They could have headed home this afternoon instead of spending another night in the forest, but both men felt the need to get away from their people for a while.

Red Fox studied his white friend's face through the leaping flames. Fletch didn't have his old fervent zeal for life anymore. He had gone through a big change the past year and a half. Most of the wildness had gone out of him, and a brooding darkness replaced the crooked smile that used to hover over his lips. And where had the devilish gleam in his dark eyes gone?

What had caused all of this? the Indian wondered. Had something happened in Canada that had changed him so, or had it come about when he returned to Big Pine?

Watching Fletch through lowered lids, he said, "I saw Laura and her daughter the other day. The little fair-headed one has certainly grown."

The way Fletch's body stiffened at his remarks gave Red Fox the answer to his friend's radical change. As he had half expected, Laura was the cause of the pain that lurked in the depths of his dark eyes. His friend loved his father's wife. A heavy burden for a white man to carry.

Red Fox mentally shook his head. Palefaces took everything so seriously, always reluctant to let go what couldn't be changed. The red man, however, accepted what blows he was given and got on with his life.

"Do you remember my first wife, Bluebird?" Red Fox broke the short silence that had fallen.

"Yes, I remember her," Fletch answered, seeing the feisty little wife in his mind's eye. "She was very beautiful, and you had a hard time not to act the besotted fool over her."

"Yes." Red Fox's lips curved in a sad, crooked smile. "She was my whole world. For a time it ended when she died giving birth to Little Fox. But after a while the Indian bows to the dictates of his god. The Great Father had a purpose in taking Bluebird away from me, and after a month of grieving her loss, I replaced her with her younger sister, Rippling Waters.

"She had been taking care of Little Fox since he was born and she loved him very much. Being his aunt, she would be good to him, I knew. That is not always so when you put a woman over another woman's children. When their own come along, they might neglect the ones who came with the marriage. I could not let that happen to Bluebird's son."

"So you didn't marry for love the second time?" Fletch looked questioningly at his friend.

Red Fox shook his head. "I had an affection for Rippling Waters. I had seen her grow up. She is gentle like her sister was, but unlike Bluebird she is very biddable. She bows always to my wishes." He grinned ruefully. "That doesn't put much excitement in our marriage, but it is a peaceful existence. There was never much peace in my wigwam married to Bluebird, as you know."

"What about . . . you know . . . in bed?"

"It is good," Red Fox answered, then added slyly, "I have trained her well."

Fletch recalled how he had guided Laura in the acts of lovemaking, how eagerly she had responded to him. He was lost in the memory of her soft body clinging to his, her long, slim legs wrapped around his waist, when Red Fox spoke.

"There is no truth to the rumor that you will marry the woman who has slept with so many men, is there?"

Fletch's face clouded indignantly. "I'm surprised you'd ask me such a question, Red Fox. Do you believe that I'd want such a woman to be the mother of my children? Hell, I don't even sleep with her anymore."

"It pleases me to hear that. You have been very lucky. She is the type of woman who would purposely get a baby in her belly with another man, then point the finger at you."

Fletcher's face showed the shock that Red Fox's words had given him. It was just such a stunt Milly was capable of doing. He looked at his longtime friend and demanded, "Why didn't you give me that advice when I was sleeping with her occasionally? As thickheaded as I am, that possibility never entered my mind."

"I can't teach you everything, Fletcher Thomas." The Indian's eyes gleamed with amusement. "A man must learn by his mistakes. Sadly, sometimes it's a hard lesson."

Fletcher knew that all too well. He'd made a big mistake with Laura, one he would pay for the rest of his life.

"My son, Little Fox, left the village this morning in search of his manhood," Red Fox said at the end of a long yawn. "I worry about him. Isle Royale is a rough place for a young teenager to spend a month on."

"Isle Royale?" Fletcher swore softly. "That island is downright dangerous for an untried teen. It's overrun with wolves and bears, I've heard."

"I know this," Red Fox said solemnly, "but for years that's where the thirteen-year-olds are sent to spend a month, to kill their first big game."

"I'm sure he'll be all right," Fletcher said, seeing the concern in the father's face. "I'm sure you've taught him well in the use of the bow and arrow, and to always be on the alert for danger."

"I have done my best," Red Fox said, "and now I must leave him in the hands of the Great Father."

He rose and added more wood to the fire; then he and Fletcher rolled up in their blankets, their rifles lying beside them. A distant pack of wolves had serenaded them as they sat around the fire.

Chapter Twenty

Laura's fears of the night vanished with the rising of the sun. Its bright rays striking her face had awakened her. She leaned up on an elbow and looked down at her sleeping daughter, one dimpled fist tucked under her chin.

Wondering when in the night the rain had stopped, Laura rolled out of the blankets and almost tripped over the big dog that lay watching her, his tail thumping on the needle-strewn ground. He had faithfully watched over her and Jolie during the night.

She stepped out from under the tree and stood a moment looking out over the mist-shrouded lake, then turned her back to it to gaze at a sunny meadow some hundred feet away. She had seen several such open spaces as she rode along yesterday, scattered among the dense forest of pine and spruce, wildflowers blooming profusely.

Laura slowly stretched her back and arms, working out the knots from sleeping on the ground. As she made her way to the lake to wash her face and hands, she shaded her eyes against the rising sun and looked around to see if she could see Little Fox.

She saw him quite a distance away, standing on the shore, holding a pole and line in the water. Seeing him fishing for his breakfast reminded Laura to check on her snare.

When she had finished washing her hands and scooping water onto her face, Laura went to find out if she and Jolie would have fresh meat for breakfast. Her eyes lit up when she saw the fat rabbit caught in her snare. She cut the rabbit down and dressed it out the way Taylor had taught her when she was young.

Laura found Jolie still sleeping on her return, and after stirring up the fire and hanging the spitted rabbit carcass over it, she went back to the lake to rinse out the baby's soiled underclothing.

This time she tied a rope to Brave's collar to keep him near Jolie. She couldn't chance his spotting his playmate and running off to him.

Laura found her daughter beginning to stir when she returned with her wet laundry. She tied the clothes to the saddle lying on the ground. They would dry as they rode along. The aroma of the roasting meat wafted to her enticingly.

While she waited for the rabbit to cook, she changed Jolie into dry clothing, then spent some time stretching her little arms and legs and gently massaging her neck and shoulders. She imagined that from lying in the cradle board for so many hours yesterday the baby would be stiff also.

After strapping Jolie back in her cradle board Laura checked the rabbit and found it ready to eat. The baby waved her legs in approval as her mother fed her tiny bits of the meat. The dog showed his appreciation of his breakfast by wagging his tail when he got his share of the rabbit.

Laura ate quickly and hurried to saddle the mare. She didn't want to lose sight of Little Fox. While she was letting Beauty drink her fill of the clear lake water, she saw the Indian lad's back disappearing among the trees. She hung the cradle board with Jolie on her back, mounted Beauty, and rode out, keeping well behind Little Fox's trotting figure.

Fletch, too, was awakened by the sun striking him in the face. He had dreamed about Laura last night. Not his usual erotic dreams but those that made him uneasy. In one he saw her in a thick fog astride the mare. He thought Jolie was with her but wasn't sure. However, he could make out the wolf dog running alongside Beauty. His heart began to pound when he saw the gray shape of a wolf following her at a distance. He held his breath when the beast came closer and closer to her. He saw the animal stiffen, and he braced himself for when it would spring at her. He opened his mouth to call a warning to her, but no sound left his lips.

The wolf was at Laura's throat when Fletch awakened in a cold sweat. The dream had been so real his body was shaking, and it took him a long time to get back to sleep. And then only to dream of her again.

This time she sat before a campfire, again surrounded by a mist in the darkness of the forest. She was crying and he wanted to go to her, but his feet only moved by inches and she seemed to be moving farther and farther away from him. He called her name but she didn't look up.

Why couldn't she hear him? he cried out silently. Was it only her spirit that sat there, gazing sadly into the flames?

Sometime in the early morning Laura ceased to haunt his sleep and he rested peacefully.

But now, as he and Red Fox set out for home walking at a fast clip, he relived his dream. He couldn't shake the feeling that all was not well at home, either.

The sun was setting when Fletch and the Indian came to the fork in the trail. Red Fox lifted his hand in farewell, and Fletch walked on toward the post.

He heard raised voices while still some distance from home. When he walked into the clearing, he found half the village men gathered around his father. He hastened his steps, calling out, "What's wrong, Pa?"

He received only a stony look from Taylor as he joined the men, and it was Daniel who answered, "Laura is gone. The men have been searching for her since yesterday."

For a moment Fletch couldn't breathe. He thought his heart had stopped. Finally he managed to say, "Gone? Gone where?"

Daniel made a helpless gesture. "Nobody knows. She left a note for Taylor but didn't say where she was going."

A look at the men's grim faces told Fletch that they had found no trace of her.

Daniel gave an unhappy shrug of his shoulders. "I'm sorry, Fletch, they found nothing. The rain washed away any tracks she might have left. Taylor says she was riding her mare."

There was near panic in Fletch's voice when he asked, "Do you have any idea where she might have gone, Daniel? Maybe she said something to Maida."

"I'm sorry, friend. Maida is just as surprised as everyone else."

"I've got to find her, Daniel. You know I do."

"I do, Fletch, and me and the fellers are goin' out again tomorrow as soon as it's light."

"I'm going out myself. I'll take Red Fox with me. He's the best when it comes to tracking."

"I'm gonna get back home now." Daniel squeezed Fletch's shoulder in silent sympathy. "I have to tell Maida that we didn't find her friend. She's beside herself with worry. I'm afraid she's gonna make herself sick, cryin' and carryin' on."

Daniel walked away, and when Fletch turned around he found that the other men had left also. Only he and his father remained standing in front of the post. He walked up to Taylor, started to ask if he knew why Laura had left, then quickly snapped his lips closed when he received a look of sheer ice from his father.

"Come on inside, Fletch," Taylor said, his voice matching the chill in his eyes. "I have something to say to you."

As soon as they stepped inside the store, Taylor wheeled and faced a confounded Fletch. "I've found out who Jolie's father is," he said, wasting no time in coming to what was on his mind.

"You did? Who? How?"

"Don't act the innocent with me, you damn pup!' Taylor almost shouted. "You're Jolie's father!"

"What! Are you crazy?" Fletch looked at Taylor as though the older man had gone stark, raving mad.

Taylor limped across the room and stood behind the counter. "You're the crazy one for thinking you could get away with it," he shot out at Fletch. "Blood always tells in the end."

"I don't know what in the hell you're talking about." Fletch's voice rose. "Hunter O'Hara is the baby's father."

"The hell he is!" Taylor's voice rose too. "First you let people think that Adam Beltran fathered Jolie and now you blame Hunter. But you are the father! I'd never have expected it of you. I still don't want to believe it."

"Then don't believe it, for it isn't true." Fletch forced himself to calm down and lower his voice. "Tell me what makes you think the child is mine. Did Laura say that Jolie belongs to me?"

"No, she didn't. I discovered it on my own."

"How?"

Taylor looked at Fletch, trying to decide whether his son's behavior was sincere or if he was putting on an act. A tic appeared on Fletch's strong jaw. His next words would answer his question. "Jolie always reminded me of someone. The other night I realized who. Your mother. You probably don't remember, but Mavis was fair with blue eyes."

Fletch's legs grew so weak he had to sit down. His head in his hands, he said, "Pa, I swear to you that I had no idea. I truly believed what the neighbors were saying about Laura and Adam until one night Beltran came to me and convinced me that the people were wrong. Then Laura became real chummy with O'Hara, and I decided that he was the one."

He looked up at Taylor, a hopeless grief in his

eyes. "Why do you suppose she left after so long a time?"

Taylor's whole body sagged with relief. His son hadn't been pretending a lie. He wasn't a scoundrel, thank God. There was a softness in his gruff voice as he said, "She left because she could no longer bear the wagging tongues of the gossiping bitches in this village." His big hands clenched into fists. "If anything happens to my daughter, every last one of them will pay."

Fletch stood up and went to stand in the doorway, staring out into the gathering wet darkness. The cry of a hunting wolf pack sent shivers down his spine as he remembered his dream. Were Laura and his daughter out there in the forest somewhere? Were those animals following them?

"Did Laura take the dog with her?"

"Yes, she did, and I take comfort from that. He'll be a big protection for them. She also took her rifle."

"Do you think she's trying to make her way to Detroit?"

"That thought crossed my mind," Taylor said. "I can't think of any other place she'd have in mind to go."

Fletch turned back into the room, his big frame shaking with the sobs he could no longer hold back. "God, Pa," he choked out, "what if she's been set upon by a pack of wolves? That dog of hers is a fighter, but he couldn't take on a whole pack."

Taylor swallowed the lump that rose in his throat. "I won't let myself think about that. I tell myself that everything is going to turn out all right, that she will come back to us."

"I'm not going to depend on her returning on her own," Fletch said, his lips firming determinedly. "After Red Fox and I comb the area tomorrow, I'll go to Detroit if I don't find her."

As Fletch started to leave, Taylor said, "You might as well move back into the cabin. It's gonna be lonesome there all by myself."

It was nearly dusk when Fletcher and Red Fox turned wearily toward home. They had covered a radius of 20 miles since starting out at first light.

They hadn't expected to find the mare's hoofprints in the needle-strewn forest, but had hoped they might find a scrap of cloth where a dress had caught on a brush, or a dropped handkerchief, or even horse droppings. But they had come up empty-handed.

"Will we search again tomorrow?" Red Fox asked when they came to where he would leave Fletch.

"I don't think there's any use," Fletch answered with drooping shoulders. "I'm heading out for Detroit tomorrow. I can't think of anywhere else to look."

"I guess it's logical she would think of going there so she could raise the fair-headed one."

Fletcher looked at his friend and said soberly,

"The fair-headed one is my daughter, Red Fox."

The big Indian made no response for a moment, only looked at Fletcher with probing black eyes. When he did speak, there was a hint of reproach in his voice.

"Why is it you're not her mother's husband? Why are you not married to this woman you claim to love so much?"

"Because I'm a damn fool, that's why," Fletcher answered, staring off into the forest. "When I went off with those men to Canada I foolishly thought I was doing the right thing by Laura. I was the first man to be with her and I wanted her to have time to think clearly about what had happened between us, to decide if she truly loved the *man* or what his body had made her feel. It didn't enter my mind that my seed had taken root inside her."

"So that is why Taylor married her," Red Fox mused. After a pause, he asked, "Does Taylor know that you're the father of the little one?"

"He didn't at first; then a couple of days ago he realized that Jolie looked like his first wife, my mother. Until then, he thought Jolie got her fairness from Adam Beltran, since he was the only real blond in the area."

"Hah!" Red Fox snorted. "That is an insult to Laura, suggesting she would have anything to do with that little weasel. She would only love a man of strong character like herself."

"I guess that lets me out," Fletcher said with

a thin smile. "My character hasn't looked too strong lately."

"No, friend, you are an honorable man, you only acted foolishly where Laura was concerned," Red Fox said. "Do you want me to go with you to Detroit?"

"Thank you for offering, but I'll go alone. I may be gone for a long time, and your people need you."

"May your White Father be with you, then." Red Fox shook Fletcher's hand, then took the path leading to his village.

Chapter Twenty-one

The sun was setting when Laura came in sight of the narrowest and shallowest spot in Lake Superior where Little Fox had said he would cross to Isle Royale. It had not been an easy task to follow the boy all day, but she had managed. Now she looked out over the lake and saw the lad kneeling in the bottom of a canoe, the sun glistening on droplets of water falling from the paddle as he moved toward the shore of Isle Royale.

When the lad landed and dragged the bark vessel onto the shore, then disappeared among the trees, she urged Beauty into the water.

When the little mare reached the center of the narrow strip, the water was up to her belly, and Laura kicked her feet clear of the stirrups and tucked them up behind the saddle. The water was smooth here, and they moved slowly but steadily.

Beauty lunged onto the shore, water streaming off her flanks. Laura reined her in and gazed around, wondering in what direction to ride. She saw no sign of the canoe; the boy had hidden it well. But she saw his tracks leading off to the right.

"I'll not go that way," she said to herself, for it was doubtful he would go to the cabin that Butterfly had mentioned. In his search for manhood he would shun all comforts.

She nudged Beauty with her heels and turned the mount's head left. The great firs were filled with bird song as Beauty stepped daintily along, but Laura was barely aware of it. Her attention was on the forest that seemed to move in on her. She had remembered hearing about wolves and bears on the island, and a film of anxious sweat had formed on her brow.

Laura had just glimpsed the shadowy figures of two wolves slipping through the trees when she came to a small clearing and saw the log cabin glowing in the light of the setting sun. She urged Beauty into a full lope, then moments later pulled her in sharply only a few yards from the sturdy building.

It was hard to say who was the most surprised and alarmed, she or the old Indian who sat on a large, flat rock near the porch. He was old and wrinkled, and most of his teeth were gone, she noted when he stood up and grinned warily at her.

She urged the mare forward, stopping within a few feet of the old brave. "Who are you?" she asked in the charged silence, her voice breathless from her unease.

"I am called Spotted Horse," came the answer in a cracked voice. "I have not damaged your home," he hurriedly added. "I will get my blanket and move on."

He looks so frail, maybe even ill, Laura thought as the bone-brittle Indian stepped upon the porch. He had wrongly assumed the cabin was hers. Actually, he had as much right as she did to be here.

"Where will you go?" Laura asked on impulse as she swung from the saddle. "Do you have people to go to?"

The black eyes that were dimmed with age clouded over. "My wife and children are gone, taken away by the white man's disease, pneumonia. The killer wiped out half our village. I wasn't told to leave my people, but food is always scarce in the winter and I could sense that food was given to me begrudgingly, especially when a child was crying from hunger.

"So, one morning in December I paddled my canoe across the lake to this island. I told myself that it was in the Great Father's hands. Either I would survive or the wolves would make a meal of me."

"It appears that you have survived." Laura smiled at the old one.

"Yes," Spotted Horse answered gravely, "but only because I found your cabin empty. There was enough wood chopped to see me through the rest of the winter, and I was fortunate enough to send an arrow through a deer's heart. Only once did I have a narrow escape with a wolf."

When Spotted Horse continued on into the cabin, Laura stared thoughtfully at the ground. It would be lonely here with just Jolie for company, and she was sure the old fellow had nowhere to go.

When Spotted Horse came outside, his ragged blanket rolled and tucked under his arm, a much-used bow and quiver of arrows slung over his bony shoulder, Laura said, "The cabin is big enough for both of us, old brave. Tomorrow we will plant a garden patch." She patted the dog on the head. "This fellow will keep us safe from the wolves while we work."

Thanksgiving flashed in the Indian's eyes, but that was the only sign he gave of his relief. When he answered, "If that is your wish, I will stay with you," Laura had difficulty not to laugh out loud. What a proud old fellow he is, she thought.

"What is the age of your papoose? he asked as Laura removed the fussing Jolie from her back.

"She will have her first birthday soon," Laura

answered, stepping up on the porch, taking note of how the old man's black eyes stared at her daughter's blond hair. Little Fox had done the same thing until he grew used to the color.

She stepped through the door that Spotted Horse had left open and stood a moment to accustom her eyes to the dim interior. When articles of furniture began to take shape, she moved purposefully into the room as though she were familiar with it. She must keep up her deception of owning the cabin, otherwise the old man might chase *her* away.

The large-sized room had a musty, alien odor of meals Spotted Horse had cooked over the winter. As she walked across the floor to the hand-crafted bed, she said, "Would you please open the shutters and raise the windows?"

When bright light flooded the room and a fresh breeze wafted inside, Laura laid Jolie down on the bed fastened to the wall next to a large fieldstone fireplace. The bed was so neatly made up it was clear the old Indian had preferred sleeping on the floor, curled up before the fire.

After taking Jolie out of the cradle board, Laura straightened up and took stock of her new home. Beneath the window was a good-sized table, its top made of handhewn boards, and along each side of it was a half-rounded log bench. In its center was a lamp, its bowl nearly full of kerosene. Grouped around it were a jar of matches, a salt and pepper cellar, and a narrow wooden box just big enough to hold knives, forks, and spoons. On each end of the table there had been placed tin plates with matching cups. They were clean but dusty.

Completing the furnishings were two chairs, rudely constructed like the other pieces but comfortable-looking with seat and back padding made from a colorful Indian blanket.

All in all, Laura decided, she could be much worse off. The cabin was sound, and there were plenty of deer to supply meat and the lake to give up fish. There was also the garden she and the old man would make. Above everything else, she could at last live in peace. There would be no more whispering behind her back, no more sly, knowing looks.

Jolie fussed and as Laura picked her up Spotted Horse said, "The papoose is hungry. I will pull down the deer haunch from where I hung it in a tree and make us a fine stew."

Laura smiled at him and said, "Make a big pot of it, would you please, for I am very hungry too."

Spotted Horse nodded, and she thought that his footsteps were more sprightly as he left the cabin. He's as happy as I am to have company, she thought.

Chapter Twenty-two

Laura plopped down beneath a young birch, her body crying out for rest. She twisted the toes of one bare foot in the cool green grass as she looked out over the large garden patch she and Spotted Horse had toiled over. They had taken turns with the spade the old Indian had purchased at the trading post five miles down the lake.

The soil was virgin and rich, having never before nourished man's vegetable crops. The seeds she had thoughtfully brought from home, beans, corn, peas, onions, turnips, squash, and pumpkins, had quickly taken root and now were sturdy, flourishing plants. Last night for supper she and Jolie and Spotted Horse had enjoyed their first meal of sweet peas. How good the first fresh vegetables of the season had tasted after the long, cold winter.

Laura looked up in the branches where Spotted Horse had suspended a contraption he had put together to hold Jolie while they worked in the garden. The little one was safe from any wolves that might sneak up on them. She was quite content looking up at the leaves and blue sky.

Laura glanced at the mare staked nearby, then looked down at the rifle lying beside her. Usually the dog guarded Beauty, but at the moment he was off in the woods somewhere chasing rabbits and squirrels. Spotted Horse had left this morning to paddle his canoe down to the post.

What a godsend that post had been for her. When she had learned of its presence she had sent the old man off with a shopping list without much hope of it being filled. But he had returned with all the necessary ingredients to make bread, along with a pail of lard, a slab of bacon, a tin of crackers, a round of cheese, and a bag of coffee beans. And to her delight, canned milk for Jolie. Spotted Horse had paid for the items with some beaver pelts he had trapped along the lake over the winter. He had not set a line in the forest for fear of being set upon by wolves. He had gone to the post today because she was low on milk and kerosene.

Laura leaned back against the tree trunk.

Looking up at the sky, she thought that the last three weeks had passed much better than she had expected, due to the old man's presence. She depended on his wisdom, his company, and Jolie adored him. Many times when he talked to the little one in his language, Laura saw a softness in his black eyes.

Her lips twisted ruefully. Jolie was beginning to chatter back to him in his tongue. Wouldn't that tickle Pa if he knew?

Sadness settled over Laura's face. How upset Pa must be, how worried. Had she been wrong to run away from home? When she remembered all the reasons that had sent her to Isle Royale, she knew she had made the right decision. She was content here. Her daughter and the old Indian were all she needed. She had loved and trusted a man once but would never be so foolish again.

She was thinking of lowering Jolie down from her perch and returning to the cabin to fix lunch when the dog came running out of the forest, barking furiously. He came to a bracing stop in front of her, whining and yipping, trying desperately to tell her something.

"What is it, boy?" she asked. When she stood up, he ran a few feet away from her, then stopped and looked back, plainly telling her to follow him. The thought went through her that something had happened to Spotted Horse as she looked up in the tree to check on Jolie. The old man's contraption was motionless, telling her that her daughter was sleeping. She grabbed up the rifle, freed Beauty from her stake, and swung onto her back. Grasping the mare's mane and gripping her belly with her knees, she raced after the dog.

He had run but half a mile when he stopped before a jumble of rocks and boulders and nudged at a slender figure lying facedown at their base.

"Little Fox!" Laura gasped, sliding off the mare, her eyes glued in horror to the buckskin tunic that hung in shreds on the boy's back and shoulder. She didn't have to be told that the teenager had been attacked by a bear, and that Brave had driven the animal away.

"Please, God, let him be alive," she prayed as she ran to kneel beside the crumpled figure. She picked up his limp wrist to feel for a pulse.

She had almost given up hope that there was still life in her young friend when finally she felt a flutter of movement like that of a baby bird. "I must get him to the cabin before wolves smell the blood," she whispered frantically.

She led Beauty up close to Little Fox, chastising her severely when she sidled away at the scent of blood. In her anxiety to get the lad onto the mare's back she had a strength she wasn't aware of having before. At any normal time she would have been unable to lift the sturdy body and lay it over the mount's back. With one leap, she was mounted and was sending Beauty racing toward the cabin.

Laura gave a breath of relief when she rode into the small clearing and saw Spotted Horse coming up the path from the lake. If anyone could help Little Fox, it would be the old Indian. She jumped to the ground at the same time as Spotted Horse came hurrying forward. He saw the torn garment, the blood dripping off the dangling arm, and asked no questions. He slid the boy onto his shoulder, and Laura followed them into the cabin.

"Put him on the bed." Laura hurried forward to turn back the covers. When she had helped Spotted Horse ease the unconscious boy onto the leaf-filled mattress, the old man pulled his hunting knife from the top of his knee-high moccasins and began to cut away the tattered buckskin. They were both appalled at the long, deep gashes that had been visited on the tender flesh.

"Get me a basin of water and a cloth," Spotted Horse ordered. "Then go take Jolie out of the tree."

Laura heard her daughter's angry cries then and hurried to fulfill the old man's request. It took but a minute to bring Jolie into the cabin, and Laura kept an anxious eye on Little Fox as the little one used her chamber pot.

The boy was moaning weakly as his ugly gashes were bathed, and she said, "Poor little brave, he must be in a lot of pain."

"He is"—Spotted Horse nodded grimly—"but I must make sure all the dirt is out of his wounds. Otherwise infection will set in and we could lose him."

"Do you think you can save him?" Laura asked hopefully as she set Jolie into the chair that Spotted Horse had raised the seat to her height at the table. She gave her a piece of skillet bread liberally sprinkled with sugar.

Spotted Horse looked up at her, concern in his eyes. "I will do my best, but it is in the hands of the Great Father. Watch over the boy while I go into the forest to gather special roots and leaves. They will make a tea that will draw the poison out of his system." When he straightened up he looked at Laura and said, "Something tells me that you know this lad."

"Yes, I do," Laura answered, but didn't go into details why she was acquainted with her young friend. The Indian might ask questions that she didn't care to answer. She was taking no chances that anyone from her village might learn of her whereabouts.

Spotted Horse didn't press her for any more information, and when he left at a trot she hadn't known he was capable of, she took the seat he had vacated.

Lying on his stomach, his head turned to the side, Little Fox began to fret and move about. He whimpered in his native tongue, and Laura had no idea what he was saying. She wondered if he cried for his father or the aunt he now called Mother. She gently smoothed the long black hair from his forehead and felt his brow.

Did it feel a little warm? She chewed thoughtfully on her lower lip. When she felt the pulse in his wrist, she was certain it beat faster than normal.

"He's going to be all right." She patted the dog's head as he nosed up beside her and sniffed his playmate's face. "Spotted Horse knows how to doctor him."

Laura prayed that her promise would come true, for the angry-looking slashes on the slender back were still oozing blood. She stood up, and taking the basin of bloody water she exchanged it for a pan of clean water, along with a clean cloth.

She was carefully bathing the wounds and softly crooning a song mother Marie had sung to her as a child when Spotted Horse entered the cabin. In one hand he carried a branch from a bush she had seen many times in the forest but did not know the name of. In his other hand he grasped some roots that still had dirt clinging to them. Laura watched the old man strip the leaves off the branch, then wash them thoroughly in a pan of water. When the leaves were cleaned to his satisfaction, he brought them to the bed and carefully laid them over the deep gouges.

When every inch of the bear's claw marks was covered, he looked up at Laura and ordered, "Scrub the roots clean; then put them in a pot of water to simmer over the fire. The juices from the roots will help keep the fever down that is beginning to build inside him."

"How long should it brew?" Laura asked as she walked over to the table and picked up Spotted Horse's knife that lay there.

Spotted Horse looked at the mantel clock. "When the long hand points to three it will be long enough," he answered.

"Fifteen minutes," Laura said to herself, for it was now one o'clock. She busily cut off the limp stem and leaves from the three different kinds of roots, scrubbed them with a rough piece of haversack, transferred them into a pot of water, and placed it on a bed of red coals. To hurry the heating along she laid wood chips against the coals, which immediately caught hold and flamed around the cast-iron vessel. When the water began to bubble, she raked the chips away and the water settled down to a gentle brewing.

When fifteen minutes passed, Laura removed the pot and carried it to the table where she ladled the greenish juice into a tin cup. She picked up a spoon and hurried to the bed with the cup.

Little Fox was quite restless now, making it necessary for Spotted Horse to forcibly hold him down so that he wouldn't disturb the poison-drawing leaves on his wounds. All the time Spotted Horse talked soothingly to the lad in his native tongue. When he sensed that Laura stood beside him, he looked up and said, "If you will hold his head steady I will spoon the liquid into his mouth. He will fight it, for it is very bitter."

Laura climbed over the foot of the bed, and positioning herself at Little Fox's head, she gently but firmly placed her hand on his head and held it steady. Spotted Horse filled the spoon from the cup, blew on the liquid to cool it, then held it to the boy's dry lips.

Little Fox fought its unpalatable taste as it hit his tongue, but Laura didn't let him move as Spotted Horse's remedy trickled down his throat.

Twenty minutes later half the cup's liquid had been drunk, and Spotted Horse straightened up. "That will do for now," he said. "We'll wait an hour, then get some more inside him."

Laura rose stiffly from her knees, and as she crawled off the bed she looked over at Jolie, who had grown very quiet. The little one was sound asleep, her head on the table. "Poor baby," she said softly and lifted the little body and gently laid her down on Spotted Horse's bed of blankets.

"I will prepare the little brave a bed of soft pine needles," the old man said, walking to the door.

"Oh, but I wouldn't want him sleeping on the floor," Laura objected.

Spotted Horse looked at her as though her words were foolish. "Where do you think he would rest if he was home in his wigwam?"

Laura nodded and said no more. Like the rest

of his family, the boy would have a bed of furs on the floor. The old man closed the door behind him, and she set about making a pot of venison stew. It had just began to simmer over the fire when Spotted Horse returned, his arms full of soft pine tips. When he arranged them on the hearth next to where he slept, Laura took the quilt from her bed and tucked it neatly over the thickness of the featherlike boughs. When they had carefully moved their patient to his new bed, she took the top sheet and spread it over the slender body that was growing restless again.

"It is time to get more medicine inside him." Spotted Horse reached for the cup and spoon.

"Is your root tea taking effect on him yet?" Laura asked anxiously, taking up her position beside Little Fox.

Spotted Horse shook his head. "He is still in the grip of the fever, still fighting off the bear in his mind." He pulled the sheet down to examine the wounds on the slender back. "The bleeding has stopped, though. When we have finished dosing him, I will put fresh leaves on the gashes."

The rest of the day wore on, and dusk settled around the cabin. The stew was eaten, and after Brave had his share he was sent outside to watch over Beauty until morning. During this passage of time Little Fox had been forced to drink the bitter tea every hour on the hour. He no longer tossed about, but lay in a dull stupor of exhaustion from the fever and loss of blood.

It was close to two in the morning when the fever broke and Little Fox slipped off into a deep sleep. The crisis was over. Spotted Horse laid a hand on the sweat-dampened head and said, "His spirit will not pass into the unknown world. He will live to kill many deer."

"Poor little brave," Laura said softly. "The reason he came here was to kill a deer with his bow and arrow, to put his childhood behind him and become a man. He will have to go back to his village now, still an untried lad."

Spotted Horse shook his head. "You are wrong. Much will be made over him at his village. Will he not bear the scars of the grizzly? Is he not a man to have survived the mutilation of his back and shoulders? His father will be very proud of him."

Laura hadn't thought of it that way, and an amused smile hovered on her lips. She could just see Little Fox holding court, showing off his scars to his peers, boasting how he had fought off the bear. Most likely he would embroider his story by saying that he had gravely wounded the animal with his bow and arrow. Who was to call him liar?

Later when she lay in bed, Jolie cuddled up close to her, Laura remembered that the boy's month would be up at the end of the week. Her eyes flew open. If Little Fox didn't show up in the village shortly after that, his father would become concerned and come looking for him.

Laura lay awake, staring into the darkness trying to figure a way out of the dilemma that loomed ahead. Her young friend wouldn't be able to travel for at least another two weeks, and Red Fox would come looking for him way before that. Her hiding place would no longer be a secret.

The next morning Laura's eyes ached from the lack of sleep, but during those dark hours she had reached a decision. She must take Jolie and make their way to Detroit. She felt confident that Spotted Horse would help her. If not to accompany them, at least to sell some more of his beaver pelts and give her the money to buy passage to the city where she could become lost among so many people.

Chapter Twenty-three

Fletch stood on the porch of the Great Northern Hotel in Detroit, looking up and down the unpaved street. Across from him a big sign on a building read "Johnson and Bros." and beneath it in smaller letters, "Guns, Pistols and Munitions Done to Order."

The next building was the City Meat Market, then beside it a sign proclaimed "John Hurley—Loan Agent." At the north end of the street lay the disreputable part of the city where brothels, saloons, and dance halls that scarcely disguised their real purpose could be found.

Men of faint heart and decent women never ventured there, for drinking and prostitutes led to arguments, fights, and guns.

Fletch turned to look south of the gun shop.

There was a hardware store, a cigar and tobacco shop, a clothing store, and a meat and grocery store, the last building before homes took over.

On the side of the street where he stood was a restaurant, a boardinghouse, a Chinese bathhouse and laundry, and a two-story building with a doctor's office on the first floor and a lawyer's on the second. At the end of the street was a school, a church, and a cemetery.

Fletch knew this street and these buildings like he did the trees and cabins back at Big Pine. He had walked past them countless times the past three weeks in his search for Laura.

They had been useless walks, a waste of breath to question people if they had seen a tall, beautiful woman with a toddler looking for employment. He had met with negative shakes of the head.

Bleakness in his eyes, Fletch stepped down onto the dusty, rutted street. He was certain that Laura was not in Detroit and he didn't know where else to look for her. He would go home, rethink her disappearance, and hopefully come up with another idea of where she might have gone.

He refused to think that she and his daughter were not alive somewhere.

Taylor lifted Butterfly off his naked, sweating body and curled her against his side. As he stroked her damp, long black hair he said, "We can't go on this way, Butterfly, me sneaking over to your village, you slipping over here after everyone has gone to bed. I worry about you being out in the woods after dark."

Butterfly grew very still. Was she now to hear the words she had dreaded since the first time they'd made love beneath a tall pine? Had the moment come when Taylor would say it was time to end their relationship?

She held her breath, waiting to hear the dreaded words. But a long silence ensued before Taylor spoke again, and stunned her speechless.

"I think it's high time we got married, Butterfly. I am several years older than you and I want to make sure that you will be provided for when I'm gone."

Butterfly released her breath in a soft flutter. Never, ever, had she expected Taylor to voice the wish to marry her. Dare she hope that it would be the kind of wedding white folks had . . . in their church? One that was legal in all ways? The government wouldn't recognize an Indian ceremony.

When she was so long in responding, Taylor gave her hair a gentle tug and asked, "Don't you want to marry me, Butterfly?"

Butterfly raised up on an elbow and leaned over Taylor. Looking gravely into his eyes, she asked, "Will we be married by your white preacher? I will not have you called a squaw man."

Taylor gave a robust laugh and hugged her to him. "Of course Preacher Stiles will marry us."

Butterfly kept her cheek on Taylor's chest and her words were smothered as she said, "What will the village people say? Will Fletch be angry with you? And Laura? I feel strongly that she should be with you again."

"I don't give a damn what the villagers say, they can rot in hell for all I care. It was their vile gossiping that ran Laura off. Fletch and Laura won't care. They've known about us all along." Taylor heaved a long sigh. "I do hope you're right about Laura and little Jolie returning to us. I wonder if Fletch has found any trace of them."

"In time he will find her, I'm sure of it."

Taylor kissed the top of Butterfly's head, then stared up at the storage room's ceiling. "I'll talk to Reverend Stiles tomorrow and set the date for our wedding. Saturday is three days away. Will that suit you?"

"That will be fine," Butterfly answered and rolled over on her back. "So as not to have hard feelings with my people, we must have an Indian ceremony also. They would feel slighted if we did not."

"I can understand that. You and Chief Muga decide on the day."

"You are so kind and thoughtful, Taylor." Butterfly stroked her fingers across his chest.

Taylor caught her hand and moved it down

his bare stomach to where there was the beginning of an arousal.

"Should we celebrate our coming nuptials?" he whispered hoarsely, then climbed on Butterfly's willing body.

The stallion blew softly as Fletch pulled him to a halt in front of the church. He had been ridden all day without a rest in Fletch's sudden desire to get home as soon as possible. A thought had entered his mind that something was happening there, maybe that Laura had returned to Big Pine.

What was going on in the church house on a Saturday? he wondered, then thought that Hunter O'Hara and Agnes Morse might be getting married today. He swung to the ground as people started coming out of the small church.

The men looked pleasant enough, but the women, with the exception of Maida, Justine, Agnes, and Big Bertha, looked as though they had been eating green grapes. "What has displeased Big Pine's society group?" he asked himself as he stood at Buckskin's head.

And what was Pa doing with Butterfly hanging on his arm as they followed the other people outside? Had his father finally decided to let everyone know of his association with the Indian woman?

Fletch skimmed his eyes over Butterfly and thought that she was truly a handsome woman, tall and regal-looking. Her raven black hair, worn in two braids, lay in stark relief against the white buckskin tunic with bright beadwork around the neck.

And look at Pa! Fletch grinned. He hadn't seen him wear his suit in years. A person would think it was he and Butterfly who had just got married, he wore such a wide smile.

When the men gathered around Taylor, shaking his hand and slapping him on the back, Fletch said in a stunned voice, "By God, it *is* his wedding." He wanted to whoop with laughter. The old man had gotten up the nerve to marry the woman he had loved all these years. That accounted for the sour looks the women wore, especially Widow Louden. She'd had her eye on Pa ever since mother Marie passed away. To lose out to a heathen Indian must be a bitter cup to swallow.

Fletch shouldered his way through the men who stood around the bride and groom, and with a wide smile held his hand out to Taylor. "It's about time you married the prettiest woman in the area," he said and then turned to Butterfly. "Welcome to the family, Butterfly." He smiled as he leaned forward and kissed her cheek.

The new bride blushed with pleasure, then quickly sobered. "Did you find any trace of Laura?"

Fletch looked from Butterfly to his father, who waited anxiously for his answer. "I'm sorry, Pa, but I found nothing. I went over every inch of Detroit. She's not there."

All the happiness left the newlyweds' faces. They wished they didn't have to attend the party that Maida, Justine, and Bertha had arranged for them at the tavern. Butterfly slid her arm in Taylor's and said softly, "She will return, husband, I feel it in my heart. Let's go to the party and pretend to have a good time. The two young women and Big Bertha have gone to a lot of trouble for us."

"You'll be there, won't you, son?" Taylor asked as Fletch started walking toward his friend Red.

"I'll be there." Fletch grinned. "I wouldn't miss the chance to dance with the bride."

After Fletch greeted his trapper friend, Red asked if there was any news of Laura. When Fletch shook his head, Red said, "Your friend Red Fox was here looking for you yesterday. He said you should come to his village as soon as you return."

"Maybe he has news of Laura." Hope built inside Fletch.

Red shook his head. "I asked him that. He said no, that it was another matter he wanted to talk to you about."

Fletch would have liked to stay longer at the wedding party, where the three women had prepared an abundance of food and the drinks were a gift from the groom. But Milly Howard had grabbed on to him the moment he walked into the tavern and had clung to him like a burr, her eyes flagrantly inviting him to take her to bed. Her rubbing up against him, her coy looks, only made him wonder what he had ever seen in her.

Finally, in desperation, he gave Red the high sign to come help him. When the trapper came and dragged a reluctant Milly onto the dance floor, Fletch slipped out the door and into the storeroom, barring the door behind him. He was taking no chances of Milly sneaking into bed with him.

He would be sleeping in the storeroom from now on, giving his father and Butterfly the privacy they deserved. He undressed and stretched out on the narrow cot his father had slept on over most of the winter. He said a mental prayer that Laura and his daughter were safe somewhere, then fell into a deep sleep. It had been a long and tiring day.

Elisha stamping around in the store awakened Fletch the next morning. He rubbed his whiskered jaws thinking wryly that Pa had made sure he could spend as much time as he wished in Butterfly's arms today.

The position of the sun shining through the window told Fletch that it was around eight o'clock. Knowing that Red Fox wanted to see him, he rolled out of bed. It must be something important since his friend had come looking for him. It wasn't the Indian's habit to come to the white man's village.

Fletch's sudden entrance into the store startled the old man frying bacon and eggs on the potbelly stove. "You scared the bejesus out of me, Fletch," Elisha complained, picking up the fork he had dropped to the floor. "I didn't know you wuz in there."

"I'll be sleeping in the storage room now . . . for a while at least. Would you mind adding some bacon and eggs to the skillet? I'm half starved."

Elisha nodded and said, "Coffee is ready if you want some."

"Sounds good." Fletch reached for a cup beneath the counter. "I haven't had any decent brew for over three weeks."

"What do you think about your Paw gettin' married again?" Elisha asked, slapping a plate heaped with bacon and eggs on the counter.

Fletch sluiced the soap off his face, then picked up a much-used towel to dry off with before answering. "I think it's high time he made a decent woman out of Butterfly. She's a fine woman."

"Some of the wimmenfolk around here don't have your sentiments," Elisha said, digging into his breakfast.

Fletch gave a short laugh as he pulled his plate to him. "I'm sure that won't bother Pa and Butterfly one whit."

Elisha chuckled. "If Taylor hears anyone badmouthin' his new wife he'll tell them to go to hell and refuse to sell them anything."

"Do you know if Pa went to the preacher and

had his marriage to Laura annulled?"

"Yeah, he did. Had it all done legal like."

"I guess there was a lot of talk about that."

Elisha laughed. "The ole gossipers like to have talked their tongues off, buzzin' back and forth between each other's cabins."

If I find Laura and bring her back here, they'll really have something to talk about when they find out Jolie is my child, Fletch thought as he pushed his empty plate away and prepared to leave the store.

Twenty minutes later he was astride a rested Buckskin and riding toward the Indian village.

Fletch was ready to take the fork that led to the Indian village when he saw Red Fox riding toward him. He reined in and waited for the Indian to reach him.

"I can see in your eyes that your trip to Detroit was fruitless," Red Fox said as he pulled his pinto up next to Buckskin.

Fletch nodded. "I found no trace of Laura." He studied his friend's face. "I can see that something is bothering you, friend. Is one of your family ill?"

Red Fox peered off through the trees as though looking a long distance. "Those of mine in the village are all well," he finally said. "It is the welfare of Little Fox that bothers me. Night before last I had a dream of him. It was so vivid I know that he is in trouble. I want you to go with me to Isle Royale to help me look for him."

"Of course I will go with you, but are you sure it wasn't just a dream and nothing more? The lad has another week before his month is up."

"It wasn't an ordinary dream." Red Fox shook his head. "I could see my son too clearly. His limp body was lying at the foot of a pile of boulders. There was blood all over his back."

"All right then, let's get going." Fletch turned the stallion around and Red Fox led off, heading toward the lake trail that Laura and Little Fox had taken a little over three weeks ago.

Chapter Twenty-four

Laura's mind was in a turmoil as she bent over Little Fox and felt his brow. She hadn't slept at all well last night, her brain buzzing with the dread of what lay ahead of her.

She had never been to a city before and had no idea what Detroit would be like. She had heard stories about it, some of them not very pleasant. Some claimed it was mostly made up of brothels, saloons, and gambling halls. It was said that cut-throats roamed the streets and that no man, woman, or child was safe from them.

How in the world will I find employment there? she worried, finding Little Fox's brow cool and sitting down beside him.

Last night after she and Spotted Horse left the boy long enough to grab a bite of supper, she had gotten up the nerve to approach the old man about selling some more of his furs and lending her enough money to enable her to get to Detroit.

"But why would you want to go to that bad place when you have a fine cabin here and a fine garden coming on?" The old man had looked at her in amazement.

"As you know," she had answered, "I am acquainted with the lad. His name is Little Fox, son of Red Fox and grandson of Chief Muga. A week from now when Little Fox doesn't show up at his village, Red Fox will come looking for him."

"Are you afraid of this brave?" Spotted Horse had watched her closely.

"No, I am not afraid of him, but he will tell his friend, a man I don't want to know where I am. It is very important that I get away by the end of the week. And I would greatly appreciate it if you don't say where I've gone."

"You are making a mistake, Jolie's mother. You are running to meet trouble. Why don't you wait and see if something doesn't happen before it gets here?"

"Believe me, Spotted Horse, trouble will get here. I know from experience with this man. I must get away as soon as possible."

A deep sadness had come over the old man's face. "I had thought to spend my remaining years here on the island with you and Jolie. And who will teach the little one wisdom and patience? She has no father to do that, and her mother has little of either one. I do not know what will become of the little white-haired papoose.' "

"Jolie will be all right, Spotted Horse. If I find that I can't make my way in Detroit, I promise you I'll come back here." She had waited a moment, then asked, "Are you going to lend me the money?"

"I will, of course, get you the money," the old man had agreed, though reluctantly, then added, "I hope I am not doing wrong in helping you go to such a place."

And so the old man had gone off to the post this morning to sell more beaver pelts.

Laura gave a start when she noticed Little Fox looking wide-eyed at her. "What are you doing here, Laura?" he croaked.

"I live here now." She smiled at him. "How are you feeling?"

"I feel weak and hungry, and my back hurts."

"I imagine that it does. Do you remember being attacked by a bear, being clawed by him?"

The boy shivered. "I'll never forget it. If the dog hadn't come along and scared him off, the beast would have killed me."

"He almost did. An old Indian named Spotted Horse saved your life with his roots and leaves."

"Where is he? I must thank him." Little Fox raised his head and looked around. "Where is Jolie? Didn't you bring her with you?"

"Of course I did. She has gone on an errand with the old Indian."

A worried frown grew on Little Fox's brow. "How much longer do I have before my month is up?"

"One day short of a week."

"Do you think I can travel by then?"

Laura shook her head. "I'm sorry, little friend, but a week from now you'll still be very weak. You lost a lot of blood."

"But my father will be worried if I don't return to the village on time."

"I know he will, but you know that he'll come looking for you, so don't fret about it."

"Yes he will." Little Fox smiled and asked, "I don't suppose you have any cookies?"

Laura laughed softly. "Not today I don't, but I will make you some tomorrow." This morning before Spotted Horse had left with his bundle of furs, he told her that they were getting low on sugar. She had managed to keep amusement off her face. Spotted Horse liked her cookies as much as the boy did. Tomorrow she would spend much of the day making cookies. She wanted to leave a good supply for the old fellow when she left.

Little Fox leaned up on an elbow, wincing a bit. "Why have you left Fletch, Laura? He's not on the island, is he?"

"No, he's not on the island," Laura answered sharply. "And what do you mean why did I leave Fletch? It was Taylor I left."

"I didn't mean to upset you, Laura," Little Fox said quickly. "It's just that my father always refers to you as Fletch's woman."

"Your father shouldn't say that. It's not true."

"He will be surprised when I tell him. Usually he is right in all things. He is a very wise man." Little Fox laid his head back down on the pillow to ponder this rare happening.

A smile hovered around Laura's lips as she smoothed the sheet over the boy's back. When he murmured, "Thank you," she walked to the door and looked outside.

High in the blue sky an eagle soared on slowly flapping wings, ever ready to swoop down on a small, unwary prey. Laura remembered as a small child helping mother Marie be on the alert for eagles, which would grab up their baby chicks and fly away with them. How she would cry every time they lost a fluffy ball of yellow to one of the eagles.

I still miss mother Marie, Laura thought, leaning against the door frame. If she were alive today, everything would be different. She had been wise and would have known that her son was lusting after her adopted daughter and would have put a stop to it before it was too late.

It's a little late to think of that now. Laura sighed and lowered her gaze to the lake at the sound of a fish leaping out of the water to catch a fly. She watched it arch its body, then drop back down, leaving ever widening ripples in the clear water.

"Maybe I'll just go catch you for our supper," Laura thought out loud.

Riding a yard or so behind Red Fox, Fletcher noted that his friend's broad shoulders were beginning to have a dejected droop. It had taken them two days to reach the island, arriving yesterday near dark. They had started out early this morning looking for Little Fox. Every few minutes they called the boy's name but received no response. Fletcher nudged the stallion into a lope, reaching Red Fox and riding alongside him. "We still have a big part of the island to cover. We'll run across him anytime now."

"I don't know, Fletch." Red Fox shook his head. "I'm about to give up hope."

"Don't do that." Fletch smiled encouragingly as they approached a pile of large boulders, reaching a height of about nine feet. "Let's go check out that jumble of rock. It looks like a place a lad would choose to make camp."

They turned their mounts' heads in the direction Fletch had indicated, and on arriving, both swung to the ground and began searching for tracks.

Almost immediately Red Fox spotted his son's moccasined footprints. His exultant "Aha" was cut short when he saw the large prints of a bear.

"Now don't panic, Red Fox." Fletch fought to keep his own fear out of his voice. "The tracks could be days apart."

Then they spotted the bloody rocks, and a broken arrow shaft, clearly telling them what had happened. The boy had been set upon by a bear.

Red Fox's usually stoic features crumpled and his fists clenched. He had lost his firstborn, his only son, to an animal. He didn't even have a body to take home.

He turned his grief-stricken eyes to Fletch, who called out excitedly, "Come here and see what you can make of these tracks."

What Red Fox saw were the tracks of a horse that had been ridden up to a base of boulders, and prints of a man of small stature who had climbed to the ground and run to where blood-spotted rocks lay. The tracks of a dog ran alongside the booted prints.

Hope surged through the big Indian's blood when he saw the footprints return to where the man had left his horse. This time the footprints were deeper, as though made by a larger man, or a small one carrying an Indian lad.

"Come on, Red Fox." Fletcher squeezed his shoulder. "I think we're going to find your boy in just a short time. It will be easy to trace these hoofprints."

Red Fox stood up from examining the blood-stained rocks. "There's a cabin at the end of this island, but the teenagers are forbidden to use it while seeking their manhood. That's why I didn't go there right away. But from what these tracks tell me, someone has taken my son there."

In a few minutes they smelled the wood smoke

before they saw it rising from the chimney of the small cabin sitting among the pines. "Someone is living there," Red Fox said and kicked his mount into a hard gallop. He was brought to a rearing halt in front of the cabin and his rider was off his back before his front hooves came back to the ground.

"Father?" Little Fox exclaimed when the light from the doorway was blocked by a pair of broad shoulders.

"My son!" Red Fox responded as with three big strides he was across the room and kneeling beside Little Fox's pallet. "Are you all right?" His eyes scanned the narrow back with the great bear marks on it.

"I am now, but I was gravely ill for a while."

"Who has been tending your wounds?"

"An old brave called Spotted Horse. He is very wise about roots, leaves, and bark."

"Yes, I can see that. Tell me now how you came to tangle with a bear."

Unnoticed by Red Fox, Laura stood at the window peeking out at Fletch climbing off Buckskin as Little Fox began his story.

She was shocked at how Fletch had aged. Had he been ill? she wondered as he stepped up on the small porch. There was gray in the hair at his temples, and his cheeks were almost gaunt.

"But he's still the handsomest man I've ever seen," she told herself as his tall frame darkened the doorway. When he stepped inside, she stiffened her features, hiding how happy she was to see him.

Fletch started walking toward father and son when a movement at his left caught his eye. He wheeled around, wariness in his eyes, coolly prepared for anything that might happen. His jaw dropped then and he shook his head in disbelief.

"Laura! What are you doing here?" He moved toward her.

Willing her pulse to settle down, Laura set her chin at a hostile tilt. "Not that it's any of your business, but I live here."

Fletch held her eyes a moment, then looked around the room. "Where is Jolie?"

Laura hesitated before answering, "She's gone with a friend to the post down the lake."

"Oh?" A steely glint appeared in Fletch's eyes. "Is this friend male or female?"

Laura delayed again before answering, "Male."

Fletch's lips drew into a tight line as he glared at Laura. She stared back at him, remembering how that hard, chiseled mouth could turn so gentle when he kissed her.

Her own lips tightened when he sneeringly asked, "A male who came with you from the village, or a new one you've met here?"

"Again it's none of your business," Laura flared indignantly, "but I'll tell you anyway. I met him here."

"Damn you, woman," Fletch grated. "Even

here on an isolated island you manage to meet a man."

Laura gave an indifferent shrug of her shoulders. "I guess I'm like you in that respect. You always manage to find a woman."

His eyes icy bleak, Fletch said, "I've never lived with any of them."

"I've never lived with any of my men friends either . . . until now."

"So you are living with him?" When Laura nodded, he asked after a moment, "Is this one special, then?"

Laura thought for a moment before answering, "Yes, in his own way he is very special. He's kind and wise and Jolie adores him."

That last was too much for Fletcher. It was bad enough that this stranger had the woman he loved, there was no way in hell he was going to have his daughter as well. Jolie would adore no man but her father. He reached for Laura, and she shrank away from the anger in his eyes.

Fletch dropped his hands when he saw the fear on Laura's face. But he didn't move away from her as he said through gritted teeth, "No man is going to take my daughter away from me. I'll kill the bastard first."

Laura stared at Fletch in dazed astonishment. How in the world had he learned that he had fathered Jolie? He's bluffing, she decided, and demanded, "What gives you the idea that Jolie is your child? Wouldn't I have told you if she were?"

"No, you damn well wouldn't. You're too damn stubborn to do what would be normal. Even as a little girl, you could be wanting a drink of water but you were too mule-headed to let anyone but Ma give it to you."

"Well, it's not true that Jolie is your child."

"Yes, she is. I have proof of it."

"How? You never could prove it before, and she still has blond hair and blue eyes."

"So did my mother."

Laura dropped weakly into a chair. Her secret was out at last. "Why didn't you mention that fact before, instead of accusing me of being with Adam Beltran, then Hunter O'Hara?"

"Because I didn't know what my mother looked like until Pa told me. When Jolie grew older, he finally noticed the striking likeness to his first wife."

Laura looked up at Fletch, her chin in the air and rebellion in her eyes. "Now you know. So what?"

"So we're going back to Big Pine and get married."

After her gasp of surprise, Laura said loftily, "Impossible. You seem to forget that I'm already married."

"Not anymore, you're not. Pa had his and your marriage annulled. He's remarried now."

Shock hit Laura, leaving her stunned. "Please

don't tell me he married that awful Martha Louden."

"Of course not," Fletch answered almost angrily. "He married Butterfly."

Laura drew a long breath of relief. "Thank goodness. I was afraid he'd never get up the nerve to make Butterfly his wife, even though he wanted that more than anything in the world."

Fletch nodded. "That, and seeing you and me married and making a home for our daughter. How soon can you get ready to leave? When is your boyfriend supposed to get back with Jolie?"

"You have an overworking imagination if you think I'll go back to Big Pine," Laura flared out, "let alone marry you. I'd never tie myself to a skirt-chasing womanizer."

Laura thought for a moment that Fletch would strike her, his face looked so furious. He took a menacing step forward and stood over her. "Maybe you won't marry me, but you'll come back to Big Pine."

"Not on your life will I come back to that place." Laura glared up at him.

"You'll come if you want to see your daughter again. I'm taking Jolie back with me."

Laura was on her feet in an instant. "It will be the sorriest day in your life, Fletch Thomas, if you try."

"Why? What are you going to do about it?" Fletch sneered. "Are you going to sic your boyfriend on me? I'd love to take a few swings at him."

It had grown quiet over by the pallet as Fletch and Laura had their heated argument. Red Fox spoke now. "I would not like for you to hurt the man who saved my son's life, Fletch."

Fletch swung around and looked at the Indian, somewhat startled. In his mixed emotions of seeing Laura—surprise, joy, then black anger—he hadn't even noticed his friend kneeling beside his son.

He walked across the floor and hunkered down beside Red Fox. "So, Little Fox," he said as he studied the red claw marks on the dusky skin, "I see you've met up with a bear."

"Yes. A sow. I guess she had a cub nearby. I shot an arrow in her chest, but she just kept coming after me. I was sure happy when Brave came along and chased her away."

"So actually it was the dog who saved your life?"

"Not just him. I would have bled to death if Brave hadn't brought Laura to me. She got me here to the cabin, and it was Spotted Horse who stopped the bleeding and doctored me through my fever."

Fletch tried not to show his shock that Laura's new man friend was an Indian. It would not sit well with Red Fox if he thought that Fletch Thomas didn't like the idea of Laura loving a red man, that he didn't think the man was good enough for her. It wasn't that he felt that Laura was above living with one of Red Fox's race, it was that he felt she was too delicate for the harshness of Indian life.

"I guess we owe this fellow a lot." Fletch ruffled the black hair lying on the pillow and stood up, thinking that if the brave didn't try to stop him from taking Jolie away with him he wouldn't beat him into a pulp, even though the thought of the man touching Laura's body almost doubled him over.

When Fletch stamped out of the house without another look at Laura, she walked over to the pallet and knelt down beside it. "What do you think of your son fighting a bear?" She smiled at Red Fox.

"I think he was very foolish. He should have climbed a tree. We had only hoped that maybe he could bring down a small deer."

When Little Fox didn't make a response to his father's chastising, only lowered his lids, Red Fox said to Laura, "Why did you not tell Fletch that Spotted Horse is an old man? Did you perhaps want to make him jealous?"

Laura felt her face growing red. To make Fletch jealous was exactly why she failed to mention the old man's age, and Red Fox knew it. Her wish had worked to a degree. She hadn't expected, though, that Fletch would strike back at her by threatening to take Jolie away. Somehow she must take her daughter and slip away as soon as possible. She wished she knew how long Fletch planned on staying.

She looked over at Red Fox and said, "The old

brave says that Little Fox cannot travel for a couple weeks. Do you agree?"

"I think maybe ten days," the father answered.

"Will you be staying here until then?"

"Yes. I will relieve the old one of taking care of my son."

"I expect that Fletch will be staying on also."

Red Fox knew what she was fishing for and he slid her a look of dry amusement as he answered, "Who knows about my friend Fletch? He is like the wind that blows in March. Sometimes one way, sometimes the other. He may leave today, tomorrow, or maybe he'll stay and return with me and my son."

Laura realized she'd get no information from the Indian, so she asked, "Why didn't you tell Fletch that Spotted Horse is an old man?"

"My friend is hot-blooded, sometimes has a reckless tongue, and most things come too easy to him. Especially where women are concerned. It amuses me to watch him make a fool of himself. Perhaps he will learn that anger always overrides reason."

A smile flickered in Red Fox's black eyes. "Laura Thomas, there's a lesson you could learn also. When you find your temper beginning to stir against Fletch, walk away from him. That will rile him more than anything you could say to him, and in the meantime you'll not have said words you wish you could recall."

"I don't wish to recall anything I said to Fletch Thomas." Laura sniffed. Rising, she walked away from Red Fox, her head held high. She walked out onto the porch, wondering where Fletch had gone.

Fletch had walked about half a mile from the cabin and was waiting for the man who was stealing his daughter's affections. He sat on the needle-strewn ground, his back propped against the trunk of a pine a few feet off the lake trail.

He idly picked up dead twigs and snapped them between his fingers, his mind on Laura. She hated him, and he couldn't blame her. Because of his stupidity she had had to suffer the village women's ostracism, overhear their demeaning remarks, witness their suspicious looks at Jolie's little blond head. It was all his fault that she had run here to this wild island to get away from the pain they were giving her. And he had been just as bad as the women, if not worse. He remembered his cruel taunts, his accusations, his sarcasm. He couldn't blame her if she never spoke to him again.

But, dear Lord, he wished that she would. He couldn't visualize a life without her, and one way or another she was going to be a part of it. She had cared enough for him once to give her virginity to him, and if only a small coal of that love still lived within her somewhere, he was going to fan it into flames again. If he had to steal Jolie away from her, so be it. He was desperate and would go to any lengths to get the woman he loved back to where she belonged. No way in hell was he going to leave her to live with some young buck who wouldn't appreciate her.

Fletch was so immersed in his thoughts he gave a startled exclamation when Brave was suddenly standing before him, his hackles raised, deep growls issuing from his throat. "Here, boy." He held out his hand, palm up, to the dog that had never really accepted him.

He was relieved and somewhat surprised when the growling ceased and the hair on the thick neck lay down. "So you remember me," he said softly, slowly rising to his feet. When Brave flopped down on the ground, his tongue lolling out of his mouth as he panted, Fletch slowly brushed the dirt and needles off his seat. He didn't trust the dog not to lunge at him if he made any sudden movements.

He stood waiting then. The Indian should be coming along anytime now.

Less than ten minutes had passed when Fletch heard the clomping sound of horses' hooves. He stepped out onto the path, then swore to himself. It was no young brave coming toward him, but an old Indian. But wait a minute. That was Laura's little mare, Beauty, the white-haired man was riding. How had he come to have the mount? Had he stolen it from the other Indian?

When horse and rider were almost upon him, Fletch raised his hand. Beauty was reined in and the old Indian looked at him with wary eyes. "What do you want of me, paleface?" He frowned fiercely.

"I want to know where you got that horse."

"I did not steal it if that's what you're thinking." The old man looked scornfully at him. "I have the permission of the mare's owner to ride her."

"And who is that?"

"That I will not tell you. I do not know who you are."

"That I will not tell you," Fletch threw the old man's words back at him. "I am telling you, though, that I'm taking the mare away from you." Fletch grabbed hold of the mare's bridle near her mouth. "I don't want to hurt you, so climb down please."

The old Indian was stubbornly shaking his head when Fletch caught his breath and stared. A blond curly head had suddenly popped around from behind Spotted Horse, smiling and gurgling, "Dada."

"Jolie!" Fletch exclaimed, a wide smile on his face as he lifted his arms to her.

When his daughter would have gone into his arms, the old man put back an arm, holding her fast in her carrying case. "I still do not know who you are." He glared down at Fletch.

"I am the child's father. Did you not hear her call me Dada?"

"Laura has never said to me that she had a husband."

Fletch's eyes widened a trifle. Had Laura played a trick on him? Purposely let him think that she was living with a young brave? As the

Indian continued to glower down on him, Fletch asked, "Are you called Spotted Horse?"

The white head nodded, and Fletch muttered, "I'll get her ornery little hide for this."

By now Jolie was beginning to fuss and strain toward Fletch. Spotted Horse gave him a long, thoughtful look, then removed his arm so that Fletch could lift the baby down. When he had her in his arms, he hugged her tightly and buried his face in her curls. He knew he had missed the child, but not in the same way he had missed her mother. He knew now that he couldn't bear a life without them both in it.

With Jolie nestled in his arms, Fletch walked back toward the cabin, making his plans of how and when he would slip away with his daughter. He hated to do it that way, but it was the only sure way of getting Laura back to Big Pine.

Spotted Horse, a few yards behind, hoped that he had done the right thing, letting the tall white man take Laura's daughter. As the mare clomped along, he wondered ruefully how he could have stopped the one who called himself Jolie's father.

Chapter Twenty-five

Laura walked out on the porch for the third time to peer through the trees, looking for Spotted Horse and Jolie to appear. Fletch hadn't returned from wherever he had gone. She was beginning to worry that he had something to do with the old man not returning at his usual time. She tried to comfort herself with the thought that maybe it was taking Spotted Horse a little longer this time because he had to dicker over price on his beaver pelts.

Her face was still heated from an altercation she'd just had with Red Fox. She had innocently asked him how his wife would fare while he was gone so long. He had answered with much arrogance that it was up to her to take care of herself. If she died in his absence it would be just as well, since he had no use for a woman who couldn't manage when he wasn't around.

She had stared at the handsome Indian in shocked silence a moment, then blurted out, "How sad that you are married to a woman you don't love."

Red Fox had given her a look that said she was soft in the head. "Love, bah!" he snorted. "Do you not know that there is only one true love? The love you have for your parents, your children. Have you not noticed how many times a man or woman changes partners? You never change your parents or children."

While she sought for some words that would prove him wrong, Red Fox had stood up and stalked out of the cabin.

Little Fox tried to soften his father's harsh words by saying, "My father said that when you left Big Pine, Fletch searched all over Detroit for you. Do you not think that maybe that was done from love?"

"It would seem that way, wouldn't it?" Laura smiled gently at the thirteen-year-old, but inside she knew why Fletch had gone to Detroit. Besides her having his daughter with her, Pa had ordered him to go looking for her.

She had stayed with Little Fox until his father returned to the cabin, walking straight to his son's pallet without a glance at her. She took his previous advice when she felt her anger rising and walked outside.

Laura sighed now as she peered through the

trees at the lake trail. Had something happened to Spotted Horse? She had just made up her mind to saddle Fletch's stallion and go looking for him when she spotted Beauty coming toward the cabin.

Her heart began to hammer. Jolie wasn't with him. "Oh, dear Lord," she whispered, "Fletch has taken her and left." She stepped off the porch and walked around the building to look where Fletch and Red Fox had staked out their mounts. Both horses were still there. In a panic she hurried back to the front of the cabin just as Spotted Horse drew Beauty up to the porch.

"Spotted Horse!" she called wildly. "Where is Jolie?" The old man climbed stiffly from the saddle and, giving her an accusing look, asked, "Why did you not tell me that you have a husband?"

Laura started to answer that she had no husband, then stopped. She wanted this old Indian's good opinion of her. He might think badly of her if he knew she'd had Jolie out of wedlock.

"I'm sorry," she said, "but I didn't think it was necessary. Now, where is Jolie? Has he taken her?"

Spotted Horse looked over his shoulder. "She is with her father. They come now."

Laura saw them then, the big tall man and the small child riding on his arm. How good they look together, she thought for an instant, then banished the thought. They didn't belong together, no matter how becoming it looked. Fletch had once called the little one a bastard, and that was hard to forget.

"You know he spoke in anger," her little voice inside whispered. "He only wanted to hurt you, you had him so angry." She brushed aside the words that made excuses for Fletch and hurried down the path to meet him.

Jolie smiled at Laura as she ran up to them but cuddled closer to Fletch as if she did not want to be taken from the broad, warm chest. The little one's action stung Laura, but she wouldn't let it show.

Or so she thought. Fletch knew her too well, even down to the flicker of her eyelashes. He gave her a mocking smile as if to say that his daughter knew where she belonged.

But Laura knew Fletch equally well, and she knew there was leashed anger inside him. Some of it came out when he said in rough tones, "Your taste in men has changed considerably." When she made no answer, he said, "Did it amuse you to make a fool of me in front of Red Fox?"

"You made a fool of yourself," Laura flared back. "All I said was that, yes, a man was living with me, and Jolie is quite fond of him. You jumped to your usual bad opinion of me and assumed that living together meant that I was sharing my bed with a man."

"You know damn well that you meant me to believe that," Fletch half snarled.

"Think what you want," Laura snapped. "You always do."

"Damn you, you never let me think what I want to think," Fletch grated. "You've always got me riled up, making me say and do things that I don't want to think or say."

They were at the cabin now, and before they stepped up on the porch, Fletch asked, "Are you returning to Big Pine with me and Jolie?"

Laura's only answer was a sharp, "Hah," as she stepped inside the one-room building. Wouldn't he be surprised when he learned that neither she nor Jolie was going back to Big Pine?

When Fletch followed her into the cabin he handed Jolie to Spotted Horse, who had made himself known to Red Fox and was explaining the herbs and roots he had used on Little Fox. "Keep an eye on her, would you please?" he said. "I need to talk to her mother."

The old brave took the baby, who went to him willingly. "You need to beat her, not talk to her," Spotted Horse told Fletch and gave Laura a dour look. "She must understand that her place is with her man. Laura is a fine woman, but she is very stubborn."

"Spotted Horse!" Laura exclaimed, hurt and angry. "How can you tell him to beat me? I thought you were my friend, and now you are turning on me."

"I am your friend, Laura Thomas. That is why I'm telling your man to teach you obeisance. I have thought long on the months when this island will be frozen, cut off from the rest of the world. How would you and Jolie survive if something should happen to me? My years are many. I am now like a candle burning down. I know that soon it will flicker and die out. I will rest much better if I know that you and Jolie are being taken care of by your man."

Laura felt tears burn the backs of her eyes. The old man wasn't going to help her get away from Fletch. He was like the other Indian, Red Fox. Woman must bend to the wishes of man. Well, this woman wasn't about to bend to any man.

"Come on, you heard the man." Fletch nudged Laura toward the door, sparkling amusement in his eyes. "It's time you learn to obey me."

Laura tried to dig in her heels, to stay where she stood beside the table. But the big hand on the small of her back easily propelled her through the door. Half blinded by rage, she stumbled outside, and Fletch took her arm and tugged her down the lake path.

When they were out of sight of the cabin, he drew her into a patch of willow whose lacy foliage drooped to the ground. When he released her, she spun around, wrapping her arms around her waist, on the verge of outraged tears. "You dare to take a willow branch to me, Fletcher Thomas, and it will be the last act you'll ever do."

Fletch didn't answer her. His eyes were fastened on the betraying peaks of her breasts which the passion of anger had caused to harden.

Laura wheeled around, turning her back to him. Fletch drew a ragged breath and said huskily, "It doesn't matter that you try to hide yourself from me. I can remember clearly how satin soft they felt in my hands, how sweet they tasted in my mouth."

He took her shoulders and turned her around to face him. Stark passion looked out of his eyes. "And you remember things too, if you'd only admit it. You were like a wildcat in my arms as I thrust in and out of you. You eagerly took everything I had to give you."

He drew her to him, cajoling huskily, "Please, Laura, I need desperately to make love to you, to cover your body with mine, to drive slow and deep inside you. It's been so long," he whispered, bending his head and covering her lips with his.

Laura was determined that she would stay rigid in his arms, not respond at all. Then his tongue was sliding into her mouth and his hand was in her bodice, stroking and rolling the nipple between his thumb and finger. She felt a weakness building inside the pit of her stomach, and when he pulled her breast free and bent his head to draw her aching nipple into his mouth, she gave a little sigh and melted against him, her arms coming up around his neck, all conscious thought deserting her. Her body had taken over with the driving need to be made love to.

With a sharp intake of breath, Fletch placed his fingers on the buttons of her bodice. In seconds the material separated and he was cupping both breasts in his palms, the pads of his thumbs rubbing her puckered nipples. Laura gave a sigh of intense pleasure when he bent his head and began suckling first one and then the other.

She felt him slide his hand down between their bodies and knew that he was unfastening his trousers. When he removed his hand from between them, she reached down and curled her fingers around his thick, hard manhood that jerked like a live thing.

As she squeezed and stroked him the way he had taught her, he slid a hand up her skirt, then down inside her bloomers. She moaned softly when his finger began to slide back and forth on the little nub of her femininity.

They were both breathing heavily, almost ready to reach a release, when Fletch raised his head from Laura's breast and said hoarsely, "Let's get out of our clothes."

In seconds their clothes lay scattered on the ground. Laura sat down on the shirt Fletch had spread for her, and he stood before her. His erection was strong and proud, a picture of raw physical power, a power that she knew would send her spiraling to the skies.

Fletch looked down at her, his eyes silently pleading. She came up on her knees, and grasping his thighs put her mouth where she knew he wanted it. He moaned and stroked a finger around the corners of her lips as they worked on him, whispering hoarsely how he had dreamed of her loving him this way.

A short time later when he knew he couldn't contain much longer the passion raging to be turned loose, he disengaged himself and came down beside Laura, pressing her back onto his shirt. He spread her soft thighs and climbed between them. He hung over her, waiting for her to take his glistening wet shaft and guide it inside her.

As his male strength filled her from wall to wall, Laura didn't think she could bear the pleasure of his possessing her. She could only moan her joy and cling to his shoulders as he rocked against her.

She felt like a wanton when in only a few minutes she reached the desired peak and soared away in a blinding sea of delight. Twice more, without finding his own release yet, Fletch brought her to that crest again.

The third time, as she was slowly coming back to earth, Fletch gave a hoarse cry, bucked his hips rapidly, then collapsed on top of her.

"God," he whispered in her hair, "but you're good. Already I want more of you."

Laura realized he wasn't speaking empty

words, for she could feel him swelling inside her. He came up on his elbows and rested awhile as his hard maleness was jerking and throbbing, anxious to be in motion again. He leaned forward and, giving Laura a quick, hard kiss, shoved his hands beneath her rear and lifted her up to fit her hips in the well of his.

Slowly, he began a deep thrusting.

An hour later, his body glistening with sweat, having reached two more releases, Fletch finally rolled off an exhausted Laura. Drained, they both fell asleep.

When they awakened the sun had moved quite a bit westward. Fletch stretched luxuriously, then reached for Laura. She laughed and exclaimed, "No more, Fletch. I'm completely drained."

Fletch chuckled. "So am I. I'm afraid we made pigs of ourselves." He leaned up on his elbow and, resting his arm across her waist, said, "I only wanted to hold you while we talk."

Laura became almost breathless with excitement. Fletch was going to tell her that he loved her. He was finally going to say the words she had waited for years to hear. When a long pause ensued, Laura asked, "What did you want to talk about, Fletch?"

"Well, for one thing I wanted to point out how perfectly we are matched when it comes to making love, even though otherwise we spat a lot. But I think now that we'll be living together, in time that will stop."

When Laura's body stiffened and she made no response to his spoken thoughts, Fletch frowned and said, half impatiently, "For Jolie's sake you know that we must marry." When Laura still didn't say anything, he said angrily, "What we just shared didn't mean a thing to you, did it?"

When Laura still remained silent, his fingers bit into her side. "Get this into your hard head. We will marry. I will not have people thinking that I'm the kind of man who won't shoulder his responsibilities."

Laura wanted to laugh, to cry, to smash her fist into the handsome face of her daughter's father. To get her back to Big Pine was what all the lovemaking was about. Not one word of love had been spoken, not even an endearment had passed through his lips as he made love. Not love, she amended. She should say while he spent his lust on her. He didn't care diddly for her. He was only worried about his reputation, what the people of Big Pine would say and think about him.

Laura sat up and began to get dressed. Fletch sat up also. "You haven't said anything." He caught her arm for attention. "Don't you have an opinion on what I said?"

"It's a very poor one," Laura answered sharply, jerking her dress down over her head. "I don't give a damn what people think of you.

They couldn't think less than I do. Like I told you before, Jolie and I aren't going back to Big Pine with you."

"All right, damn your ornery hide!" Fletch jumped to his feet. "Don't come. You can stay here with the bears and wolves and freeze to death this winter, but I'm taking Jolie off this island."

Laura opened her mouth, then shut it. *Don't say anything,* she cautioned herself. *Let him think that he's going to have his way, that I won't buck him anymore.* She did up her last button and walked away, leaving Fletch looking after her, puzzlement on his face. His eyes narrowed. It wasn't like her to give up so meekly.

As he climbed into his buckskins he laid his plans.

Chapter Twenty-six

Laura banged pots and pans about, slapped tin plates and flatware on the table. She ignored the cross looks she received from the two Indian men. She smiled grimly to herself. She hoped she'd make enough racket to drive them out of the cabin. She was tired of the dour, accusing looks they'd been sending her ever since Fletch stamped into the cabin, his scowling face showing that things remained the same between them.

She had a suspicion that her noisy actions were amusing Fletch as he sat rocking Jolie, keeping her entertained with a narrow wampum belt he had taken from his pocket. She had definitely seen his shoulders shaking once with contained mirth when she deliberately dropped the Dutch oven lid onto the hearth and its ringing clatter had made both Indians jump and send her sour looks.

Well, she thought grimly, let's see how much he laughs when he discovers that Jolie and I are gone. She had made up her mind that tonight when everyone slept she was going to undertake the first theft in her life. Desperation was making her do it. She planned to take the money Spotted Horse had received for his furs. The small leather pouch in which he kept his valuables hung on a peg in its usual place. It bulged with greenbacks.

Laura told herself that Spotted Horse had been quite willing for her to have the money before Fletch had turned up claiming to be her husband. She smiled without mirth. Parading as her husband, he would be responsible for repaying Spotted Horse for the money she had taken. The old man would expect him to do it.

When the evening meal of roast beef and baked potatoes was on the table, Laura picked Jolie off Fletch's lap, saying, "Come on, Mama's little pumpkin, supper is waiting." By the time she placed Jolie in her special chair and took a seat beside her, the three men had followed her. With sidelong looks at her they pulled out chairs and sat down.

The meat and potatoes began to disappear at a rapid rate as the men helped themselves, piling their plates. Laura said sharply to Red Fox,

"You'd better prepare your son a plate before everything is gone."

Red Fox lifted his head, his black eyes boring into her. "As a woman, shouldn't you be doing that?"

"If you were not here I would feed the lad." Laura glared back at him. "But I am not his mother. Since you, his father, are here, it is your duty to see to your son."

Red Fox looked at Fletch as if to say, *Order your woman to bring my son his supper.* But his white friend kept his eyes averted. Red Fox rose, picked up his plate, and before he stalked over to the pallet, growled at Fletch, "Next time beat your woman a little harder. She still has a sharp tongue and foolish ideas."

Spotted Horse grunted agreement, making Laura want to kick his bony legs under the table. She glanced at Fletch, who had kept silent, and found his face devoid of expression. She knew, however, that he wanted to burst out laughing.

The meal was quickly over, the tight atmosphere not conducive to light conversation. When everyone rose to leave the table, Fletch picked up Jolie and resumed sitting in the rocking chair. Red Fox and Spotted Horse lit their smelly pipes and sat smoking before the small fire that had been lit to break the chill of the evening.

Laura washed and dried the dishes, pots, and pans, then rolled down her sleeves and walked out onto the porch. Night had fallen as they ate, and stars were beginning to blink in the sky. A pale yellow moon was reflected on the lake, and on the other end of the island a pack of wolves were baying at it.

She sighed. She'd hate leaving this place. She had known peace here if not complete happiness. But she had been content enough, and she didn't know what lay ahead of her in Detroit. Maybe she would only find more heartache.

The hoot of an owl drifted through the darkness as Laura stretched and yawned. It had been a long day, filled with many emotions. Emotions that had ran the gamut of anger, passion, despair, and anger again.

She turned to go back into the cabin to go to bed, and found Fletch blocking the doorway. "Where's Jolie?" she asked, peering around his shoulder.

"She fell asleep and I put her to bed."

"Did you change her into her nightclothes?"

Fletch shook his head. "She was sleeping so soundly I hated to wake her up. I took her shoes off."

"I guess it won't hurt this one time," Laura said after a thoughtful pause. "If you'll let me past, I'm going to bed myself."

"Look, Laura, things will work out if you give them a chance. Just be a little patient."

"Are you trying to tell me that you're going to change?" Laura challenged Fletch. "I think not. You could no more change than those wolves out there could stop howling." With those cutting words she pushed past him and walked into the cabin.

Fletch stepped out on the porch and went to stand where Laura had stood. He looked up at the same moon, bleakness in his eyes. Laura had no intention of returning to Big Pine, he realized. Only one thing would bring her back there. He stepped off the porch and walked thoughtfully along the lake path.

Back in the cabin, Laura was forced to climb into bed in her daytime clothes. She wasn't about to change clothes in front of eagle-eyed Red Fox. He would probably think she was skinny and a weakling and would make some demeaning remark about it.

She couldn't get comfortable at first, being on the wrong side of the bed. Usually she put Jolie next to the wall so she wouldn't fall off. But Fletch had put her in front, and Laura hesitated to risk awakening the little one if she moved her.

Exhaustion overtook her finally and she fell into a deep, relaxing sleep.

Some hours had passed when Laura came wide awake, as though someone had shaken her shoulder. She lay in the darkness, listening to the snores coming from beside the fireplace. She recognized Spotted Horse's nasal rattle and supposed that the rumbling sound came from Red Fox, since she couldn't remember ever hearing Fletch make sleeping noises.

Now is your chance to get Spotted Horse's money and slip away with your daughter, her inner voice whispered. *Fletch will not be expecting you to leave so soon.*

Laura sat up and prepared to scoot off the bed, then gasped aloud. Jolie was no longer in bed with her. In a panic, she thought wildly that Jolie had fallen out of bed and cracked her head.

Her eyes flew to where Fletch had stored his bedroll next to the hearth. Her heart began racing. It was gone. He had outguessed her. He must have taken Jolie and was now on his way to Big Pine with her.

How long a head start did he have on her? her mind asked frantically as she shoved her feet into her shoes. Could she overtake him tonight? He'd have to stop and make camp somewhere along the way for Jolie's sake, and she was sure he wouldn't try to cross the lake at night.

Laura was stuffing a grub bag with tins of milk, bacon, corn bread, coffee, and rice when Little Fox hissed from his pallet, "Laura, Fletch had been gone a little over two hours."

"Thank you, Little Fox," Laura whispered back. "Please pray to your Great Father that I will catch up with Fletch."

She was out the door then, running to where Beauty was tethered to a tree and where Brave watched over her. She dug her saddle from beneath a pine and heaved it onto the mare's back.

When she had the saddle in place and secured the grub bag behind the cantle, she tied Brave to a long lead rope attached to the saddle and swung onto the little mount's back. With a kick of her heels she sent the animal racing down the lake trail.

Laura figured she had been riding an hour when fog began drifting off the lake. It came in fast, and within minutes it had thickened until she could scarcely see a foot in front of her. The fog had an ominous quality, as though it waited for something dire to happen.

Beauty had slowed to a careful walk now, picking her way, following Brave who seemingly was leading the way. When suddenly Beauty pricked her ears, a cold shiver ran down Laura's spine. Did the mare sense that a wolf was near? She peered ahead through thick gray mist, her ears attuned to any sound that a running wolf might make.

Her heart gave a great leap when in the total silence she heard a child crying. She wanted to kick the mare into a hard gallop but knew it would be a foolish and dangerous action. She had never felt so frustrated in her life as they moved along at a snail's pace.

The cries were becoming louder, bellowed out in angry tones. Laura relaxed a little. Jolie was all right, she was only cross.

Laura almost rode past the small campfire a couple yards off the trail. The only reason she spotted it was that Brave started barking and straining against the lead rope. Laura turned Beauty's head in the direction of the stand of birch where Fletch had camped and hit the ground running.

"Damn you, Fletch Thomas," she cried in mingled rage and relief as she snatched Jolie off his lap.

Jolie wrapped her arms around Laura's neck and clung to her like a little monkey.

"A fine father you are." Laura glared at Fletch as she sat down across the fire from him. "You take a baby from her warm bed without a thought of bringing any food for her. What did you plan on feeding her? Rabbits and squirrels?"

A sheepish look flooded Fletch's face. That was exactly what he had planned on doing. When Laura ordered him to bring her the grub bag tied to Beauty's saddle, he went meekly to do her bidding.

He felt helpless and stupid when a minute later Laura began feeding their daughter corn bread, washed down with sips of watered-down canned milk. In his anger at Laura he hadn't thought of anything but taking Jolie away, to force her mother to come looking for her.

When Jolie smiled happily, her tummy filled, Fletch fully expected Laura to take the baby and ride back to the cabin. He wouldn't try to stop her. He realized now that to force her to return home with him would be like keeping a wild animal penned up in a cage. All the life and laughter would go out of her.

As he stared into the flames, he decided he would take Laura and Jolie to Detroit, find them a nice small place, then send money to them every month. He could still take care of them even though they would be hundreds of miles away.

He started to speak of his decision, but Laura was lying on his bedroll, Jolie tucked close in her arms. His pulse rate increased with hope. She could have ridden back to the cabin. The fog had lifted half an hour ago. He laid more wood on the fire and stretched out on the other side of Jolie, hoping that in the morning Laura would be riding with him instead of away from him.

Laura kept her eyes closed, feigning sleep. She did not want Fletch talking to her. They would only get into a heated argument, and she had resigned herself to returning to Big Pine, and a few sarcastic words from him might change her mind. Her scare tonight had shown her that Jolie needed two parents even if the husband didn't love the wife. She would just have to turn a blind eye to Fletch's indiscretions.

I can do it for Jolie's sake, she told herself as she drifted off to sleep.

It was around noon when Laura and Fletch rode into the village, tired and hungry. Jolie rode with Fletch, sitting safely in front of him. A group of Laura's old enemies stood in front of the store staring at them, and Laura grimaced. She knew what she must look like, her clothes all wrinkled and her hair a tangled mess. How their tongues would wag when they got alone together.

She and Fletch had just drawn rein and dismounted when Taylor stepped outside. He stared a moment, then yelled, "Laura!" and rushed to take her in his arms and give her a bear hug. "I've been worried sick about you, girl." He held her away from him and skimmed his eyes over her face. "Where have you been?"

"We'll tell you all about it later, Pa," Fletch said. "Right now would you ring the bell, bring all the people in? I have something important to tell them. I want them all to know at the same time so we don't have to go through the same story a dozen times."

Taylor's roaring welcome had brought everyone out of the tavern, as well as Big Bertha and her girls. Laura didn't have time to wonder what Fletch was up to as Bertha and the young whores gathered round her, exclaiming how they had worried and missed her.

Maida and Daniel were there next, with Justine just seconds behind them. In a short time all the women and most of the men in Big Pine were gathered around the store.

"Fletch has something he wants to tell you folks," Taylor said, then stepped aside, grinning at Fletcher. "Go ahead, son, speak your piece."

Fletch's eyes singled out every woman who had ever gossiped about Laura, who had treated her shabbily, before he said in a ringing voice, "I want to clear up once and for all who Jolie Thomas's father is.

"I, Fletcher Thomas, sired her. She is my daughter."

Into the shocked silence that followed, Milly Howard stepped forward and sneered, "Why has it taken you so long to come to that conclusion? That blond-headed baby still looks the same to me."

"Yes, she does." Fletcher looked fondly at his daughter in her grandfather's arms. "And I hope that her looks never change. She looks exactly like my mother, Pa's first wife."

When the surprised exclamations of the women who had scorned Laura, mingled with the happy cries from her friends, died down, Fletch walked over to Laura and said softly, "Will you take a walk with me, Laura?"

What is he up to now? Laura asked herself, not trusting him for a moment. But everyone was watching them, and besides, she couldn't resist the pleading in his eyes. When he took her arm, she walked away with him.

They took the path along the lake, Fletcher not speaking until they were out of sight of the people still discussing his astounding news. When the path followed the bend of the lake, he motioned Laura to sit with him on a fallen log.

She hesitated a moment, then walked over and sat down. Arranging her skirt over her knees, she wondered what Fletch was going to say to her. He looked so solemn and tense.

He sat down beside her, and her nerves became more taut when he didn't speak. Whatever he had on his mind he was having a hard time saying it.

Laura sighed inwardly. She was sure it was something she didn't want to hear. Something to do with Jolie.

When Fletcher did finally speak, she was sure she misunderstood him, for he said, "Laura, I don't blame you for feeling the way you do about me. I have treated you shamefully, said awful things to you. But all along it was jealousy and hurt that made me act that way.

"I know that it is hard for you to believe, but I have always loved you, Laura. First as a child, then later as a young woman. I'm begging you now to forget what a bastard I've been and take me out of my misery. Please, will you marry me?"

Happiness and love shining out of her eyes, Laura cupped his face in her hands and said softly, "Damn you, Fletcher Thomas, you don't know how long I have waited to hear you say that you love me. Of course I'll marry you."

With happy laughter on his lips, Fletch grabbed her and kissed her until she was dizzy with it.

By the time they returned to the post area,

everyone was gone. "We'll tell them our news tomorrow," Fletch said as he opened the door to the store.

A soft smile curved Laura's lips as she walked into the room where Taylor had recovered from his broken leg. The cot was narrow, but wide enough for a couple to sleep in each other's arms.

Trapped in a loveless marriage, Lark Elliot longs to lead a normal life like the pretty women she sees in town, to wear new clothes and be courted by young suitors. But she has married Cletus Gibb, a man twice her age, so her elderly aunt and uncle can stay through the long Colorado winter in the mountain cabin he owns. Resigned to backbreaking labor on Gibb's ranch, Lark finds one person who makes the days bearable: Ace Brandon. But when her husband pays the rugged cowhand to father him an heir, at first Lark thinks she has been wrong about Ace's kindness. It isn't long, however, before she is looking forward to the warmth of his tender kiss, to the feel of his strong body. And as the heat of their desire melts away the cold winter nights, Lark knows she's found the haven she's always dreamed of in the circle of his loving arms.

___4522-2 $5.99 US/$6.99 CAN

Dorchester Publishing Co., Inc.
P.O. Box 6640
Wayne, PA 19087-8640

Please add $1.75 for shipping and handling for the first book and $.50 for each book thereafter. NY, NYC, and PA residents, please add appropriate sales tax. No cash, stamps, or C.O.D.s. All orders shipped within 6 weeks via postal service book rate.
Canadian orders require $2.00 extra postage and must be paid in U.S. dollars through a U.S. banking facility.

Name______________________________________
Address____________________________________
City____________________State_______Zip__________
I have enclosed $__________ in payment for the checked book(s).
Payment must accompany all orders. ❑ Please send a free catalog.
CHECK OUT OUR WEBSITE! www.dorchesterpub.com